Legends
Can Be
Murder

Connie Shelton

Books
by Connie Shelton

THE CHARLIE PARKER SERIES
Deadly Gamble
Vacations Can Be Murder
Partnerships Can Be Murder
Small Towns Can Be Murder
Memories Can Be Murder
Honeymoons Can Be Murder
Reunions Can Be Murder
Competition Can Be Murder
Balloons Can Be Murder
Obsessions Can Be Murder
Gossip Can Be Murder
Stardom Can Be Murder
Phantoms Can Be Murder
Buried Secrets Can Be Murder
Legends Can Be Murder

Holidays Can Be Murder - a Christmas novella

THE SAMANTHA SWEET SERIES
Sweet Masterpiece
Sweet's Sweets
Sweet Holidays
Sweet Hearts
Bitter Sweet
Sweets Galore
Sweets, Begorra
Sweet Payback
Sweet Somethings

Legends
Can Be
Murder

Charlie Parker Mystery #15

Connie Shelton

Secret Staircase Books

Legends Can Be Murder
Published by Secret Staircase Books, an imprint of
Columbine Publishing Group
PO Box 416, Angel Fire, NM 87710

Printed and bound in the United States of America
ISBN 1501071807
ISBN-13 978-1501071805

Book layout and design by Secret Staircase Books
Cover image © Maryann Preiseinger
Cover background image © cekur

First trade paperback edition: November 2014

As always, this one is for Dan, my husband, best friend and constant inspiration through all the years.

Special thanks go out to Dan Shelton, Susan Slater and Shirley Shaw for spotting my errors and helping me to make this book as good as it can be.

Chapter 1

It makes no sense to finish a journey from New Mexico to Alaska by driving south, but that's the way it is. Or at least the way it happened for me as I reached the outskirts of Skagway, scanning the unfamiliar scene—seaport, mountains, ocean vessels—looking for a heliport where my husband should be awaiting my arrival. There it was, a flat stretch of tarmac with a half-dozen helicopters sitting like inactive insects resting on bright yellow H's on the ground. I pulled over near them, spotting our JetRanger's familiar blue and white paint scheme among the others, and looked at the pickup truck's trip odometer before shutting off the engine. Three thousand and ten miles from home. It felt so good to get out of that vehicle.

The dog apparently agreed. Freckles hopped to the ground and ran circles around me. Drake had been sitting around the FBO awhile; I saw him walking toward me across the airstrip from the tiny fixed base operator's office with a shorter male figure beside him. We'd made the journey more or less together, switching off between who drove and who flew every couple of days. I will make note here that he cheated near the end, by cutting off the final big loop into the Yukon and flying straight west from Morley Lake while I drove the paved two-lane the rest of the way.

Alone with his aircraft he could have done the journey cross-country in half the time, I felt sure, but we'd plotted a course that would take us through towns where he could get jet fuel and I could count on a comfy hotel bed each night. We managed it in eight semi-grueling days, although I certainly couldn't whine about the spectacular scenery. You really can't believe this place until you've seen it.

"Hey, babe," he said. "What took you so long?"

I growled and he gave me a wink. He turned to the man beside him.

"This is Chuey Martinez, hon, head mechanic for Kerby's operation." He stood half a head shorter than Drake's six feet, and was slightly on the stocky side, with dark hair showing at the edges of his ball cap.

"*Only* mechanic," Chuey said with a smile that showed square, even teeth. "But two ships aren't all that hard to manage." He stuck out his hand and the warmth of it reminded me that my own hands, along with my arms and face, were quite chilly.

I reached back into the pickup for my fleece jacket. When we had packed our things in Albuquerque, where the June weather consisted of unrelenting sunshine and temperatures well into the nineties, it was hard to imagine that I would want thermal underwear, turtlenecks and a coat. Drake, however, had a lot of mountain flight experience and lives with a motto that you can never take too much warm clothing. Catching sight of a large round thermometer on the side of the building, I had no trouble believing the fifty-five degree reading.

Chuey caught me looking. "When the sun drops, be ready. It's supposed to be forty-five tonight."

Even Freckles must be feeling it. She'd settled beside me and was leaning against my legs.

"Have you touched base with our landlady yet?" I asked Drake.

He shook his head. "Didn't have her number. Plus, Kerby's been briefing me ever since I got here. His first group will be ready to head out in the morning."

Kerby Allen was the owner and operator of a business here called Gold Trail Adventures. We'd been shifted over to him when our original job of hauling seismic crews fell through. Secretly, I thought taking people out to look for gold sounded way more exciting than hauling loads of heavy equipment anyway. Once we settled into our rental house I would find out the rest of the details from Drake. I pulled a folder out of the glove compartment which held all our travel information.

"Roberta Gengler," I said. "That's her name, and I have the address and phone number right here."

I had begun looking for housing last fall and was a little surprised to find that many properties were already leased for the coming summer. It seemed that Skagway, where the normal population was fewer than a thousand, tripled in size with seasonal workers and gained tenfold when the cruise ships were in port. I'd snagged the first place I could get that was an actual house and allowed dogs; many of the seasonal workers were lucky to find dormitory-style housing provided by their corporate tour-company employers or a room in someone's home. Some of the brave college-aged ones tried tent camping, but I knew good and well I would not be up for that for the span of our four-month contract. It was probably too much to hope our place would be charming; we'd be happy if it was comfortable and weather-tight.

"Berta's a good gal," Chuey said. "I think you'll like her. And she's got a daughter that's not bad at all." He gave a little eyebrow-wiggle in Drake's direction.

"Let's give her a call, see if we can unpack the truck before dark," I suggested.

Chuey noticed the town map in my folder and stepped closer to point to it. "Here's Berta's place. I think the rental is also on State but I'm not sure. Grocery is right here. Gas station there."

The town was laid out on a neat grid, five streets wide and nine or ten long, with a railroad track leading from the dock area and going away into the mountains somewhere. Everything Chuey pointed out was within a few blocks, easy walking distance.

We said goodbye to the mechanic, Drake saying he'd be back in the morning, and climbed into the truck where I pulled out my phone and called Mrs. Gengler. Six minutes later we were driving up outside a low cottage on Main Street, which seemed oddly named given that the part we saw was residential. A woman waited on the walkway that led from the street. Her short-sleeved shirt and cotton capris attested to the fact that she was thoroughly acclimated to Alaska summers. She wore her chin-length brown hair in a blunt cut that framed her face with breezy curls, and blue eyes edged with laugh lines went along with the bright smile she sent our way.

"Charlie and Drake? Welcome to Skagway." She shook hands with Drake, paused a second and pulled me into a hug. I knew I would like her when she caught sight of Freckles and knelt to give the dog a hug too. Our brown and white spaniel/shepherd mix can be a handful, but at a year old she's settling down a bit. She wagged her entire body at Roberta Gengler's attention.

"Everyone here calls me Berta," the landlady said as she pulled out a small key ring. We followed as she unlocked the front door, chatting the entire time.

"It's two-bedroom," she said, "even though you said you only needed one. But I'd appreciate it if you don't take in another renter for that second room, not without checking with me first. You've got use of the whole house. The backyard is fenced for little-bit here." A gentle tickle at Freckles's forehead. "And there's a garage. I can't say what-all junk might be in there but you're welcome to move it around if you need to. I think your vehicle will fit inside if you like. Or just leave it in the driveway. Doesn't matter."

She led the way through the living room—where I noted a stone fireplace, small sofa and two armchairs, and a lonely-looking plain coffee table—into a small kitchen where the white paint seemed to have been freshly done.

"You got your basic furniture, plenty of kitchen utensils, dishes and such. I did tell you about bringing your own linens?"

I nodded. I'd even remembered to label the box. With Drake's auxiliary helicopter gear, I'd been allocated space in the truck for our two suitcases and two boxes for anything and everything else I might need. Considering that I was still somewhat on call with the private investigation firm where

I'm a partner with my brother Ron, my must-haves included a computer and an assortment of necessary business files. It didn't leave much space for household stuff, but then again, I felt sure I could get any absolutely necessary item here in town.

"I live right behind," Berta was saying, pointing out the kitchen window toward a thicket of shrubbery and a dark brown metal roof. "My house faces State Street. You need anything, you can either walk around the block or just duck through that thin spot in the bushes." She jabbed her finger. "Just left of that Sitka mountain-ash tree there's a gate."

I nodded vaguely, completely unclear which tree she meant, hoping we wouldn't have to go dashing for help anytime soon.

She turned with a raised eyebrow and placed the keys in Drake's hand. I took it to mean this was the moment to ask any questions.

"Internet service?"

"Yep. The router's at my place but you'll get a decent signal over here. Password's written on the inside cover of the phone book." She tilted her head toward the refrigerator, where an ancient wall phone hung adjacent and an actual printed telephone directory sat on the counter. "No movies on the computer after seven at night. That's my time and something about both of us trying to watch a movie at once messes up my viewing."

I assured her that wouldn't be a problem as we walked back toward the front door. Drake paused to examine the thermostat on the wall and Berta went over a couple of quick instructions. I was happy to see that we didn't have to rub sticks together or keep a woodstove burning.

Two minutes later she'd disappeared and we found

ourselves alone in our new little Alaskan abode. I stepped over to Drake and wrapped my arms around him. It felt good to be together on solid ground once again.

"Unless you really want to cook tonight," he said, knowing full well that I wouldn't, "how about if we unload the truck, get the dog settled in, and then find someplace that can fill us with food and drink?"

Well, he didn't have to repeat that invitation.

Boxes accumulated in the driveway and we separated the helicopter gear from those that would be going inside. I read labels and directed them to different rooms, the whole process taking less than an hour. It felt like early afternoon but my stomach said 'hungry' and the clock told us it was nearly seven p.m. when we finished. Drake set up the dog crate, where Freckles sleeps at home or away, while I located her food and filled a bowl. One thing about dogs, as long as they know they'll be fed, they can turn nearly anyplace into a home. Her little tummy filled, she accepted my bribe of a treat and went happily into her crate.

Freckles had stretched her legs by zooming around the fenced backyard while Drake and I unloaded the truck, but after a week on the road both of us really needed a stretch, too. We decided to walk until we found dinner. Broadway, the main commercial street through the center of town, was only two blocks over so we began by heading there. It didn't take long to find a lively spot that combined restaurant, bar and music in a long room filled with people who definitely looked more local than tourist.

There was that moment when the noise level dropped and a few dozen eyes turned toward us—the you're-new-in-town syndrome—but it quickly passed. After all, residents here were accustomed to their lives being invaded by a new crop of outsiders each day throughout a season that must begin to feel way too long by autumn.

We found a small table against a dark-paneled wall. The long bar in Zack's Place was made of the same shiny dark wood, lined with a dozen backless stools which were now at a hundred-percent occupancy, occupied predominantly by bearded men in plaid and women with tight jeans and equally tight Henleys. Beer in green bottles with a label I didn't recognize seemed the beverage of choice. Otherwise, the room held an assortment of four- and six-top tables and I noticed conversations freely taking place between them. Aren't small towns great?

"So," I said to Drake, once we'd settled and ordered drinks, "you've met the new boss ... tell me what we'll be doing."

He took a swig of the green-bottled beer he'd decided to try. "Kerby Allen started Gold Trail Adventures to appeal to city dwellers who want to try roughing it a bit and think they'll get rich in the process. When you think about it, not all that different from those intrepid souls who came up here in the 1880s for the original gold rush."

Skagway had been the starting place for the huge stampede into the Yukon. It had quite the colorful history but all I'd heard up to this point was that we would take people out gold prospecting. I'd pictured long troughs of water with a sprinkle of gold dust seeded in, although from the brochures it looked as if those sorts of touristy operations existed without need of a helicopter to take the customers very far from town.

"Kerby owns some cabins up in the mountains, various places, or maybe he's leasing them ... I'm not sure at this point. Anyway, each cabin is furnished and stocked with food and some basic mining tools. We get a GPS programmed with the waypoints, we drop the folks off. One of Kerby's guys meets them, gives a little orientation and shows them how to use their gold pans, then we fly out and leave the customers to fend for themselves for the next week or two. They buy the one-week or the two-week 'adventure' depending on their stamina and budget."

"But isn't it risky to just leave them alone like that?" My plate of halibut and chips had arrived and I had to stop a second to dip one of the crisp potatoes in ketchup.

"They'll be provided with satellite phones, in case of emergency. If they can't handle it, we'll pick them up."

I had a hard time wrapping my head around the idea of being left alone in the land of grizzly bears without something more than a phone for a lifeline, but then again I've sort of turned into a wuss as I've become a little older. My idea of roughing it now is a twelve-inch TV in a motor home. I've seen those reality shows where families struggle along, repairing their ancient tractor or generator with duct tape and paper clips, and there has never been the slightest appeal in that. But it takes all kinds.

Drake was probably reading my mind as all these thoughts flitted through, but he wisely stayed occupied with the fish, which was so tasty that neither of us had the inclination to fill the time with talk. I was nearly finished eating when I looked up to see a woman about my age approaching our table.

"Hi, you guys must be Charlie and Drake. I'm Mina."

I must have had a blank look on my face.

"Berta's my mom." She tucked a strand of straight brown hair behind one ear and held out her hand. She wore little makeup but had a smooth complexion that certainly didn't require it, and I was admiring the quality of her haircut and the golden highlights among the chestnut strands when she spoke up again. "Welcome to Skagway."

We invited her to join us.

"Just for a minute," she said, taking the third chair and setting her phone and a small spiral notebook on the table. "I'm on deadline for a piece on how to make your garbage cans bear-proof." She rolled her eyes. "Wilbur hired me for the 'crime beat' but that's a laugh. The worst crimes around here are drunks peeing in alleys and, once in awhile, somebody speeding down Alaska Street. If a real crime ever happened around here everyone in town would know about it well before the paper came out with the news."

I found myself laughing but was interrupted by Mina's phone.

"Uh-oh, gotta go." She glanced at the readout, did the eye-roll thing again, told us to stay in touch, and breezed out the door.

I turned to Drake. "Maybe we should head back. Freckles has to be wondering what's happened to us."

Chapter 2

We walked out into the evening and I looked at my watch. Nine o'clock and not even beginning to get dark yet. We strolled down a cross street and turned up State Street; I spotted a market, closed at this hour, where I would need to come soon to stock up with food. The long day was catching up with me and yet the light sky made it seem as if I shouldn't be sleepy yet. This would take some adjustment.

"I forgot to bring a book to read," I told Drake. "Something tells me I'll need a bedtime story to put me to sleep."

He wiggled his eyebrows, although he knew good and well that what he had in mind would invigorate me more than make me tired.

"We could take a look in the house and garage," he

suggested. "See if any previous tenants left reading material behind."

I didn't recall seeing any bookshelves in the house. "I suppose we should take a look at the garage anyway. If it's got space, I'm sure your truck would love to park inside at night."

The keys Roberta had given us included a small one that fit the padlock on a rusted hasp that held together double doors on the stand-alone garage. Drake worked it a bit, commenting about buying some WD-40, until he got it open. The doors swung ajar to reveal a decent-sized space. There were shelves along one wall, while the back was crowded with a clutter of gardening tools, a battered wheelbarrow and a lawn mower that didn't look as if it had run since 1953.

"I'm hoping yard work isn't expected of us," Drake said, eyeing the assortment.

"By the layers of dirt and rust on this stuff, it doesn't look like any of it has been used in ages."

"Well, the yard is in good shape, so Berta must have somebody who comes by."

I began perusing the shelves while he pushed the lawn mower aside and estimated whether there would be room for his vehicle. One shelf contained a warped paperboard box with a floral pattern and a flap with a short piece of cord wound around a bead to keep it closed. It was the only thing on the shelf that seemed promising, everything else having to do with killing mice and bugs or consisting of ancient life jackets and other boating gear. I pulled the box down and blew off a thick layer of dust.

The cord crackled as I unwound it but the lid of the box seemed to have protected the contents well. It contained a stack of letters tied with a length of blue satin ribbon, along with a couple of small, bound books. The postmark on the top letter was visible but I couldn't read it in the dim light.

"Look at this," I said, without taking my eyes off the box. "I don't know if it'll be as gripping as a Ludlum novel but it might keep me entertained."

"Charlie, that could be private family stuff that belongs to Roberta."

He was right, although clearly she didn't care enough to keep it at her house. But I should ask her before I delved in too deeply. I *should*.

I tucked the box under my arm while Drake re-secured the doors, commenting that he thought he could move enough of the junk around to get his truck inside. The sun had dipped below the hills and, true to Chuey's prediction, the chill in the air intensified. We scooted inside, and while Drake started a small fire in the fireplace I made the bed in the larger of the two bedrooms. Luckily, I had brought plenty of blankets.

The crackling flames felt good as we curled up together on the little couch, and I soon dozed. About the time we could have thrown on another log, Drake got up to close the fire screen.

"You look tired." Taking my hand, he led me to the bedroom. He was right—this was way past my normal bedtime and it had been a very long day. I snuggled next to him under the covers. The mattress was wonderful and I didn't know another thing until the sun rose—at 2:57 a.m. I groaned and rolled over. We must get some room-darkening curtains right away.

When I awoke the second time it was nearly six and I actually felt refreshed. I brushed my teeth but couldn't find my shampoo, so I pulled on yesterday's clothes and resolved to finish unpacking later this morning.

In the kitchen I rummaged through my small stash of provisions and came up with instant coffee and some sugar packets swiped from various restaurants along the journey. One of the lower cupboards gave me a tea kettle and the water from the tap tasted icy and clean. I filled the kettle and set it on a burner, wondering whether any of the cereal bars remained from our pantry in New Mexico. Sadly, the box contained only one, which I dutifully broke in two to share. A grocery trip would be another must—soon.

Drake appeared at the kitchen door, looking far fresher than I. He'd showered and shaved, and when I showed him the scanty breakfast offering he even offered to take me out again. On top of that, he said he would take Freckles for a walk while I showered. Okay, I'll admit that I needed one desperately. I used his shampoo and even managed to find clean clothes before my sweethearts returned.

Two blocks from our new little home we found a café with the perky name of Tootie's Place, which looked like the spot to be in the mornings. The smells of coffee and bacon wafted out the open door, and most of the tables were full. I spotted Mina at the counter where we were to place orders; she was dressed in layers of outdoor clothing and sturdy boots.

"Hey, Charlie!" She greeted me as if we'd known each other for ages, and turned to introduce me to her companions—Zack, Ross and Marta—all similarly dressed. "We're heading out to do the Icy Lake Trail today. Wanna come along?"

I couldn't admit to her that nothing about an icy lake or a trail sounded all that appealing to me, so I pleaded work and unpacking and such, leaving her with the impression that, otherwise, I would have loved to come.

"They seem nice," Drake said, as we grabbed a table after the others had left the café. "You sure you didn't want to go?"

I caught the gleam in his eye. He knows that my outdoor scenery fix is best done from the seat of a nice, warm helicopter.

"So, we meet with Kerby this morning to get our assignment. I think he said something about today's group being a family of three—mom, dad and a son."

I felt my plan to start nesting begin to fall apart. He recognized the look of dismay.

"We can't keep eating in restaurants every meal," I said, with a tilt of my head toward the prices on the overhead menu. "We'll spend the whole summer working and still not take home any money. A grocery trip is a must, so shall I do it this morning or we can both do it this afternoon?"

He's used to my bottom-line attitude; some of my accounting background is starting to rub off on him. Plus, he feels about shopping the way I feel about hiking to an icy lake.

"Drop me off to report for duty with Kerby, you get things settled at the house. Come back out to the heliport by, say, ten o'clock and we'll be ready."

By the time we finished breakfast, the schedule gave me less than two hours but it wasn't as if I had a long commute to work or anything. Still, it wasn't that I was really needed in order for Drake to fly three people to a cabin in the mountains. I grumbled to myself a little, but realized that this was really a training flight for me. I would be on my own with future flights, and I needed to know the situation.

I dropped Drake off near the FBO building, made as quick a trip through the grocery market as is possible in an unfamiliar store, got home, stared longingly at my suitcase full of rumpled clothing but left it for later.

Once the food was put away, I headed back to the airport, a routine that wasn't unfamiliar to me. I found Drake and another man in a pilot briefing room, standing in front of an aviation sectional map pinned to the wall.

Kerby Allen was about sixty, with salt-and-pepper hair, sideburns a touch long by today's standards, and the kind of sincere brown eyes that meant he was probably really good at selling things. His handshake was warm and his manner professional. Drake had told me Allen had been an Army pilot toward the end of the Vietnam war, which gave him high marks among other pilots. That was no easy assignment, over there. Not to mention that he'd survived a bunch of years flying this rugged Alaskan terrain.

"We want this to be the kind of adventure experience that folks will go home and tell their neighbors about, they'll give glowing reviews on our website, they'll rave it up on Facebook and Twitter," Kerby said as we settled around a conference table near the wall map. "In the old days, men left home and family behind and came up here to look for gold in the Yukon. The desire for riches—that thing they call gold fever—it's powerful and strong. It still is. We haven't lost that yearning for adventure, it's just that today we basically fall into two camps—those who get their 'adventure' from a cruise ship, TV or video game, and those who hire a Sherpa to climb Everest. Short-term fun or a real risk of dying.

"Here at Gold Trail Adventures I want to provide all of the real life experience, but minimal danger. That's why our clients have a way to contact us—the satellite phones—but they'll be living out at our cabins without electricity or Internet. It's a great way for families to bond. Plus, there's the very real chance for them to actually discover and take home some gold. Each of the properties has a running stream for panning, and several of them have nearby caves or mineshafts to explore. My men have shored up the old mines and we've blocked off tributaries and secondary tunnels where someone could get into trouble. We don't tell them, but we've seeded the sites with enough real gold to get them started. Then they get excited and have a blast just getting in there and going for it."

I got the feeling some of this came straight from the sales brochure.

"Last summer the gold adventure was so successful that I was flying almost non-stop. It's why I decided to add a second ship, yours, this year."

The fact that he had two helicopters working was reassuring. One of us would be backup for the other, in the event of mechanical problems or simply needing some time off. I still wasn't sure that a seven-day-a-week, four-month contract wouldn't wear our butts out completely.

"So," Kerby said. "Here are your coordinates for the first flight, and the family should be arriving soon. Barney's your contact this time, already waiting up at the cabin. He'll do the orientation with the clients and then you'll fly him back here."

It all sounded so very organized; of course, assuming that nothing can go wrong is usually the precursor for exactly that.

Drake and I walked out to the flight line. He had started the pre-flight inspection on our ship, so we completed the few remaining tasks and were just considering a cup of hot chocolate when a car pulled to a stop at the FBO's front door.

Out stepped a family of three, all dressed in Gorsuch or some other upscale clothier's idea of what gold-panners in Alaska would wear. Clearly, none of them had ever donned a pair of pac boots in their lives. I watched in amazement as they pulled three gargantuan duffles from the back of the vehicle. All of this gear would have to be weighed; an aircraft, any aircraft, can only hold so much and a helicopter is especially sensitive to the restrictions. We cannot manage the monster luggage airlines allow.

Luckily, Kerby Allen was there to meet them at the door and he introduced us. I caught the surname—Mikowski—but the rest went by in a blur. Kerby eyed the heavy luggage and instructed the passengers to bring their things inside. As each bag went on the scale, I was surprised to see that only one was overweight. A laptop computer had to be pulled out. Joe Mikowski grumbled, but Kerby explained that there would be no Internet service at their cabin and he might as well leave the device locked away safely at the office. The wife gave her husband a look and opened her son's bag, where she found some kind of video game. She added that to the computer that was staying behind.

"But, Mom ..." the boy whined.

"Chandler, we all agreed. We're doing this adventure to spend time together, not to go off in our separate corners and play with electronics." Her eyes were on her husband as she said it.

I was doing my best to think ahead to the flight itself. Drake would be at the controls for this one, but soon I would be taking other groups out on my own. Those mountains were steep, rugged, and topped with snow. I couldn't let my attention waver.

Drake and Kerby stowed the passengers' bags, alongside our own survival gear. I'd already received the reminder about how something as simple as a faulty fuel pump could result in having to spend a night out on a mountainside until help could come. And that was the best-case scenario. A crash landing didn't even bear thinking about.

In ten minutes the bags were secure in the cargo compartment and the Mikowski family was belted into the three back seats of the JetRanger. Drake and I were up front and I watched carefully as he programmed coordinates for the destination cabin into the GPS. That done, he gave a quick safety briefing over the intercom headsets—simple things like don't open the doors while the aircraft is in flight. I pictured the look on Junior Mikowski's face as his mother had taken his video game away and thought the reminder was well timed. The father seemed pretty subdued, considering he was heading out on the adventure of a lifetime, for which I was sure they had paid big bucks.

A few last checklist items and Drake pulled pitch and we rose above the airstrip, the other helicopters and planes growing smaller as we gained altitude. I watched as he made course adjustments, tracking the headings shown on the GPS. He flipped an intercom switch so that only I would hear his voice.

"We're only about ten minutes from the cabin if we fly a straight line but we're supposed to give a little bit of a tour too. The extra waypoints I programmed will take us over a glacier and a long waterfall, and after we've circled those we'll come around."

I couldn't complain—there must not be one ugly thing

in this whole state, I decided as we spent thirty minutes flying what amounted to a large circle, with snowy peaks lined up in ranks as far into the distance as we could see. I had the sectional map on my lap, following along, and I spotted the trail where Mina and her friends were even now hiking to their lunch-spot destination. Soon, with Mount Clifford as a landmark, Drake sighted the cabin and began making a descent into a tiny green valley. Amazing how fast you can cover territory by air; reaching this cabin by trails from town probably would have taken hours.

Brilliant green grass showed in contrast to the mountains that rose all around us. A narrow stream ran out of the hills, flowing toward the larger river we'd flown over, joining with it to eventually reach the sea behind us. A man in dark pants and red plaid jacket stepped into sight and began waving. His thick beard and the fur-lined trapper hat gave him a real mountain-man appearance. He pointed toward some orange cones set up on the ground, our landing zone, and Drake positioned the JetRanger into the wind and set her gently down precisely in the middle of the demarcated area.

The red-coated man approached as Drake let the rotor blades spool down, introducing himself as Barney, the Gold Trail Adventures event coordinator.

"I'll be about twenty, thirty minutes giving the orientation," he told Drake through the pilot-side open door. "You and your wife can get out and walk around with us, if you want, or just wait here. Kerby did tell you I'll be flying back with you?"

He asked the question as if the idea of staying behind with the Mikowskis was scarier than dealing with a grizzly.

Drake nodded and we climbed out. It took a few

minutes to get everyone out of their seatbelts and to unload their gear.

"The cabin is fully stocked with food, fuel and plenty of warm bedding," Barney was saying to the husband and wife. Young Chandler had immediately zipped away to the stream and was on his knees, dipping an arm into water that had to be only a degree or two warmer than an ice cube.

Barney picked up two of the duffle bags and I grabbed the third, curious to see what the 'adventure' living conditions would be like.

The cabin looked surprisingly comfortable. A main room held a modern woodstove with a handy stack of split logs nearby. The chairs and couch looked like the nice, soft kind you'd want to sink into and a full bookcase solidified the idea that I could be one happy camper here. A small kitchen filled one end of the room, and Barney was giving Mrs. Mikowski a quick primer on the use of the propane stove and refrigerator.

He waved in the direction of the two bedrooms, then led everyone to a sort of service porch-slash-storage room.

"Put your garbage in this sealed metal bin," he said with a firm look on his face, "and never, never leave any food outside around the cabin. Not a cooler, not a half-eaten sandwich, not a candy bar. Once the bears smell anything edible, you'll have 'em prowling around and they can take that front screen door off with one paw."

I might have imagined that both Mikowskis went a little pale. The missus glanced out toward the stream to be sure Chandler was still in sight.

"Now here's your satellite phone," Barney was saying. "We fully charged it at the office but you got no way to recharge it out here. It's for emergencies *only*. The numbers are right here on this label on the back. If you get on it and start gabbing away, you'll run it down and then you'll have no way to reach us. You know, for when that bear shows up."

Mrs. Mikowski reached for the phone and tucked it under her arm. I wondered at the wisdom of mentioning the bears again, but maybe Barney's experience showed that people don't follow instructions unless you give them a scary reason to.

He went through a little Q&A with the guests, reassuring them that everything they needed was right here, pointing out the supplies and how to light the woodstove. Neither of the adults seemed to have much clue and I wondered how soon before they would decide they'd had enough adventure and be calling for their ride home.

As it turned out, that happened a lot sooner than even I could have guessed. By eight a.m. on day two, Kerby Allen was calling Drake's cell phone, interrupting what would have been our first great sex in the state of Alaska.

"That family of three that you delivered to Cabin One?" he said. "They'll need a ride back. Oh, and you'll be taking the police chief up there with you. Looks like they've found a dead body."

Chapter 3

Every thought in the world went through my head. Did Kerby say they'd found a dead body? Or was one of our intrepid adventurers now deceased? I was pretty sure he said *found*. I held onto that thought while I threw on some clothes and brushed my teeth. I couldn't stand to think of someone we'd delivered to that remote spot, now mangled by a bear, drowned in the creek, or whatever else might befall a city slicker in the wilderness. Was this such a great idea after all?

But by the time we arrived at the heliport, Drake had talked reason to me. Surely Kerby would have sounded a lot more stricken if he'd just lost a client, not to mention the negative publicity this would cause. And he *had* said the family would need a ride back. I took a deep breath as we walked into the office.

A uniformed policeman approached—tall, clean-shaven, gray-haired, going a little soft around the middle.

"Drake Langston? I'm Chief Sam Branson." He held out a hand, and Drake introduced me, throwing in the fact that I'm a partner in a private investigation firm back home. Sometimes that gets a little uncomfortable; law enforcement types don't usually want anyone else mucking about in their cases. But Branson only gave a nod.

"Kerby already took off," Branson said. "We should get there as soon as we can. Before anything gets moved."

Drake was already leading the way to the JetRanger, so I tagged along and helped Chief Branson into the front seat, untangling the shoulder harnesses for him before climbing in and buckling myself into the back. Drake finished a quick pre-flight inspection and joined us. As he'd told me the previous day, flying directly there we sighted the cabin within ten minutes.

Kerby Allen's own red and white A-Star sat on the ground, rotors unmoving, and a few people milled about. As we set down, I was surprised to see that one of them was Mina Gengler. I approached her and saw that she was scribbling furiously on a notepad.

"Hey, Charlie! Didn't know you'd be here," she said. "How about this thing? Most exciting story of the year. Probably the decade! I can't think of the last time someone found a skeleton around here. Well, one *not* inside a crashed airplane."

My expression probably went blank as I processed all that. How often *did* they find skeletons inside old plane crashes, I wondered. But that, of course, wasn't the real story today.

My attention was drawn to a hubbub on the front porch

of the cabin, where Rhonda Mikowski was fluttering about and jabbering like her Chatty Cathy string had become jammed.

"I can't handle this," she exclaimed, for probably the twelfth time as I walked toward the porch. "Chandler, poor baby. He's going to need counseling. We need to get professional help. Now. I just have to get us home—I don't know how we'll ever get over this."

Chandler, meanwhile, in his inimitable ten-year-old way, was equally wound up. "It was *so* cool!" he said to Chief Branson. "It was, like, all these bones and a skull and everything. And it's laying there on the ground like this."

He threw himself to the grass, taking a position on his side, making his arms and legs look stiff and adopting a fierce toothy grimace.

Chandler jumped back up. "When I get home I'm gonna post it on Facebook. My friends are gonna be *so* jealous! I *knew* Alaska would be cool."

Personally, I didn't think the kid looked traumatized at all. He was on his way to fame and fortune at home because of his find. But then, being childless myself, what do I know?

Sam Branson knelt near the boy. "Can you show me where you found it?"

"Oh, sure. It's up in that cave." The kid pointed vaguely up a hill behind the cabin. "I got up this morning and went exploring."

Kerby had said that all caves and mines had been checked for stability and dangerous areas blocked, but surely his crew didn't know this one existed or they would have found the skeleton themselves. I may have just spotted the first chink in the armor of his sales presentation. And if Rhonda Mikowski needed to panic about something in today's events, maybe it should be more along the lines of the fact that her son had wandered into a cave at six o'clock in the morning, unsupervised. But I kept my mouth shut and just followed along as Chandler led the police chief through thick bushes up the steep mountainside. Mina hustled to catch up, and Rhonda Mikowski finally had to shut up as the altitude became too much for her to breathe and talk at the same time.

The entrance to the cave was obscured by leafy undergrowth—it would never be spotted from the air—but once the boy pointed it out, we discovered an opening, low but wide enough for an adult to easily walk through, bent at the waist. And once inside, the ceiling rose to where three adults could all stand up.

"There it is," Chandler said, pointing as proudly as a cat who'd laid a dead mouse on the doorstep. "Just like I found him."

"Thanks, son. You did the right thing, telling your dad and having him call me," said Chief Branson.

Mina snapped a couple of pictures before Sam gave her a look. "I'll be keeping those for my files, for the time being," he said.

She sent him a frown.

"Chandler, why don't you go on outside with your mom," Sam Branson said gently.

I put an arm around the boy's shoulders and guided him back toward the daylight. Once his mother had taken charge, fussing over him and insisting he go back to the cabin to lie down, I scooted back into the cave to see what the chief and Mina were doing.

By flashlight, Branson was studying the bones. It was

gruesome in a distant sort of way, but I could handle it as long as I didn't dwell on the reality. Better, for now, to keep it in the perspective that this was just like watching a show on the Discovery Channel.

The bones had darkened to a brownish-tan. Clothing covered most of it except the skull, hands and part of the forearms. The bell-bottom pants and boldly patterned shirt—even with a thick layer of dust—made me think of the fashions of the 1970s, garish and somewhat gender neutral. Could the person have been here that many decades?

Chief Branson had asked Mina to take some notes, cautioning her that they were for his official use and not to be repeated in the newspaper. From what he was saying, my observations were validated.

"Poor sucker probably got off the hiking trail that runs along the top of this ridge," he said. "Maybe it was getting dark and cold, he came in here for shelter. Could have starved to death."

"Was that cabin here years ago?" I asked. "You'd think he would have gone there, rather than into a cave."

"Nah. That place was built only about five years ago. Kerby's leasing it from the owner for the summer. I don't think there's another dwelling for miles in any direction out here." He stood up and brushed dirt off the knees of his uniform. "Well, let's get this done. Ladies?"

It was his polite way of escorting us out. When we got back to the cabin, Drake had already gathered the Mikowski family and their belongings into our helicopter and was lifting off.

"He's bringing Jerry back with him," Kerby said as Sam, Mina and I approached the cabin. He turned to the chief. "Look, I better get to my office and make sure I pacify those folks. Doubt I can talk them into taking one of the other cabins, so I'm probably gonna have to refund their money." He looked none too happy about that. "You'll be okay here until Drake and Jerry get here with a body bag?"

Branson nodded. "I might ought to go back up there and shine the light around, see if there's any other evidence that goes along with our John Doe. Then I suppose that's my first order of business—find out who the guy was and notify someone."

Kerby gave a little gesture toward us, indicating that he would give Mina and me a ride back to the airport. When we got there, he rushed off to speak to the Mikowskis, who were enviously eyeing the cruise ships at their nearby docks, and I saw that Drake was about to lift off again with a uniformed officer in the front passenger seat.

A little at loose ends all at once, I looked around. Mina had trailed Kerby into the office, hanging to one side but clearly listening to his conversation, gleaning tidbits to flesh out her news story. I didn't believe for a minute that this wouldn't end up on the front page of Thursday's edition.

I supposed that Kerby might have another assignment for me. I could, after all, fly his ship to one of the other cabin sites if anyone needed pickup or delivery. I probably shouldn't leave until I knew for sure, so I walked into the employee break room where we'd been told we could get coffee anytime or buy snacks from the vending machines.

"So, I heard that you're a private investigator," Mina said, coming up behind me, startling me into sloshing coffee onto the countertop that already enjoyed a sprinkling of sugar and a few other spills.

"Uh, not really," I said, going on to explain that I'm the financial partner in the business; my brother Ron is really the PI. "Once in awhile I get in the middle of things, but it's not usually my idea."

"But you've been to crime scenes before, right?"

Suddenly I could see where this was going, and although I liked Mina and wouldn't mind becoming friends, I really didn't want my name in the local paper my second day in town. I stalled by taking a sip of coffee.

"Ugh, this stuff is awful," I said. "How about we find something that doesn't stand up by itself? I bet you know who has the best coffee in town."

Either Mina also wanted a friendship, or she knew the only way to get me to confide was to chum up. I chose to believe that the smile she sent my way was genuine. I dumped the bitter brew down the drain, tossed the foam cup in a trash can and we walked out.

"Mina?" Kerby Allen was alone in his office and signaled to my reporter buddy. "Can we talk a minute?"

I detoured right along with her.

"Listen, Mina, I know this is a big story for you, and Wilbur's going to be wetting his pants to run it ..." Kerby shifted in his seat.

"But you don't want me to embarrass you or the mayor," Mina said, her chin jutting out just a little defiantly.

"Well ... yeah." He dropped his normal salesman smile. "All I'm asking is that you don't name the location or say that my company is involved."

"Because all the locals won't book trips with you? Come on, Kerby, it's the tourists you're after anyway."

"Yes, but you never know where that kind of information goes. These days, with the Internet—"

"Plus," Mina taunted, "it's an election year and your wife likes her job. A dead body associated with your business just brings this all a little too close to home, doesn't it?"

He visibly squirmed.

"Come on, Charlie, let's go." Mina was really enjoying his discomfort.

I held up my index finger. "Kerby? You don't have another flight for me, do you?"

He shook his head.

"You can call me if you get one, you know." I had to be careful not to be seen as taking sides. For all I knew helicopter pilots were plentiful here, and Drake and I could be fired on a whim. On the other hand, I somewhat doubted that. We'd been brought all the way from New Mexico for a reason, and it had to be that Kerby Allen didn't have anyone else lined up to work for him—for whatever reason.

Standing out on the apron, I watched the other tour operator's machines take off and land. From brochures, I'd gathered that one company held contracts with all the cruise lines and had a steady business taking their passengers on a variety of excursions up to the nearby glaciers, a dog-sled camp and to view the coastline. Perhaps Kerby Allen had come in as competition and when he couldn't break into their market had devised the idea of the gold-search adventure packages. And maybe he'd pissed off somebody important in the process.

The sun warmed the pavement so Mina and I decided to walk down to a coffee house she liked.

"Let's cut over on Fourth," she suggested. "If you read any of the Gold Rush history you'll find that a lot of the streets went by different names back then. Fourth used to be Bond, Sixth was once called Holly. Broadway has always been the same and these days it's usually jammed with visitors."

Sure enough, a block over I could see that about a million tourists had come off three cruise ships, which sat at the docks this morning. People were walking along like ants pouring out of an anthill, most not finding their way past the jewelry and souvenir shops.

"We love it when they come," Mina said. "We love it more when they leave."

I remember a friend who lived in one of New Mexico's popular tourism areas saying the same thing. One town even had bumper stickers made: *Welcome to Chimayo! Spend Your Money. Go Home.* It really changed the dynamic of a town when the population quadrupled or more in the course of a day. Ordinary activities such as having lunch often became monumental tasks.

"The seasonal workers are another story. At least you're here buying food and paying rent and integrating with us a bit. Aside from tour businesses like the railroad and a few locally owned gift shops, most of the cash from the day-visitors stays in the hands of the cruise lines. At least we get some hefty docking fees and a whole lot of taxes out of the deal."

We had reached the coffee house and although the place was packed Mina assured me the offerings here were fabulous. I pulled off my jacket in the warm room and draped it over the back of my chair at a little corner table for two.

"I was curious about that—your conversation back there with Kerby. I got the impression he wasn't exactly in your good graces."

She waved it off. "It's not Kerby I dislike, and it's one of those things that's hard to explain. His wife and my mother go way back. Mom and Lillian both grew up in Skagway, and now Lillian is mayor of the borough. It's an old feud and not worth mentioning, but there's been a lifetime of little digs and insults. This morning it was all about having a little fun because, for once, I'm the one with something to hold over them."

I supposed Lillian Allen couldn't be completely unpopular if she'd been elected mayor so it must be a personal thing, as Mina said. At least the topic had turned away from her earlier questions about my private investigation connections, and the latte that arrived a few minutes later was absolutely every bit as great as she'd promised.

The coffee house teamed with activity as people in T-shirts breezed in and grabbed something to drink, gulped it down and left—in a hurry to rush through that vacation without actually savoring it. No one seemed to mind that we held onto our table for close to two hours, chatting about all those subjects people cover when getting to know each other. We'd graduated high school the same year and finished college at the same time—me at UNM in Albuquerque, Mina heading to the lower forty-eight to experience school in San Francisco but beating a path back to her quiet hometown after graduation. She'd lost her dad in a fishing boat accident only a year after both of my parents had died in a plane crash. It was no wonder Mina and her mom were so close.

"I just like the pace here so much better," she said. A glance at the clock on the wall. "But, speaking of pace ... even in a small town editors like you to check in and show some signs of work. I guess I better get back and write up this story."

"Will you name Kerby's company in the article?" I asked

as I picked up my shoulder bag and jacket.

"I doubt it." She delivered that line with enough of a smile that I knew she'd considered it. I also had the feeling that a spiteful move wasn't really part of her personality.

Outside, a few clouds had begun to build with a single puffy one obscuring the sun just enough to throw a fresh chill into the air. I slipped my jacket on, noticing that most everyone else had done the same. Mina pointed out the newspaper office, which was just across the street.

"Stop in anytime," she said. "I'm always up for a coffee break." She crossed the street and disappeared inside the wood-sided building with its Old West façade.

I looked both ways, getting my bearings. I was nearly as close to home as to the airport. Unless my cell phone should ring, I seemed to be free as a bird at the moment. I could go back to the airport and see what Drake was up to, but odds were that I would end up hanging around listening to the always-present round of stories that happened anytime you put two or more pilots into the same room. Or, I could head for the house and finish unpacking and settling in. Plus, I felt sure the dog would love a break by now. She might even convince me to take a long walk with her this afternoon.

As it turned out, on my own I went into a little frenzy of efficiency. I located the stacked washer-dryer in a utility closet and did two loads of laundry—somehow during the week on the road we'd managed to go through half the clothes we'd brought. I organized kitchen cabinets to my liking and put away the food I'd bought, and even planned a casserole for dinner. After a call from Drake saying that he was taking another flight, I clipped Freckles's leash to her collar and we marched our way the entire length of Skagway—and back.

With clean laundry stacked neatly in the dresser drawers and the casserole ready to go into the oven, I settled onto the sofa and picked up the box of letters I'd found in the garage.

The pasteboard box was designed with a hinged lid that opened like the cover of a book. Once I had released the short length of silk cord that held it closed, it swung open with a creak of the old paper covering to reveal a compartment about four inches deep. I had brushed off the layer of dust with a tissue; now I wondered whether I'd found a treasure trove or merely aggravated my lungs with who knows what types of grime and mold.

Inside were neat stacks of letters tied in bundles with white satin ribbon, somewhat yellowed with age. I picked up one of them and saw a small, bound book beneath. The top envelope was addressed to Mrs. Maddie Farmer in San Francisco, California, in beautiful script of the sort that hadn't been taught in school in a long, long time. The postmark was dated October 14, 1898. I slipped the envelope from its ribbon binding without untying the bow; somehow it felt less like prying.

The paper inside was thin and crackly, some type of onionskin, I supposed, although I hadn't seen anything like it since poking around in my ninety-year-old neighbor's house as a child. I began to read.

My Dearest Wife,

I hope this letter finds you well and our little Isabelle happy and healthy. I have good news ...

I scanned downward. The letter was signed *Your Loving Husband, Joshua.* A glance back at the packet showed that the next letter was dated October 1, and each successive envelope went a little further back in time. Mrs. Farmer evidently added each new letter to the top of the stack as it arrived. I made the quick decision to read them in the order they were written, so I slipped this one back into the envelope and put it into the ribbon binding. This was, after all, a story and I'm not one to skip ahead and spoil the ending.

May 12, 1898.

My Dearest Wife,

Arrival in Skagway, Alaska, at last! The sea voyage felt far too long and I am already lonesome for you and our dear daughter. But, oh, the excitement here in Alaska. Men are returning from the Klondike with incredible tales, and the newspapers are filled with stories of the fortunes to be made ...

Chapter 4

Joshua Farmer pulled the lapels of his jacket together across his chest. San Francisco could be chilly, even in summer, but the breeze off Taiya Inlet as it swept over the ice-covered mountaintops went straight through his clothing. He owned a warmer coat. Why hadn't he put it on when he set out for the post office this morning? It seemed so important to get his letter off to Maddie, to reassure her that he had arrived safely, and the morning sky was clear for the first time since the steamer docked three days ago. He simply must adapt to this new way of life, to the realization that his every move must be carefully thought out because, here, the weather meant life and death. He looked ahead, down the row of hastily constructed wooden buildings, at the long line of men standing in the muddy road where the queue formed for service at Skagway's tiny, one-room post office, and he patted the pocket of his jacket to reassure himself the letter was still there. Once she heard from him, Maddie would write back, and he knew the connection would sustain him through anything.

"Just got here, eh?" said a voice behind him. "Eager to join the Gold Rush stampede, I suppose?"

Joshua turned. The man wore a thick hide coat and a cap with flaps over his ears, making Joshua aware that his own bowler hat and woolen jacket were entirely inadequate. A full beard would probably be warmer than the fashionable handlebar mustache worn by virtually every man in the city these days. He could adapt to that; shaving had always been a chore anyway. The man's bright eyes were waiting for an answer.

"Oh. Yes, I came in on the *Portland,* Monday. Joshua Farmer."

"I'm Harry Weaver. Pleased to meet you." They shook hands. "Got your kit organized yet?"

Joshua had seen the enormous list of equipment required before he could start the trek along the Chilkoot Trail into the Klondike. Over a thousand pounds of clothing, food and gear for each man. He had a dozen questions about how one would physically manage such a load, but at this moment it seemed more prudent to act as if he had already figured that out. He nodded.

"Have you been there and returned?" he asked Harry.

"Partway," the man said, enigmatically.

Before Joshua could inquire further, a disturbance erupted near the head of the line. Oaths flew, fists were raised.

"Happens every time the mail comes in," Harry said. "They don't have enough help in there, so they'll sort part of it, hand it out, close up to sort some more. We could be out here three or four hours."

Joshua had never heard of such an inefficient system and his surprise must have showed.

"They hire four men but pay only enough for one. No one stays long and it's a thankless job because the patrons are always angry over something."

Such as being locked out in the cold while the mail was sorted. He sighed, debating whether to ask Harry to save his spot in line while he went back to the rooming house for his warmer coat. He again touched the pocket with the letter.

His companion must have sensed Joshua's discomfort. "If you have the money for your stamp, I'd be happy to mail that letter for you when I get inside."

Joshua felt his brows rise.

"Just figured. You been here four days, you want to get word back home to somebody. You won't have mail waiting for you, like the rest of these fellows because there's been no time for her letter to reach Skagway."

Joshua smiled. "You know what, Harry? You could be a detective."

The man smiled and Joshua instantly trusted him. He pulled out the letter to Maddie and placed it, along with two pennies, into Harry's hand.

"Thank you so much, sir." He tipped his hat. "I'm sure I will be seeing you around."

Joshua took a shortcut through a field behind a large building, where even at nine in the morning rowdy music from a piano could be heard through the walls. Dirty snow, melted now to clumps of ice, lay in sad piles on the north sides of nearly every structure. He wondered at what point the days would warm enough to melt the last of it.

A woman emerged from the doorway of a tiny shack that had been appended to the back of the dance hall. Strands of yellow hair fell from the knot at the top of her head and the strap of her cotton chemise had slid off one shoulder. She started to hike it back into place but when she spotted Joshua she sent him a coy smile and left the strap hanging.

He stared at the ground and quickened his pace. Bachelors, and probably some of the married men who'd been in the gold fields a long time, undoubtedly visited these women in their cribs but Joshua was determined to get quickly to the Klondike, make his fortune, and send for Maddie and Isabelle as soon as possible. He would not have them living at her parents' home forever.

Mrs. McIlhaney's house with its sign, Rooms For Rent, appeared on the next block and Joshua hurried inside. In the parlor, the early morning fire in the woodstove was dying. Mrs. McIlhaney had been one of the first women to join her husband (God rest his soul) here in Skagway, and she was probably in the kitchen starting dinner preparations as she schooled her two children in reading and writing at the kitchen table. She'd bragged to him when he rented the room that theirs was one of the early families to arrive after the initial influx of men, a bit less than two years ago. She recalled that Skagway had consisted of Captain William Moore's log house, a couple of other wooden buildings, and a few hundred tents when she disembarked. Now there were close to ten thousand people, mostly men; virtually all of them were on their way up the White Pass Trail, or they would be as the snow melted and the summer days grew long. Including Joshua himself.

He stood in front of the woodstove, stretching his

hands toward it, nearly touching the black iron surface in an effort to draw any warmth he could manage. When his fingers would flex again he climbed the stairs to the tiny room he'd rented in the attic, a place he was thankful to have although he couldn't fully stand up except in the very center of the room and his neck got a severe crick in it if he walked around in there for more than a few minutes. On the plus side, most of the heat from the ground floor came up here; despite the uninsulated walls and spaces where daylight showed, at least the sleeping quarters were tolerable. Besides, he would soon be on the trail.

He sat on his bed and picked up the paper he'd been given aboard the steamship, the list of supplies. Too bad he hadn't checked this before he left San Francisco, where the prices would have been so much lower. He'd assumed that outfitters here would be compassionate toward their fellow stampeders and that there would be ample stock of anything a potential gold miner would want. He was only now learning the sad truth. He stared at the neatly typed list, which had been compiled as the bare minimum for two men:

4 barrels best flour, at $6..$24.00
200 pounds granulated sugar, at 6 cents...............................12.00
200 pounds navy beans, at 4 cents...8.00
100 pounds of cornmeal..2.75
250 pounds of breakfast bacon, at 12.5 cents......................31.25
3 boxes yeast, 25 cents; one-half tin of matches 0.75

That was only the beginning. Then came the items such as candles, a Yukon stove, and of course he must have mining tools. He scanned down the list: dried onions and potatoes, rope, clothing. Nails, pitch and wood to build a boat—he'd had no idea. Files, a coffee pot, shoe thread, twenty-four pounds of raisins, blankets, an ax, rubber hip boots, mosquito netting, goggles and snow glasses, buckets, pans, a tent, and of course a revolver and a rifle, each with its necessary ammunition. The list went on and on, a vast array of items for travel and survival.

It amounted to nearly four-hundred dollars! Even at half that amount, assuming one man would pass the inspection at the Canadian border with half the goods, it was more money than he'd ever seen in one place. He began scratching off items. Surely he could get by without dried fruit—he didn't care for it that much anyway—and he didn't need the "best" coffee. There must be something less expensive that he could get hold of. On the other hand, where two men might share the cost of the guns, one man couldn't very well take half a rifle.

He checked off the items he already owned—primarily clothing—and he had already purchased a gold pan from a fellow at the docks in Seattle. Huh—the one item shown on the list at a lesser price than he had paid. A wave of disillusionment threatened, but he shoved it back. He pulled a small pouch from inside his undershirt, dumped the money out on the coverlet and began counting.

Chapter 5

Drake's footsteps caused the wooden porch of our little abode to vibrate and I realized with a start that it was after five o'clock. I set the box of letters aside and dashed to the kitchen to put the casserole into the oven.

"Kerby's got his hands full," Drake said as he poured glasses of wine for both of us. "Rhonda Mikowski threw such a fit—screaming 'lawyer' and 'trauma'—that he ended up having to book a cruise cabin for them, but it was that or reimburse all their money and pay extra for rescheduling their flight home."

"Maybe the cruise will be just the therapy little Chandler needs," I said, unable to keep the mocking tone out of my voice.

He opened a bag of chips and gave one of his what-will-I-do-with-you smiles. I set the timer on the oven and we settled on the sofa while dinner baked.

"So, meanwhile, he's got two flights lined up for me tomorrow. One is to take Chief Branson and a couple of forensic people back to Cabin One so they can poke around in the cave. Unless you'd like to take that one? You know the way, and it would be some additional mountain flight time for you."

Not to mention my insatiable curiosity whenever there's something mysterious to puzzle over. I told him I'd love to do it.

I woke up at 4:37 the next morning, partly because we still hadn't done anything to darken our windows and partly because I couldn't help feeling anticipation over talking to the police chief about that skeleton from the cave. I slipped my clothes on and brushed my teeth as quietly as possible, letting Drake take advantage of the fact that he can actually sleep with a blanket pulled over his head.

Tiptoeing out to the kitchen, I started coffee and it began to brew while I let Freckles out of her crate and turned her loose in the backyard. We really should try to get a long walk done before I had to go off to helicopter work. She raced around the perimeter, nose to the ground, already claiming the property as her own in traditional dog fashion. Within two minutes she was back at the door, tail waving and ears perked in anticipation of breakfast. It doesn't take a whole lot to keep a dog happy.

I poured my coffee and stood at the window, watching the clouds, feeling a moment's trepidation about flying across mountains so vast that a small aircraft is nothing but a speck against the firmament. But wasn't that what we did all the time? The sky was no more infinite here than anywhere. I let out a calming breath, causing the coffee-steam to ripple in tendrils across the surface of the mug in my hand. Everything would be fine. I clipped the leash on Freckles just to prove it and we set off down Main Street.

There's something about being awake early and having full daylight. People were out in their gardens, where flowers were already beginning to bloom even though the days still felt pretty chilly to me. Someone had said that the short growing season was offset by the long hours of daylight, providing just the right conditions for bumper crops of vegetables that made our own desert-climate offerings look puny in comparison. Freckles pulled me along, stopping to touch noses with every other dog we encountered.

By the time we circled a few blocks and walked back into the house I could hear signs of life from the bedroom. I mixed pancake batter and put a few slices of bacon into a skillet.

"Wow, look at you, Miss Domesticity," Drake teased as he walked into the kitchen and planted a kiss on my forehead. "And it's not even six o'clock yet."

"I know, can you believe this?" While I'm a fairly early riser at home, I can't say that once *ever* have I been flipping pancakes at this hour.

He poured coffee for himself and set silverware and plates on the kitchen table. I put the platter in the middle and we got busy with the whole butter-and-syrup routine.

"So, any words of wisdom for my flight today?" I asked, once we'd satisfied our initial hunger.

"Trust your instruments."

He had told me this before, during my training and on occasions when weather was a factor. But I didn't mind that he repeated it now. More pilots get in trouble by not believing what those gauges say, thinking they are somewhere they aren't.

"And, wear your lucky socks." One corner of his mouth edged upward. It was an inside joke with us.

On a job in Scotland a couple years ago I'd had a very close encounter with the North Sea; later, as I was wringing salt water out of my clothes I told him I had known I would be fine—I was wearing my lucky socks. Since then, I've never gone on an out-of-town job without them. Now, I pulled up the leg of my jeans to show him that I did, indeed, have them on, even though they were becoming a bit threadbare by now. I should add a heavier pair over them before heading out this morning.

By nine o'clock I was standing beside the aircraft, eyeing a bank of clouds that hovered at the mountaintops, when Chief Branson and two others in uniform parked and walked toward me. I recognized one of them as Jerry, the officer who'd been on the call yesterday. Branson looked fairly chipper but the third guy barely grumbled a greeting. Definitely not a morning person.

"I'm just going to finalize the flight plan," I told him, "and then we're ready."

I watched the clouds again as I walked toward the FBO's office where Drake was getting the weather report for me. Instruments are great, but a GPS is only going to put you on the right path; it's not going to improve your visibility. All I had to do was pay attention to the elevations of all these peaks and be sure I cleared them with plenty of room.

Drake handed me the printed forecast and winds aloft report. "It's not a storm system," he said. "Just some localized clouds. You should be able to fly around it."

I gave him my bravest smile.

"I'll be out with Kerby, taking a group to Cabin Two and delivering more food to some folks at Cabin Three. Thought it would be a good chance for me to get the bigger picture. We should be back by noon and we'll be on frequency 123.02 while we're in flight. You've got a spare satellite phone in the cargo compartment, there's the ELT ..."

"Honey, it's fine. It's a very short hop." Sheesh—*surely* I wouldn't be needing the emergency locator.

Across the parking area a van had rolled to a stop and three bearded men emerged. Decked out in full mountain-man regalia they looked like extras from some reality TV show. One of them actually snapped his suspenders. A colorful group for Cabin Two, no doubt.

"I'll be fine," I told Drake. "You be careful too."

Chief Branson and his forensic team had buckled themselves into their seats, so I went around and rechecked that their doors were secure before I climbed into my own seat and put on my headset. While I went through the start-up and the turbine engine came up to speed, I gave the standard safety briefing although I doubted any of them would attempt to take pictures outside the windows, fiddle with the door latches, or get out of the helicopter until I'd told them it was all right.

The flight path to Cabin One was already programmed into our GPS; I gave my surroundings one final check, radioed the office to open my flight plan and lifted the collective.

Drake was right about the weather. Once airborne, I could see that the imposing cloud bank was really only a layer that didn't extend beyond the inlet. I found a ragged-looking spot and flew through, coming into clear air on the upwind side of the ridge. The creek was easily visible and in only a few minutes the cabin came into sight. Piece of cake.

I set the aircraft lightly on the grass outside the cabin, in nearly the same spot we'd occupied yesterday, shut down the engine and waited as the rotor blades spun down. Chief Branson waited for my signal before exiting the helicopter, then he guided his men toward the hillside where the cave awaited their scrutiny. They carried flashlights and kits that looked like toolboxes full of vials and baggies and other assorted mysterious things.

I pulled on the rotor brake, flipped the last few switches and unbuckled my harness. Outside, it was incredibly quiet. I breathed air so pure it sent a wave of energy into my lungs. With no idea how long the police would be here, I realized I should have brought along a book. But then, I hadn't purchased one yet. Drat. I could have brought that old box of letters; the reading was proving to be fairly interesting. For the moment I jogged toward the cabin, following the now-trampled path to the cave behind it.

Branson was standing at the opening, where he'd strung yellow tape the previous day, a gesture that seemed pretty silly out here, but I suppose you just never know who might come along. As I approached, he pulled the tape down and shined his light inside to indicate where the team should look for clues. The other two men ducked through the opening and disappeared from sight.

"Think they'll find anything?" I asked.

"No telling," the chief said. I noticed he was breathing a little hard from the incline. If he spent less time at a desk, he might lose some of that tummy. "This is mainly a faint hope that we'll find something that leads us to the guy's next of kin. It'd be great if there was a wallet lying on the ground in there, with a photo ID and the names of his family members."

Apparently, yesterday's discovery had not included any such items.

"We've sent the bones to the crime lab in Anchorage, so maybe we'll get some useful data there. Meanwhile, nobody in the department remembered any specific missing person cases so I've got an officer and my secretary starting to pull old records, seeing if we can come up with any cold cases from way back." He didn't give the impression that there was much hope for that. "If we don't come up with anything locally, I'll put out statewide alerts. You never know."

"Have you been with the Skagway police for a long time?"

"Nah. I retired from Denver PD six years ago. Thought I'd kick back and do a lot of fishing, but that lasted six months before I got restless. My wife had passed away two years earlier and the kids have got their own lives now. I couldn't see myself going back into big-city law enforcement, and then I saw the job listing for a police chief here," he said with a shrug, "so I came."

"How is it? Living here year round."

"I like it. The town is quiet—*real* quiet in the winter. There's a few locals who get unruly when they drink and, believe me, there's lots of time to drink during those long winter nights. So, we have a couple cells we throw 'em into. Otherwise, it's a nice little place to be."

I had to admit that he did seem like a contented kind of guy. My own antsy nature must have showed.

"We'll be at least an hour or so," he said. "You don't have to hang around."

He probably thought I'd just want to buzz back to town for a cappuccino or something, clearly not understanding what the operating costs of that machine were. It's hard to justify spending five hundred dollars to dash out for coffee.

"Maybe I'll walk farther on up the hill, stretch my legs a little," I told him. I glanced at my watch so I wouldn't lose track of time.

I found a game trail that switch-backed upward and began to follow it, but as soon as I was out of sight of the cabin and Chief Branson I began to get a little uneasy. Heavy forest blocked the view beyond twenty feet in any direction. It would be incredibly easy to get lost out here where there were no marked trails, no other hikers. And without GPS, extra gear or knowledge of the area I could see that I was just asking for trouble. I turned back and followed my own tracks back downhill.

The stream that ran through the meadow near the cabin entertained me for another twenty minutes, as I watched small fish dart among the rocks. The water was so clear that the bottom looked about a half-inch away, although I suspected from the depth of the banks that it must be at least two feet deep. And icy cold, as verified by a quick dip of my fingertips. I stood up to return to the helicopter, thinking I might reread the operations manual to occupy my time, or perhaps I would attempt a little breaking and entering on the cabin—it did have those shelves of books ... but then I noticed the deck chairs out on the cabin's front porch. One of them showed up in a shaft of sunlight and all at once that looked like a good spot to be. I plopped myself into it and stretched my legs out into the warmth. In a moment I felt my eyelids droop.

A shout caught my attention and I jumped, unsure how long I had dozed. By my watch, it couldn't have been more than five glorious minutes.

A second shout and male voices in discussion pulled me to the edge of the porch. They came from the forest in the direction of the cave. I hopped off the porch and headed that direction, only belatedly thinking that this would be a very stupid move if the men had encountered a bear.

"I don't know what made me go that far in ..." the forensic man was saying, a guy Branson had addressed as Reed.

I edged closer, noticing that no one sported teeth marks or gushing blood.

"... probably thirty yards farther in than the first one," Reed said. "I didn't touch it, wanted you to take a look."

"So two of them wandered in there?" Branson asked.

Jerry shrugged.

"Okay, let's see what we got." Branson tugged his belt a little higher around his gut. He looked over and saw me standing there. "Come along if you want."

"What's—?"

"Reed says we have another skeleton." He turned toward the cave entrance where Jerry waited for him to lead the way.

I debated for a long moment. At least there wouldn't be blood and guts—I'm not big on that stuff. And this situation was getting, as they say, curiouser all the time. Clearly, Branson thought the two dead men might have been together, which added a whole other dimension to his case. It might be a lot easier to find old missing-person reports if two men had disappeared at once.

Reed led the way, followed by Chief Branson, and Jerry had now ducked his head to get through the opening. It was now or never if I wanted the benefit of their flashlights. I hurried ahead and followed them in.

Chapter 6

With all three men and their flashlights ahead of me, I stumbled almost immediately. Jerry was at the rear so he stayed back and let me catch up, shining his light for me and falling in behind. It made the pathway much easier, but there was no way out of this now.

We passed the place where the first body had lain, the dirt floor now scuffed with boot prints from all the people who'd been in and out since yesterday. Ahead by twenty feet or so, Reed aimed his light around a slight bend in the path; he and Branson both halted. Since Jerry was behind me I had no choice but to catch up and stand beside them at the wide spot that formed a small chamber. With morbid fascination, I looked. This skeleton sat with its back against the wall, its gruesome grin facing us.

As far as I could tell, a stiff coat of some kind was the

only thing holding it in this semi-upright position. Not that I'm much up on skeleton behavior—it just seemed logical.

The chief sat on his haunches next to the remains. When he reached out to touch the coat, Reed spoke up: "Maybe we should get a few photos before we do anything else."

Branson stood up, looking a little chagrined because he hadn't made the suggestion himself.

Reed handed his flashlight off to me and proceeded to snap pictures of the skeleton, its position, and the surrounding area—from every angle. Seriously? It wasn't as if they could pinpoint a time of death or line up some ready suspects. By the accumulated dust on that coat, this one had been here a very long time too.

"So, what on earth prompted these two guys to come in here?" Branson was muttering to himself more than looking for an actual answer. He looked at Reed. "We can't tell much here. Do we have another body bag?"

Jerry said he would go get one he'd left in their larger kit in the helicopter. Without his flashlight the cavern dimmed considerably. I tried not to make it obvious that I was edging closer to the others.

Reed shined his light directly into the face of the skeleton, in close for a good look. "These bones seem quite a bit further deteriorated than the other one," he said. "The lab would have to verify that, but I'm guessing they didn't arrive at the same time."

For the first time I noticed that the skinny bone-legs ended inside a pair of boots, high ones that laced up with metal grommets and leather laces that seemed hand made. The coat, too. It was a lot older style than the '70s-era clothing on the other man. This one had dressed for warmth and the rugged outdoors and the clothing was now mostly in tatters. The first guy's clothing was in better condition but a lot more insubstantial, more like someone would wear on a day hike in summer. I voiced all this, a rambling narrative as I noticed each thing.

Branson nodded, his jaw shifting side-to-side as he considered my observations. Reed seemed to notice me for the first time.

"So, if they didn't come in here together," Branson said, "it seems odd that it's where they both ended up."

No kidding. There wasn't exactly a host of trail-side signs out here that said "Lost and Cold? Nice Cave Over Here!"

Jerry came back with the vinyl bag for the body, and I pressed back against the opposite wall to give them room. After a few minutes of watching them struggle, I saw that I was just in the way. Using the flashlight I still held, I scooted on out of there.

I stood outside the cave, sucking down some more of that fresh air, only then realizing how dank and stale the cave had felt. After a few minutes I heard their voices. Branson emerged and told me they would be ready to fly back to Skagway as soon as they loaded the slack bag into the cargo compartment. I dashed ahead to open the doors, feeling ready to get back to town and people and, hopefully, Drake.

Once we were in the air I left the intercom channel open so the men could talk. Of course, I listened shamelessly although I had to piece some stuff together because the conversation had apparently started back in the cave.

"A blunt instrument of some kind," Reed said. "And anger. It takes a good, hard swing to make a dent that size in a skull."

Okay, so now they were talking about a murder.

"A murder that happened way before any of our time," Branson said, finishing my thought.

"Taking bets, I'd say the coat and boots are over a hundred years old. We haven't seen that kind of gear in the past fifty years for sure. I was on a case my rookie year where some old stampeder was dug out of the ice. These boots look more like his than anything I've ever seen."

Sam Branson grunted. "I'm not looking forward to this one." He had slumped in the seat beside me, his shoulders bearing the weight of a task he really didn't want to perform.

I kept my mouth shut and concentrated on my controls. Eight minutes later I was setting the JetRanger down on my assigned yellow H on the ground. Kerby Allen's ship was still out, so telling my story to Drake would have to wait.

While Jerry walked to the parking lot to retrieve and bring the police department vehicle around, I made my logbook entries and waited for the turbine engine to cool. Drake would want the blades tied down for the night, but since I'm a little too short to grab the leading blade with the strap, it would be okay to leave that task to him.

Jerry backed the SUV fairly close and the three men grappled with the bag of bones and got it inside. Reed checked the passenger cabin for their kits and gear, and a few minutes later they were driving away. Interesting morning.

I closed my flight plan and debated what to do next. In the glass-fronted conference room I spotted Kerby Allen, having an intense-looking conversation with a stocky gray-haired man. He saw me before I got outside so I figured it would be rude not to at least say hello.

"Charlie, how did it go this morning?" I glanced at the other man, who seemed distracted by whatever Kerby had been saying. "Oh. This is my brother-in-law, Earl Thespen. Earl, Charlie Parker. She and her husband are taking some of our Adventure flight passengers."

Earl didn't seem to give a whit about who I was.

"Flight went just fine," I told Kerby.

"What was that outside, something the police loaded into their vehicle?"

With a half-dozen people milling around in the lobby, I didn't think this was the best place to give details. "I suppose you could talk with the chief about that."

"Was it to do with, um, what happened yesterday?"

I dropped my voice to just above a whisper. "Yes and no. You really should ask Sam Branson."

The stocky brother-in-law cleared his throat, clearly wanting to get back to their earlier conversation, so I used the moment to scoot on out to the parking lot. In a futile attempt to reach Drake I dialed his cell phone, but it went immediately to voice mail. What had I expected? He couldn't possibly be getting a signal; Cabin Two was the most remote of the locations Kerby had leased for the season.

Without any other plan, I decided to take the truck and shore up our grocery supply. The market's parking lot was nearly empty so I snagged a cart and was perusing the bread choices when a familiar voice called out my name.

Mina wore a chic sweater with her form-fitting jeans and had a silky scarf with some kind of sparkly threads draped across her shoulders.

"Wow, you're certainly dressed up," I said. "What's the big occasion?"

"*I* have a lunch date."

"Ah—he must be somebody special." It had been so long since I'd prepared for one of those first-date occasions that I really felt old and married at the moment.

She didn't take the bait. Instead, she moved in closer and talked in a low tone. "What I wanted to ask you was about this morning. I hear through the grapevine that the police were out at the airport this morning, right beside your helicopter."

Again, how much information to divulge? Especially since this little source could easily print anything I said in the newspaper.

I glanced up and down the aisle but there was no one else in sight. "We went back up to the cave. Beyond that, you'll have to get your information from Chief Branson."

"So there *was* something found!"

"Mina, don't make me say," I whispered urgently. "I don't know how much information they want to release, or when. Please, just talk to him."

She rested a hand on my forearm. "I already called his office. He told me that I can run the story about the skeleton and put out a call for information to see if anyone knows of a male in his thirties who went missing in the 1970s. *Not for publication* is the fact that the lab found dark stains on the shirt and they tested positive for blood. They think the man was stabbed."

I hoped she was a bit more discreet in all her other conversations and was only telling me this because I'd been there. As if reading my mind, she placed an index finger up to her lips. Her expression changed, and with a smile she flipped the scarf back over her shoulder and headed out.

I had to assume that Branson had not told Mina about the second skeleton—surely she would have mentioned that. But it was nice to know that my original observations were validated by the era in which the first man went missing. Now we could only hope that leads would come in and the missing man's family would have closure after all these years. The other side of it was, unless one man had bashed himself in the head and the other just *happened* to have stabbed himself, there were now two murders to be solved.

As the possibility of two accidental deaths didn't seem too likely, I had the feeling I would be pestering Chief Branson until the answers came out. I'm like a dog with a bone, that way.

The final few items went onto the checkout conveyor belt and I picked up a local paper while I was at it. What other interesting tidbits could I learn about our adopted town?

Drake called just as I was signing the credit card slip, so I detoured back to the airport to pick him up before going home to put the groceries away and make ourselves a sandwich for lunch. He entertained me with stories of the trio of lawyers he had delivered to Cabin Three.

"I thought they were a bunch of rugged outdoorsmen," I said, spreading mayo on whole wheat bread. I piled on some sliced ham as he continued.

"You didn't get a close look. The beards were all started within the past ten days, and the clothing probably came from a massively expensive trip to Cabela's. One guy kept staring at the screen on his phone with this wistful look on his face. The other two nearly panicked when they learned there was no satellite TV at the cabin."

He carried our plates to the table, where Freckles waited with ears cocked toward the food.

"Lawyers, you said? I thought they were all about billable hours and working crazy-long weeks."

"They booked the seven-day package, but I'm betting they don't even make three." He chuckled over that and I pictured Kerby with his hands full as the men tried to wangle a partial refund. Hopefully, our boss had written his customer contract in iron-clad terms.

I quickly filled Drake in on my own morning's little adventure, giving him far more details that I'd revealed to either Kerby or Mina.

"She was all decked out when I saw her at the grocery," I said. "Had some kind of lunch date, and I gathered it must be a new guy."

"Yeah," he said, "Chuey. He finally got up the nerve to ask her out."

"Well, she seemed to really be looking forward to it. Maybe they'll be a match made in heaven." Who knew?

"There's one more flight this afternoon," Drake said as he cleared the table. "Delivering a second week's worth of food to a group that's been at Cabin Two for a week already. I guess that bunch has been having a grand time on their adventure."

He turned to me. "Kerby offered the flight to us, so do you want to take it or shall I?"

Truthfully, I was more than a bit distracted by everything that had already happened today so I begged off. He was happy to go; he delivered a nice kiss and left a few minutes later. I wandered to the living room, debated whether a nap would feel better on the sofa or the bed, then picked up the newspaper I'd just bought.

Mina's story about the skeleton did make the front page headline, but the piece itself was skimpy on details. She described the approximate location of the cave, honoring Kerby's wish not to mention his company. The information from the Scientific Crime Detection Laboratory in Anchorage, including the part about the stabbing, had come in too late for her deadline, so the rest of the story consisted of the fact that the remains had been in place for 'an estimated thirty years or more' and a call for information from anyone who might be able to provide the identity of the body.

I occupied myself for another whole ten minutes by skimming the ads and community news. My gaze fell to the box of letters I had begun reading yesterday.

Chapter 7

The second letter from the bottom of the stack was dated two weeks after the first.

May 26, 1898

My dearest Wife,

The snow has begun to melt in earnest, leaving the streets a mire of mud. But my situation is looking better here in Alaska ...

* * *

Joshua stared at the pile of money on the bed and wondered how he would manage. Maddie had made him promise to hold back the cost of a return steamship ticket in case this new venture did not turn out well. Although jobs were not exactly plentiful back in the city, at least his family was there and he could find some type of work. But he refused to think in those terms. He was here to strike it rich. He would not leave Alaska until he could do so wearing a suit of the finest serge and with a pouch of money to make life better for Maddie and Isabelle. Perhaps he would send for them or start a business.

He counted the money once again—still woefully inadequate for his requirements, despite the rosy picture he painted when he wrote to his wife. He had considered looking for work as a way to earn money to make up the shortfall, but too many others had the same idea. He'd also thought of trying to start the journey with less than the required goods, which would weigh nearly two thousand pounds. But several men had been sent back from the Canadian border checkpoint for that reason. The Mounties did not want to be sent to rescue those who found themselves in trouble. Increasingly, it became apparent that he would have to partner with another man or two in order to afford the supplies. Last week he had seen another provision list, this one even more extensive than the first. Articles in the newspaper were recommending that four men team up; with a four-man tent this plan made the most sense. They could share cooking utensils, as well, and a team wouldn't need a shovel, a pick, or a gold pan for every man. He looked at the small stack of items he had already acquired and began to feel excited again.

Harry Weaver had proved to be a good friend after the day they met in line for the post office. Harry kept saying he didn't plan to join the stampede to the Klondike—he had some means of support here in town, although he never quite said what that was. But Harry had his ear to the pulse of things; he might be able to recommend some traveling partners for Joshua. He hid the money back in his concealed belt, pulled on his wool overcoat and left the rooming house.

On Broadway a wagon passed, the poor horse struggling to pull its heavy load through deep ruts in the mud. Spring weather created havoc. Warmer temperatures had begun to thaw the frozen ground, then a fresh storm would leave a few inches of new snow. Within a day, the snow melted to mush and the muddy ground became even more slippery, the mud churned into mounds with the steady flow of traffic from the nearly fifteen thousand residents. Every time a ship arrived, it disgorged a new crop of fresh-faced young men, eager to join the stampede, and the population had grown by a good thirty percent since Joshua's arrival.

A council of leaders had convened and ruled that at least one side of each street should be lined by a board sidewalk. Joshua noted that the side chosen for the walk on Broadway was the same side where three of the men's businesses happened to be located. Unfortunately, his rooming house was on the opposite side and there was no way to avoid the ankle-deep mess once he stepped off the small porch. Mrs. McIlhaney had installed scraping boards and shoe brushes in a small attempt to get the boarders to clean their shoes before entering, but it was a losing battle.

Joshua spotted Harry Weaver fifty yards up the street, entering a saloon. He hurried through the crowd to catch up with his friend. The Red Onion was quiet this time of morning, but it was one of those establishments that could get rowdy at night. Harry turned from the bar, a glass of beer in hand, as Joshua entered.

"I'm sitting with some men over here," Harry said. "Join us."

Joshua had hoped for a private conversation and some

advice from Harry, but perhaps they would have a chance for that later.

"Alastair Connell, Peter Gariston, Mick Thespen ... my friend Joshua Farmer." The others had near-empty glasses in front of them but Joshua hesitated to spend money for liquor. He would wait and see how long the others stayed. He nodded a greeting to each and took the chair Harry had pulled out for him.

"Next week," said the man named Mick. "That's when I'm heading out. Got on with Riley McDonald's team."

The others nodded appreciatively at this news.

"What about you—Joshua, was it? You heading out soon?" asked Alastair Connell.

"I'm not certain," Joshua admitted. "I'm hoping to join with some others as well."

"Maybe we should talk," said Gariston. He drained his glass. "Anybody want another?"

Joshua felt a surge of hope. Connell and Gariston looked fairly well fixed, both with an air of confidence. "Let me buy a round," he said.

Before anyone else could override the offer, he walked to the bar. Each coin he handed over felt like one less pound of flour or sugar to fill that supply list, but he justified the drinks as an investment in getting on with a good team.

"… last fall, made a mint!" Connell was saying as Joshua came back, his hands full. "Summer's the only time to do it, though. Did you see that photograph somebody put up at the barber's shop? A string of men hiking the Chilkoot last October, like a line of ants on sugar, steady up that trail without hardly a spot of white space between 'em. Snow's up to their knees and at the base of the trail section, there's literally tons of goods. They say if you go it alone, you'll make thirty, forty trips to move your gear. It's thirty-three miles, Dyea to Lake Bennett but you figure out the math, you'll walk close to a thousand—with sixty pounds or more on your back."

Joshua swallowed. The most weight he'd ever carried was probably fifty pounds. Still, he supposed a man would get used to it in short order.

"What about the White Pass Trail?" he asked. "Save the ferry ride to Dyea, just start out from here?" Truthfully, he didn't know much about either route.

"No choice about that now. It's the only way," Thespen snorted.

Connell gave Joshua a hard look. "You didn't hear about the avalanche on the Chilkoot last month?" *Fool.* "They're still up there, digging out bodies and gear. You'd go miles out of your way, if you can even find a way through. The Chilkoot might be shorter but it's a helluva lot steeper."

Joshua covered his embarrassment by taking a long sip from his beer. Harry sent him a sympathetic look.

"Too bad the railroad ain't done yet," Mick said. "I'd be going that way myself."

"Hell, it ain't even started. Be lucky if it can get you halfway there by *next* summer."

"Won't that be something? Get all your provisions aboard and make it in one haul ..."

"Don't waste your time dreamin'. That gold's all gonna be gone. You just gotta get your stuff together and go with a buddy or two. Somebody watches the gear at the bottom of the hill, the others carry as much as they can. Trade off so each guy gets a break now and then. Besides, you don't guard your stuff, somebody's gonna steal it. Only way to go." With that, Mick got up and left the table.

Joshua let the others talk. He felt like a rube; it seemed everyone in Skagway knew more than he did about this venture. He glanced hopefully at Gariston and Connell but got the feeling they'd already written him off as a greenhorn. They finished off the drinks he'd paid for and left the saloon. At least he finally had Harry to himself for a conversation.

"Harry, I've been thinking. What Mick said. It makes sense, going with a partner. So, what do you say? You and me on the trail?"

Harry tapped a fingernail on the tabletop. "I haven't changed my mind, Joshua. I can't go."

Joshua felt like a pitiful, whining boy as he asked why.

Harry pulled a small piece of paper from a pocket. It was a newspaper clipping, folded twice, which he held out to Joshua. The man in the grainy photograph had a thin face and a scar across his left cheek; his eyes were nearly obscured by the low brim of a western hat.

He lowered his voice. "The company I work for, the Pinkerton National Detective Agency, pays me a good salary to find criminals. This one—Jessie Durant—he's robbed two banks in Washington. Witnesses saw him getting on one of the northbound steamers and we know he didn't get off at Ketchikan, Wrangell or Juneau. I'm fairly certain he intended to lose himself in the crowds of Skagway. He may try to ambush men coming back from the Klondike and steal their gold."

"Detective?" Joshua felt a newfound awe of his friend.

Harry discreetly touched his lips with an index finger. "I'm keeping that information very quiet. Hoping to spot Durant and apprehend him. Don't say anything, please, and don't utter that name. It'll give me away."

"How will you catch him? Every street and saloon is packed with men." One glance around the room showed any number of men who might have been the robber, especially if he had grown a beard to cover that scar.

"Durant has a distinctive limp from a wound he received during the second robbery. So many witnesses described it to me that I feel sure I will know him if I see him on the street. In addition, I've showed the picture to both of the barbers in town. If Durant goes to one of them for a shave or haircut, they will notify me."

"And you can nab him! Then you'll put him in handcuffs and take him back?"

"That's the plan." Harry folded the paper and put it back into his pocket. "At any rate, that's the reason I can't go with you."

Joshua struggled for a compelling argument. "Maybe he's gone up there—you would see him on the trail."

"Sooner or later, every man who goes up that trail has to come back down. My chances are better here." He downed the remainder of his beer, then held the glass between his palms. "Joshua, if I might offer some advice? The stories that tell of the amount of gold coming out of the gold fields ... they've been vastly exaggerated. Most of the men are coming back dead broke."

"That can't be! I've read the papers. I've heard them talking around town."

Harry shook his head. "In a boom town like this, be careful what you believe. I know you will always hold out hope. But please consider this a friendly warning."

Chapter 8

By our second week things were beginning to fall into a routine and with blackout curtains in the bedroom I was actually getting some sleep. Drake and I took turns flying to each of the three cabin sites, although I must admit to skirting the work a few extra times in favor of browsing the shops and trying out Mina's favorite lunch spots. Roberta had joined us twice and I found the mother-daughter interaction interesting. I spotted a few slight digs, motherly advice not taken, daughterly cracks about her mother's lack of formal education and career. But they shared a lot of inside jokes, something which I must admit made me more than a little envious.

In our work, the customers became predictable, the flight routes familiar—but the scenery never failed to delight me and the weather was always an unknown. Each of the cabin sites was different: Cabin One with the nearby stream and, of course, that cave (which Chief Branson had insisted be blocked until his investigation was concluded in case some minute piece of evidence might still be there); Cabin Two, a hundred-mile roundtrip flight, sat on a mountainside with bighorn sheep as the nearest neighbors and lure of riches being inside an old mine shaft where only a hint of sparkle revealed that a vein of gold had been dug away in the days before chemical mining techniques of the smash-and-leach variety existed. One client had come back with two decent nuggets of gold and a smile that wouldn't quit.

Then there was Cabin Three, another quick flight with enough waterfall side trips to make it interesting. It sat within hiking distance of the colorfully named Dead Horse Gulch. If the customers wished, they could have easily caught the narrow gauge train back to Skagway or hitchhiked the highway back home, but they didn't know that.

The places all felt remote and once they settled into any one of the cabins most were thrilled to be away from civilization, and all wanted to believe they might be experiencing something close to what the real gold rush stampeders did. The accommodations themselves were similar in size and amenities. After each set of guests checked out we flew in a cleaning crew and a supply of food for the next batch. The crew left neatly stacked firewood and fresh bedding, something those old stampeders would have given their you-know-whats for. For guests who had opted for the two-week stay, we flew out some more food, any mail they might have had forwarded to Kerby's office, and we took their trash away—more conveniences those men would have loved in the olden days.

For myself, I could easily see settling into small town

life, preferably one without quite the influx of pastel-clad septuagenarians whose idea of adventure was that they'd booked that cruise in the first place.

However, life on the fringes of the population—living there but not belonging—left a bit of a hole in the social fabric that we normally enjoy at home. Other than the little get-togethers with Mina and her mom, my chief entertainment had become my nightly peek into the life of Joshua Farmer through his and his wife's letters. I had taken everything out and looked for some clue as to the ownership of the box itself, but it didn't have one of those handy tags that read, This School Box Belongs To:_____. I had asked Berta about it, but she had no clue where it had come from and told me I was free to read it, keep it or throw it away. Deciding on the former, I had just settled into the armchair that I'd discovered to be the most comfy when I heard Drake's truck.

Where did the time go? I dashed to the kitchen, working on my excuse for why I'd not planned dinner and hoping that a nice dry martini would keep him going until I came up with said plan.

"Hey, hon." I heard him call out even though most of my head was in the refrigerator. "Do we have any plans for tonight?"

Uh.

"If not, we've been invited to a party."

Seriously? That certainly saved my rear.

"There's not a thing that can't be saved for later." Technically the truth.

I heard him move into the bedroom. "I'm going to grab a quick shower and fresh clothes."

I arrived on the scene just in time to catch him dropping his Nomex flight suit on the floor and peeling off every stitch of clothing underneath. Hmm ... nice. But the word 'party' still hung in the air and I needed more info. I followed him into the bathroom.

"Some kind of art gallery thing," he said as he waited for the hot water to arrive at the shower head. "Kerby invited us, said it's an informal wine-and-cheese deal. He and his wife know the gallery owner and I thought it might be a chance to get to know some of the locals. Unless you'd rather not go."

By this time he was behind the plastic curtain and that last bit got a little lost as the spray hit his face. I wasn't going to waste a moment, though. When he emerged from the bathroom ten minutes later I was wearing my only non-jeans, a pair of black slacks, and a summer sweater that might be a little too lightweight. I was in the process of rummaging through my clothes to see what type of covering I might add. In another few minutes we were out the door.

Arctic Art sat at the corner of Broadway and Third, smack in the middle of Skagway's bustling downtown. Luckily, it was a lot less bustling now that the tourists had returned to their ships to rest their feet, recover from shopper's sticker shock, and partake of another sumptuous free meal. The gallery owner welcomed us and introduced herself as Donna Rae. She had a warm smile and a certain glow that meant she'd either had a great sales day or a couple glasses of wine. Either way, she told us to look around and help ourselves to food and drink at the long table that stood, conveniently, beneath a wall of breathtaking mountain landscapes.

I spotted Kerby Allen and a silver-haired woman talking to another couple. Roberta Gengler stood over a jewelry display, oohing at something the woman next to her pointed out, and I saw Mina and Chuey strolling in front of a wall of Native Alaskan art but mainly looking at each other. A budding romance—how cute. I was beginning to feel like quite the insider, with my own little collection of friends already.

Chief Branson was among those at the food table, loading a plate with smoked-salmon appetizers and a big assortment of cheeses, fruit and crackers. We said hello as Drake and I filled wine glasses, deciding to mingle a bit before sampling the food. He gravitated toward Kerby, that tendency we all seem to have where we go to a party and spend most of our time with the people we already know.

The other couple drifted away as Kerby greeted us.

"Drake and Charlie, I'd like you to meet my wife," he said, placing an arm around the silver woman.

Well, okay, that was my impression. The dazzling cap of boy-short gray hair was played to maximum effect by a silver satin blouse and silver jewelry. Lillian greeted us with a practiced politician's smile that would always look good on camera. The mayor.

"How are you enjoying Skagway?" she asked, the first question from the mouth of anyone who lives in a place heavy in visitor traffic.

I gave the answer she probably expected—the town's frontier atmosphere was charming and the surrounding scenery stunning. Drake mentioned the 'little excitement' we'd encountered our first day on the job.

Lillian's gaze slid side-to-side, her smile glued in place, as if she were at a press conference and someone had farted, making sure no one noticed.

"It was an unfortunate thing, but so long in the past." She waved away the reference as if the gesture would also sweep the sets of bones off into obscurity. "Have you visited the botanical garden yet? The outdoor plants are already doing quite well, and the garden club is working on producing some of the state's record-setting vegetables again this year."

Nice switcheroo on the subject, but even though it wasn't one of those chamber of commerce high points, she wasn't going to make the murders go away. I would simply ask the police chief about the case.

Lillian was about to go on about gardens and flowers but a lady stepped over and diverted her attention, and the two moved off to confer on some committee subject. I'd already lost interest, anyway. Drake and Kerby talked helicopter, so I moved toward the food table.

"You have to try this smoked salmon spread," Mina said as I stepped in beside her. Chuey had moved to join the other helicopter men, a loaded plate in hand. "Well, assuming you like salmon. Up here we thrive on the stuff."

She didn't have to mention it twice—it's one of my favorites too. I scooped a generous spoonful of it onto a paper plate and grabbed a handful of crackers as accompaniment. And while I was at it, I added a few pieces of melon and some strawberries ... and then there were tiny meatballs ...

"Have you talked to Chief Branson yet?" she asked while I basically made a pig of myself.

I shook my head. She was right about the salmon spread and I stuffed a second cracker into my mouth right after the first.

"This week's deadline is tomorrow and I'd like to add to my story on the skeletons if he's gotten more information from the crime lab."

I didn't dare speak with my mouth so full but I tilted my head toward the other end of the table where the chief had taken up a new plate. I eyed his oversized belly and slowed my own pace. This one plateful had to last me the entire evening. Mina bided her time and soon Branson reached our end of the table. Now that he had another full plate he wasn't going anywhere soon.

"Charlie and I were wondering," Mina began, "whether the crime lab had come through with any new information on the two skeletons in the cave."

We were a team now?

Branson didn't seem to care that she'd included me. "Is this for publication?" His teeth plucked two of the little meatballs off their toothpicks.

"Sam, you know I need what I can get for my story, but if you tell me something's off the record it will stay that way."

He nodded and finished chewing. "Okay. On the record: The first set of remains have been DNA tested but without something to compare to, we can't make an identification that way. If anyone believes he or she might be related to the man and is willing to have us test their DNA as well, that will go a long way toward helping. We don't have the budget to do one of those clay facial reconstructions so, for now, we're hoping that friends or relatives will step forward and give us names—a white male in his thirties who went missing in the 1970s. I want to withhold a description of the clothing, as that may help us rule out false claims."

He gave me the eye. "You saw the scene. Don't talk about it."

Sheesh—give me *some* credit.

He turned back to Mina. "The second body most likely dates back to the gold rush. Carbon dating loses accuracy on something less than a hundred-fifty years old, so we can't rely on that. But the clothing is of the period, both the heavy coat and the boots. And the deterioration is consistent." He bit down on a carrot stick in what was probably a small effort to include vegetables in his dinner. "That much can be on the record."

Mina had pulled a notebook out of her purse and was jotting down the gist of what he had said.

"Off the record, we're not really going to look into solving the older case. I mean, if someone wants to come along and identify the remains by the clothing or something I suppose we can let them have a go at it. But it's a real longshot at this point."

"But the man was murdered," I said, careful to keep my voice low. "I thought there was no statute of limitations on murder."

"There's not. But what would be the point? If this man died around nineteen-hundred, his killer would have to be, at a guess, at least a hundred twenty-five years old. I suppose I can't rule out some kind of deathbed confession in the nursing home, but I can't spend law enforcement time working on that one."

He had a valid point.

"The lab will save some bone material and preserve a DNA sample in the evidence archives, just in case a long-lost relative should come along and want verification. Frankly, I don't see it happening. We will give the man a proper burial in one of the old gold rush cemeteries, though. It's the least we can do."

"But your department is actively looking into the death of the younger man, you know, the one from the 1970s?" Mina asked.

"Off the record: When we get time, we will *try* for answers on that one. But I just had another case come in today and it's taking all our resources, not to mention the perpetual summer-visitor calls concerning lost purses and hiking-trail mishaps."

"Oh? What's the other case?" Mina was off on a tear and I edged toward the salmon again, justifying the indulgence with the feeble excuse that I don't get this yummy stuff at home.

"Did you hear that, Charlie?" Mina whispered as Branson's phone rang and he moved to the edge of the room to take it. "He gave us the go-ahead to work the case of '70s Caveman. I'm going to call it that."

I swallowed a cracker crumb and choked for a minute or two. "What?"

"See, I figure we're sort of the dynamic duo. You've got the investigation experience and I'm the reporter with sources." Her eyes lit with a newfound sparkle. "We could break this thing wide open and it could be my ticket to a Pulitzer."

I eyed her skeptically. "You're sure he *wants* us to solve the murder?"

"His exact words were 'knock yourselves out.' Okay, it's probably not going to be award-winning material, but let's give it a try. Please?"

She looked like the girl who used to play Nancy Drew's

sidekick on the TV series, staring at me with a look that was both gung-ho and wistful. I didn't have the heart to tell her that real-life murders don't get solved in an hour. If they get solved at all.

Chuey walked over and touched Mina's elbow. Apparently they had dinner plans. A second date. Hmm. I smiled and said good night, but not before Mina had leaned forward to tell me that she would call me about this tomorrow.

Across the room I could see that the crowd was thinning. Donna had apparently made a few sales; she was happily writing out a receipt at her desk. Lillian Allen had glad-handed long enough; she plucked at Kerby's sleeve and he became the puppy on the leash. Alone, Drake looked around and spotted me. I tilted my head toward the diminishing supply of food and he walked over.

"I forgot to tell you earlier that I ate a hefty burger for lunch, sort of on the late side," he said, declining my offer to fill a plate for him.

So I wouldn't have had to make dinner after all. He took my smile as flirtatious and suggested that we could go home any time. I dropped my empty paper plate into a waste basket and drained the last of my wine.

By nine o'clock he was into the pleasant sleep of the satiated and I was still awake. I padded in stocking feet to the living room and pulled out the box of letters.

Chapter 9

June first. Joshua watched daily as the flood of men heading north increased. Two men he'd met last week left this morning, shaking their fists in the air with triumphant whoops as they bade goodbye to the crowd in the Red Onion. If Joshua had to guess, he'd bet that more than a few rounds of drinks had been shared before he arrived in time to see the departure. For himself, he'd still not found anyone willing to partner with him; those with more money and provisions felt no obligation to take on a man who could not contribute an equal share.

Despite Harry's warning about exaggerated claims, Joshua felt certain that great fortunes were being made. He was eager, ready and willing—all he needed was a chance to get there. With a pang of envy, he walked away from the Red Onion and the scores of smiling men who hung around its doors. Ahead, next to the fire station, he spotted Jeff Smith's Parlor. It wasn't as lavish as the Red Onion and some of the others, but he'd heard tales of the games of chance played there. Maddie disapproved of such pastimes and Joshua had little experience with them; still, he felt himself being tugged toward the small wooden structure.

"Joshua Farmer?" Peter Gariston, one of the men he'd met in Harry's company, had stepped out of the Holly Street Market. "How are you, sir?"

Joshua hesitated. How to answer? It was unseemly to describe one's lack of funds. Gariston didn't appear to expect a reply. He kept talking.

"Alistair and myself have now purchased the last of our food supply," he said. "We plan to hit the White Pass Trail in the morning. For a hundred dollars you could join us."

Joshua felt his heartbeat quicken. It was double what he had in funds, even if he spent the money for his steamship ticket home, but maybe there was a way. He glanced at Jeff Smith's sign.

Gariston didn't notice. "All the major provisions are in place—three-man tent, cook-stove, pots and pans. Buy your share of the food ..." he cocked his head toward the Market "... and have it delivered. We leave at six in the morning. What do you say?"

Joshua felt a grin spread across his face. "I'll do it!"

Gariston patted him on the shoulder. "Don't forget your mackinaw and boots and plenty of warm socks and underwear, too. There's a lot of snowy country to cross up there." With another slap on the back, the man was gone.

He tugged at the door of Jeff Smith's Parlor but the place wasn't open. No matter. He could get organized first. He raced back to Mrs. McIlhaney's and took the stairs two at a time to his tiny attic room.

Sorting his clothing, he counted fewer pairs of socks than the list called for, but he figured he could wash them more often. He helped himself to the bar of soap Mrs. McIlhaney had provided, stashing it under other items in his valise. He left the bag on the bed and went downstairs to give notice.

"I'll be leaving in the morning," he told the landlady.

She looked up from the cook stove where a pot of soup simmered. "You've found a partner, have you?"

"Two men. They've already been to the Klondike once, so they know the way and I think they have a claim awaiting their return. They have all the equipment, so I only have to provide my food and personal gear."

She nodded. "That's good. Have you known them long?"

"A few weeks," he hedged. "Peter Gariston and Alastair Connell."

She sent him a wary look. "I've heard of them. Joshua, they've not been up the trail yet. They only arrived in Skagway a week or two before you came. They came to me for lodgings. I distinctly remember it because your room was available at the time, but it was too small for two. My friend Sally rented one of her rooms to them."

"They have a lot of money, and they talk about the ruggedness of the trail. Perhaps they went last year, found their fortune, and came back to Skagway for another run at it now."

"That may be." She turned back to the soup but he caught the look of skepticism on her face.

"I have to go out now," Joshua said, "but I will return tonight for supper and to say goodbye."

I cannot listen to doubters, he told himself as he hurried toward Holly Street. Running through my money while staying here in town is no good. If I don't take Peter up on his offer I will be here in Skagway a month from now, with even less money to get by. His mood brightened when he saw two men in bowler hats enter Smith's place. He quickened his pace and followed them inside.

The small bar had only a couple of rooms, the largest neatly wallpapered and a painted design dressed up the wooden floor. A short bar ran along the length of it, with a white-jacketed bartender standing behind it. The two men he'd followed were talking to a man in a tweed three-piece suit with a gold watch chain draped across the vest. He had gentle, dark eyes and his beard had been trimmed in recent days. His tan felt hat rested far enough back on his head to reveal a slightly receding hairline. In his left hand he held a fat cigar, which he puffed occasionally as the other men talked.

Joshua reckoned this was Jeff Smith. He glanced into the small adjacent room where several men in dungarees were watching a card game in progress. On the table was a layout with thirteen cards, one of each number in the suit of spades. A player set a coin on one of the cards, hoping for a match. As he watched, the dealer dealt two cards from a wooden box and paid some money. Two more, another win. As the final three cards were drawn the player shouted with joy. The dealer pushed two gold coins toward the winner. The man's face glowed with excitement as he stood.

"There's my stake, boys! I'm on my way to Dawson City!" He practically danced a jig as he headed toward the door.

The card dealer looked around, his gaze settling on Joshua. "Play?"

He glanced toward the others who had been there first, but both of them shook their heads. Well, Joshua wasn't going to let this opportunity pass him by. He quickly took the recently vacated chair.

"Okay, son, ready for your chance to buck the tiger?" the dealer said with a friendly smile.

It seemed simple enough. Clearly, the final draw of the round paid a much higher rate so he would bet cautiously at the beginning. Joshua swallowed hard and nodded. He started with a bet of ten cents and within two hands had doubled it. Next time he put down fifty cents. Doubled again. He began placing bets of a dollar—lost one but won two more. By the end of the round, Joshua had increased his cash by twenty percent. He took a deep breath as they started a new round.

This time two of the other men decided to join in and place bets along with Joshua. Clearly, they knew a winner when they met one. His confidence grew with each draw of the cards and he soon had increased his holdings from a bit over fifty dollars to well over seventy. His mind worked out the mathematics as the dealer shuffled the cards and placed them back into the shoe. He needed only thirty dollars more, then he would walk away just as the previous player had done.

He boldly bet twenty dollars on the next draw. By this time the man in the tweed suit and two of his friends were standing by, watching Joshua's growing skill at the game. The twenty dollar bet would turn into forty. So close now. He could see the money coming his way. He would purchase an ample supply of food and some extra clothing, then be ready to join Gariston and Connell in the morning. Why stop at twenty? He bet it all.

His card was a seven—his lucky number. The dealer's card was a queen. Both of the other men sided with Joshua and placed their bets. The dealer drew from the wooden shoe. The queen of hearts showed her loathsome face. The dealer quickly gathered all the bets from the table.

"Sorry, son," he said. "Here—we have a few more rounds to go. You'll catch up."

But Joshua had nothing left to bet. He rose from his chair, the world closing in around him as if he had suddenly stepped into a fog bank and couldn't see or hear a thing. He stumbled toward the door and as his feet hit the sidewalk outside he could hear the men laughing.

He jammed his hands into his coat pockets, feeling numb, and his fingers encountered one lone silver dollar. How could he have been so reckless? Inexperienced at gambling, he'd lost all sense of perspective. He lectured himself all the way back to Mrs. McIlhaney's. At the door he couldn't bring himself to go inside. The landlady had shown skepticism toward Joshua's two traveling partners; to admit now that he'd lost all his money in a gambling parlor—he couldn't face her.

He needed to walk around and get his wits together. He continued up the street, a thousand thoughts jumbling his mind. What would he tell Gariston and Connell? God above, what would he tell *Maddie*? His stomach lurched and he ducked between two buildings just in time to vomit on the muddy ground.

At the far corner of the whitewashed building a woman,

barely clad in her chemise, stared at him in pity. Just another drunk, she must have assumed. He hung his head and turned to avoid her critical gaze. While he wiped his mouth with his handkerchief, she opened the door to one of the cheap cribs and went inside. For one flash of a second, Joshua debated following, spending his last dollar for an hour of her time. The thought sickened him and he retched again.

He leaned his back against the whitewashed wall, breathing hard, working not to scream or to beat his head against the building and punish himself. He gave in to the urge and cried out in pain as the back of his skull contacted the board-and-batten siding.

"Joshua? What on earth?" Harry Weaver was at his side. "Man, what is the matter?"

Harry gripped both of Joshua's shoulders. Joshua felt himself redden. First the humiliation of losing at cards, now he'd been seen in compromising situations by two people.

"I—" He couldn't say it.

"Come on, son."

Another embarrassment. Harry treating him as a boy. But Joshua had no will to argue. He allowed his friend to lead the way. They walked into a respectable tea house where Harry considerately found a table in an empty corner and took charge of ordering tea and sandwiches. Now, topping off the humiliation, he would have to admit to his friend that he couldn't afford lunch.

No lunch, no rent, no ticket home. He felt his eyelids prickle. Blinking quickly he swiped the tear away with a fingertip, pretending to have a speck in his eye.

Harry returned to the table and spoke in a low voice. "All right now. What's happened?"

Joshua tried to come up with a story but his thoughts

were still in a tangle. He glanced around the room, saw only three other customers—ladies who were laughing among themselves at something one had said. He took a breath and the whole story tumbled out. The invitation from Peter Gariston, the deadline to come up with a hundred dollars in time to purchase his food and go with them, the foolish decision to acquire the money by gambling. Once he began talking the words came easier. It was true what they said about unburdening your soul.

"This was Jeff Smith's place you went to?" Harry demanded through clenched teeth as soon as Joshua paused in the narrative.

He nodded.

"That crook!"

"I was so foolish," Joshua said. "I didn't understand the game and I bet too lavishly."

"And they cheated you out of every cent."

Joshua stared at his companion.

"I wouldn't be surprised if every man in the place was in on it," Harry said. "Was there a man in a tweed suit? And several others, nicely dressed? Fancy tie pins and such?"

Joshua remembered admiring the pearl pin in the owner's tie.

"That was Soapy Smith. Jefferson Randolph Smith. He's notorious. You hadn't heard of him?"

"Well, yes, but I never realized Soapy was this Jeff who owned the bar."

"You're not alone, Joshua. Don't be embarrassed."

Which was like saying 'don't be tall.' There was no way around the humiliation he was feeling right now.

"Soapy Smith runs every possible confidence game there is. No doubt the man dealing the faro game was cheating. The other players could have been in on it, raising bets, cheering you on, making you think they were losing or winning every bit as much as you did."

The sandwiches arrived but Joshua could not contemplate putting food into his roiling stomach.

"The man acquired the nickname 'Soapy' by selling bars of soap which supposedly had bank notes between five dollars and fifty dollars enclosed in the wrapping. His own men would *buy* a bar, reveal a big prize, convince others to purchase them too. They worked a crowd and then vanished before people figured out that most won no prize at all and no one ever won a prize larger than the price he'd paid for the bar of soap."

"But he seemed so nice."

"Confidence men always do," Harry advised. "And this one is a pro. He's even got the newspapers on his side. A reporter in New York called him most gracious and kind-hearted. One in Seattle swore that most of the stories about Smith were untrue, were only vile rumors. Smith owns politicians and has taken advantage of successful businessmen. No offense intended, Joshua, but he has scammed men far more sophisticated than you."

Harry bit into his sandwich. Joshua could barely look at his. Despite the reassurances, nothing in what Harry said had changed his circumstances.

"I shall report this. The police will arrest him."

Harry wiped his mouth with his napkin. "Provided you find a policeman who hasn't accepted Soapy's bribes. This town is pitifully short on law enforcement personnel."

"Can you help me?"

"I'm a private detective, Joshua. I can talk to lawmen

and make recommendations, present evidence when I have it. But it is up to them to follow through."

Joshua thought hard, but what evidence did he have? None. Smith would simply say that the young man was unskilled at the game and had legitimately lost all his money. He grew angry, caught himself grinding his teeth.

"Be careful. His reach is far," said Harry. "There was a case of a man who came into town with a significant amount of gold, which he unwisely bragged about. People recommended that he have it stored in the vault at his hotel, for his safety. The next morning he inquired at the desk and was told they had no idea what he was talking about—there had been no gold stored in their vault and the clerk swore he'd never seen the man before.

"And what does the town do about this sort of lawlessness? Smith paid to organize and outfit a regiment of guards, and the next thing we know he's serving as grand marshal in the parade; he befriends important businessmen and politicians alike. You will never know if you are talking to someone who has Soapy's cash in his pocket."

Joshua's anger settled like a cold stone in the pit of his stomach.

Harry pulled out a clean handkerchief and wrapped Joshua's sandwich in it for him. "Let it be. Men like Smith may seem all-powerful, but they usually come to a quick end. One day, someone will shoot that man."

Chapter 10

collective

I gently lowered the ~~cyclic~~ and the JetRanger set down on the springy carpet of grass and dandelions that comprised our landing zone at Cabin Three. After flying the cleaning team here this morning and back to Skagway an hour ago, my duty now was to transport a lovely family of four—and their nanny!—for a week of roughing it.

Cabin Three was the best we could offer in terms of size and furnishings, but already the Manhattan-born wife had quizzed me about the state of the kitchen and was appalled to learn that, not only did it *not* have gourmet features, there would not even be a microwave oven. Hello?—no electricity, no microwave. She also complained that she'd been unable to get a nail appointment in town before the flight. I really couldn't see the point—her designer outfit would be in shreds long before the nails went.

The mister had crossed the helipad with cell phone to his ear, continued a conversation with his broker throughout my safety briefing, and let out a curse as we crossed the first hilltop and he lost the signal. I could feel his foot tapping impatiently against the back of my seat throughout the flight.

The two children, bless their little hearts, clearly had not had parental supervision in years. After roaring about the heliport and now having to touch every single thing inside the helicopter with their inquisitive little grubby hands, both of them were about to get a smack from me. It was the nanny I felt for. The poor girl had her hands full. If she should, by chance, discover the way to the highway and freedom, it wouldn't surprise me a bit to learn that she'd gone over the hill.

Barney stepped forward to meet the group. Thank goodness he was the sort of man who faced challenges with a sense of humor. He chuckled his way through the questions they tossed at him during his standard orientation talk, and I had the aircraft ready for liftoff the minute he walked toward it. From twenty feet off the ground, he gave a final wave to the three adults who looked as if it was only now hitting them. They were not in Central Park this time.

"Interesting, huh?" I asked him as we circled the small meadow and headed toward town. "Personally, I'm ready to go back to the office and take bets as to how long they'll last."

"Oh yeah. For my money, I figure the batteries on their emergency satellite phone will be gone in less than a day. Then things will *really* get interesting."

"The first group I flew—the ones with the kid who discovered the skeleton—they were more outdoor-oriented than these. And *they* ended up on the cruise ship."

Barney chuckled. "Some people don't watch those survival TV shows."

Or, my guess, they'd done every vacation spot imaginable and couldn't resist the lure of bragging to their friends back in New York that they had prospected for gold in Alaska.

Back at the airport I shut down the aircraft, ready to make my bets and take some of Kerby's money. But he had the door closed and seemed to be in the midst of an intense phone conversation. I looked around for Drake but spotted Mina first. We started for the break room, remembered the horrid coffee and decided to stroll down the street instead.

"I can't wait to start working on the identity of that set of bones," she said with a gleam in her eye. "So, what does a private detective do first?"

This chase wasn't going away, so I decided I might as well get in the spirit of it. "Missing persons these days? Well, Ron usually gets online and starts searching databases. If it's believed the person is still alive he'll question their friends and check out their home. He's even found people who had skipped out but were still posting on their Facebook and Twitter accounts. Obviously didn't want to stay *too* lost, I guess.

"However, it's probably a long shot to find information about someone who's been gone since the 1970s in a modern online database—at least outside of law enforcement. And posting fliers around town isn't exactly going to work in our case. This happened more than forty years ago, so if he had lived the victim would be in his seventies now. We have to assume his siblings or friends would also be in that age range, and odds are that they gave up looking for him a long time ago."

She paused on the sidewalk and chewed at her lip. "I wasn't even born then. It seems so weird to think in these timeframes, doesn't it? Anyway, I did some checking in the archives of the newspaper. The mid- to late-70s was the height of the pipeline construction. It was huge in this state. They hired people from all over, more than seventy thousand of them before it was all done."

"But wasn't all that construction pretty far north and west of here?" I asked, trying to put my fuzzy knowledge of the state map to work.

"It was. But parts of it run close enough to highways to give access to Skagway. And we've always been reachable by plane or boat."

"That's a lot of strangers wandering around," I mused. "And surely some of them went missing, maybe even finished their jobs and planned to go home but never made it."

"And in the days before computer databases and law enforcement agencies having access to each other's information ..."

"It's going to be a huge task." I wondered if it was even worth the effort. Maybe '70s Caveman ought to be buried and left peacefully alone.

I thought of the colorful shirt he'd worn and pictured someone back home who had that as their last image of a loved one. Even a sibling or wife in his or her older age would want answers. And the poor man *had* been murdered—the killer could still be around, thinking he'd gotten away with it.

"I'm going to ask Chief Branson if he can let us look through his missing person files from that era," Mina said. "He said there were no matches, but there might still be clues. Something he was too busy to notice."

I doubted that—police are usually pretty good at reading their own reports. However, Branson had been awfully busy these past few weeks, distracted now by the second set of bones and by his new case. Maybe Mina had a point.

"Meanwhile, let me call my brother. He has access to a few national databases, and he might give us some leads or ideas of where to find some."

Her eyes brightened again. "Excellent! This detecting stuff is fun."

Yeah, well. Wait until you've spent a week in front of a computer screen with no results. I thought it but didn't say it.

Mina and I parted at the corner of Broadway and Seventh Avenue; she headed for her office and I, with nothing else on the agenda for awhile, walked home. Freckles was eager for a walk and I was happy to indulge her. We covered a mile or so, striding at a good pace to stretch our muscles. When we made the final turn onto our own block, I saw that Drake's truck was in the driveway.

"Hey, sweetie," he greeted. He rubbed Freckles's ears and I wasn't sure whether he was addressing me or the dog.

"Done for the day?" I asked.

"Looks that way. Kerby's got a flight booked later, but he said he would take it. I think I'm a free man for awhile. What would you like to do?"

I was momentarily at a loss. I had told Mina I would call Ron and start trying to dig up information on our cave guy, but spending an afternoon with Drake sounded like a lot more fun.

"There are tons of trails to hike," he said, "or Chuey offered the use of his kayak. It's a two-place. Might be fun to paddle along the shoreline."

Seeing as how I'd just finished a walk with the dog, I opted for the kayaking experience. Drake called Chuey and got instructions for finding and retrieving the boat from his backyard. We had it loaded into Drake's pickup in just a few minutes and found the spot where Chuey had recommended we put it into the gentle water of the inlet. It took a little while to get ourselves familiar with the rhythm of paddling together but soon we were skimming along.

There's a whole different perspective at the waterline than what you feel even standing on a dock. That extra few feet puts you right there with the shore birds, and you can see fish darting away from your paddle. Gulls floated across our path but soon realized we had no food so they continued toward the commercial areas we had left behind. Along the rocky shoreline two river otters played before one chased the other into the water and they both glided away like silk. An eagle sat quietly on a dead tree limb, its white head turning as we glided by within twenty yards. I tapped Drake's shoulder and pointed. He nodded and pointed out a tern's nest.

Rounding a bend, the port now completely out of sight, the sounds changed. No motors, no shouts from people, no vehicles. A seal called out and an answer came across the water. I pulled my paddle up and could hear only slight swishes as tiny wavelets hit the bow. Something inside me let go, as if my soul had come free of the bonds of tension that constantly clench away at every city dweller.

Piloting can be tense work. It's offset by the joy of soaring above the countryside, with no traffic lanes and few places where absolutely specific routes must be followed. But this, floating along surrounded by nature ... it was a completely different type of pleasure. My mellow mood stayed with me right up to the moment we came back to the harbor area and I spotted Kerby Allen pacing the small ramp where we'd launched.

He greeted Drake with, "You don't have your cell phone on?"

My dear hubby merely acknowledged that we had taken some time off. I would have launched into all the reasons, such as the fact that Kerby had said he was taking the afternoon flight himself.

"We got a call from Cabin Three, but the signal died before we could really assess the situation. I need you to get up there. Take the A-Star, in case you have to bring the entire party out. I'll take yours and get to my meeting in Juneau." He hurried off, while Drake and I worked to get the kayak ashore and loaded into our truck.

All the while I was thinking that both Barney and I probably won our bets—the New Yorkers were giving up early *and* they'd used up all the battery power on the satellite phone.

"Do you want me to—?" I began.

"No, I'll take it," he said. What he didn't say, but I read into his expression, was that there could be a true emergency. In that case, I was happy to leave him to the controls.

I drove him to the heliport and he pulled his survival pack from the back of the truck before giving me a quick kiss and an assurance that he would call when he returned. I watched him preflight Kerby's aircraft and soon the blades began to turn. Chuey walked out of the hangar and I told him I would offload the kayak at his house.

"Don't worry about putting it around back," he said. "It's pretty heavy for one person to handle."

I nodded.

"By the way, thanks for encouraging Mina to go out with me. She's a lot of fun."

Did I do that? I might have mentioned his interest but I certainly hadn't done any matchmaking. I suspected it was a case of two small-town people who'd known each other their entire lives, then suddenly a whiff of pheromones hits the air between them and the magic just happens. I wondered whether the feelings would hold through the summer or if I would still be around to witness the end.

Chuey had already gone back to his work, and the A-Star was a speck on the horizon now. I drove the kayak to its home and realized I was hungry. I went back to our place and made myself a peanut butter sandwich, which I shared with Freckles while I calculated the time difference back to New Mexico. I dialed my brother's cell phone.

He didn't sound the least bit surprised to hear from me. Hm. Am I really that predictable?

He gave me a quick primer on missing person searches and suggested I try something online called name us.

"No, it's N-A-M-U-S," he said when I botched the web address. "Dot gov. They maintain databases of missing person reports that can be submitted by civilians or law enforcement. Coroners can also input data about human remains that have been found but not identified. If your skeleton has a family who's looking for him, someone may have submitted the information."

While he talked I found the site. We chatted a few minutes about things going on back at the office, most of which I already knew because every time he couldn't answer a customer's question about their billing or payments, he had generously given them my email address. Luckily, I had

all the records at my fingertips and there'd been no crises
yet.

"Just start your search with the basic information you
have," he suggested. "If that doesn't turn up any results,
maybe the local police or the medical investigator can
provide more data."

"Yeah, well, we've already kind of been through those
avenues. The remains are so old and the department so
small that the chief isn't exactly making this one a priority.
I'm kind of helping out a reporter friend who's bucking for
one of those stories that will boost her career."

"Plus, you're putting yourself in the position of that
family who never knew what happened to their loved one.
You feel for them. I know you, little sis."

Yeah, he did.

"Well, if the online search doesn't get you anything call
me back. I'll see if I can come up with any other connections
for you."

We ended the call with my sending good wishes to his
kids, whom I could hear arguing in the background, and his
fiancée who was probably the most patient woman on the
earth.

I began following links on the website, amazed at
the detailed types of information one could provide—
dental anomalies, tattoos, scars and markings—in addition
to the standard questions about gender, race and age.
Unfortunately, all I really knew about our set of bones
were those very basics. And the fact that he had somehow
ended up in Alaska in the 1970s. Not surprisingly, the search
turned up nothing. All I could guess was that either Alaskan
law enforcement had been slow to add info, or not many
missing person records go back that far in time.

I tried a few other angles, adding data for the possibility that the man had come from a nearby state. Washington, Oregon, and California turned up too many results to fathom. In British Columbia and the Yukon Territories nothing really matched up with the dates. I changed the "date last seen" field from 1979 to 1989, thinking maybe our guy was a fashion outcast. I was placing a lot of trust in his clothing to help with the dates. It didn't make much difference.

If our guy had come to the state to work on the pipeline, he was only one of thousands. Likely one of hundreds who decided to stay and live here after the job was finished or who had no one back home who would expect him to return. If no one had reported him missing, we might never know the answers.

I stared at the screen, dimly hearing a vehicle stop in front of the house. Drake came in a minute later, smelling of jet fuel.

"So, what was the huge emergency?"

"Ha—I'll fill you in after I grab a shower."

I was ready for some down time so I turned off the computer and sank back into the sofa cushions, pondering the efforts we were putting toward this search. Mina was investing a lot of work and staking her professional reputation on building a big story here. I wondered if she was prepared for the very real fact that the murder might never be solved.

Chapter 11

Harry Weaver's words resounded in Joshua's head as he dragged his feet toward his rooming house. Someday, someone would shoot Soapy Smith. If Joshua only had a gun—he would be that man! He would rid the city of that vermin. His anger flared once more and his teeth began to grind. Suddenly he was hungry.

Mrs. McIlhaney's soup smelled good, but her designated supper time was six o'clock and it was nowhere near that yet. Joshua made his way quietly up the stairs and unwrapped the sandwich Harry had sent home with him. A five dollar bank note floated to the floor.

It was another debt to repay but for the moment Joshua felt nothing but profound gratitude for his friend's kindness. He would give Mrs. McIlhaney two dollars for another week's rent on the room. The other three would keep him fed. He weighed his options:

One, beg a shipboard job to cover his passage on the next steamer to San Francisco.

Two, get his money back from Soapy Smith. If necessary, kill the scoundrel to do so.

Three, with the recovered money head for the Klondike gold fields.

He sat on his bed, gulping down each bite of his sandwich and feeling his energy return. What would be wrong with all those options? Rid the town of Soapy Smith and then head for the gold fields, return quickly enough that he could get aboard a steamer before anyone realized that he, the killer, had come back. As Harry had told him, the local police had few resources and even if Harry's company assigned him the job of bringing Joshua in—unlikely, since he was on another quest already—surely Harry would take pity and look the other way. Smith *was* a con man and thug, after all. Maddie's gentle face appeared to him, shocked at the evil thoughts racing through his head. He shook off the vision as a nugget of icy resolve formed deep inside him. Getting rid of Smith was the right thing to do.

Joshua looked down at his lap. The handkerchief lay there, empty, the sandwich completely gone. He brushed off some breadcrumbs and stood up, bumping his head on the ceiling. He suppressed a curse.

"Mr. Farmer? Are you all right up there?" came Mrs. McIlhaney's voice.

"Yes, ma'am. Just fine."

"You don't want to miss the parade," she called out. "It starts in a few minutes." He heard the front door open and close.

Parade? Right. It was the Fourth of July. He looked out his tiny window and saw a crowd gathering on the street. It would be the perfect time to catch Soapy Smith unaware. He folded Harry's handkerchief and stuffed it into his pocket, intending to return it as soon as he saw his friend.

Looking around the room, he wished again for a gun. He had come unprepared for this journey in so many ways. The closest thing he had to a weapon was his razor and he reached into his bag, belatedly remembering that he had left his old one at home and had only brought the new safety razor Maddie had given him last Christmas. As a weapon it looked ridiculous and would perform even worse, barely causing a slice in the skin—*if* he could get close enough.

He wondered if Mrs. McIlhaney had a gun in the house. He took the stairs carefully, making no sound, but she and the children had left for the parade. He peered into a few drawers in her small sitting room, then made his way to the kitchen. A wooden board sat on the worktable and, on top of it, a long knife. He tested to see whether it could be concealed inside his coat. Barely. He wrapped a dish towel around it to avoid cutting himself and carefully tucked the package into an inner pocket.

Out on the street the crowd had thickened—men, women and children gathering to line the street. At the north end he could see the horse-drawn fire wagon with flags fluttering from the harnesses. Spectators began to cheer.

He looked up and down the street, searching for the tan hat Soapy had been wearing this morning. Nearly everyone else wore black hats, but he didn't spot a tan one in the crowd. He ran across the street ahead of the approaching wagon, ducking through the gathering and edging his way toward Holly Street.

Piano notes and laughter, catching on the breeze, came

from Jeff Smith's Parlor. Apparently, gamblers didn't care much about parades. From the sheer volume of male voices, Joshua knew it would be folly to enter the place and confront Soapy now. There were too many of the man's cronies around. He crossed the street and tucked himself between two buildings, watching the entrance to the gambling house. His mind replayed the faro game, seeing now how the dealer must have cheated and how the other men had egged Joshua on in his bets. No wonder that miserable scum had a smile on his face all the time. He loved to watch innocent men lose their money. A flash of hot anger crawled through Joshua's gut.

On the next street over he could hear the cheers of the crowd at the parade. No one would come to investigate one more scream. He gripped the knife's handle and freed it from its towel wrapping. He practiced a few times, pulling it out quickly, but when he nearly sliced his own wrist decided that it would be better to keep the weapon handy but out of sight. He gripped it in his right hand, holding it carefully down beside his leg.

The front door to the Parlor opened. Soapy Smith! Joshua tensed, and adjusted his grip. But before Smith moved onto the street, three other men appeared. They positioned themselves around Smith, to all appearances just a casual group of friends taking a stroll. But no matter how Joshua looked at it, he would not be able to stab his prey without at least two of the men getting him first.

They walked along three abreast, Soapy with a man on either side, then the third companion behind, guarding his back. Joshua watched them from across the street for a moment then fell into step behind them.

Just as he was contemplating what it might require

to disable the third guard and attain access to Soapy's unguarded back, a woman stepped up to Soapy. She was gray haired and short, wearing a lavender dress and cream colored shawl; he thought he had seen her in church a few weeks ago. He ducked his head and rubbed at the bridge of his nose with his free hand, while the woman exclaimed that she was so happy to see Mr. Smith. She inquired whether he was doing well, and he gave a gentle laugh with a soft-spoken answer.

A minute later, when the lady passed Joshua, he looked up to see that Soapy and his men had rounded the corner and were now within reach of the parade-crowded street. He debated following but knew that the men would tightly surround their boss and Joshua himself would be quickly taken down if he got near and drew the knife on Soapy.

Perhaps a better idea ... he eyed the Parlor where piano music still rang out although the voices were quieter. Without Soapy and his thugs on hand, he could simply walk in, brandish the knife, and demand his money. The dealer knew how much Joshua had bet on the last hand. He was cheated! He could rightfully demand that money back!

Holding the knife down at his side, he slipped across the street and glanced both directions to be sure Soapy was not returning. He edged toward the door and pushed it open with his left hand.

The white-jacketed bartender was pouring whiskey for a lone man who sat at the bar. The musician was staring dreamily at a painting of a scantily-clad woman above the piano. Voices from the small betting room proved that the game was in progress. Joshua leaped toward them and gripped the knife.

"Faro dealer! I want my money back!" he shouted.

The music stopped dead. To his left Joshua caught sight of the bartender moving slowly to set the bottle down. Two players at the game table turned toward him, stunned, while the dealer just looked at him calmly.

"I don't believe I can accommodate that request," he said softly.

Joshua stepped forward. "I was cheated! You know it and all the men here know it. I don't want to hurt anyone. I only want my money back."

"Well, see, son, that's where we have a difference of opinion," the man said, slipping his hand beneath the table. "You may feel you were cheated, you may not wish us any harm. But you see, unless you back out of here right this minute, several us *will* begin to wish you harm. A lot of harm."

The hand came upward with a pistol.

Joshua spun around, intending to wield his knife at the closest person, but three more guns appeared, including a long .30-06 rifle from behind the bar. He nearly soiled himself.

"I'd suggest you go on home, boy, and forget that you ever showed yourself here today."

Joshua felt his face go crimson and he nearly tripped over his own feet getting out the door. Laughter roared behind him. He stumbled down the single step to the sidewalk and felt arms close around his shoulders.

"Whoa, whoa there," said a familiar voice in his ear.

"Harry?" His heart pounded so loudly Joshua could hardly think.

"What've you got yourself into now?" his friend demanded, steering him west on Holly Street.

Joshua allowed Harry to take the knife and they didn't

stop walking until they were two blocks away.

"What were you thinking back there?" Harry asked.

"I need my money back. I went to ask for it."

"With this?" Harry held the knife out of Joshua's reach. "A kitchen knife?"

Joshua's embarrassment went all the way to his toes.

"Look, man. You can't handle it this way. You won't get justice from Soapy Smith or any of his thugs and you'll be the one who ends up dead."

Joshua stared at his shoes. After all Harry had done for him, to be caught at such a despicable thing.

"Let's return this to the poor lady you took it from. No doubt she'll be needing it to prepare dinner tonight. Then let's figure out a better answer for your situation."

"A better answer! What would that be? I came here to find gold and so far all I've found are merchants who charge a fortune for supplies, rooms higher than big-city prices, and cheaters on every corner. How am I supposed to finance my journey with those obstacles in my way?" His voice grew louder with each accusation. "I'm damned, no matter what I do!"

A family passed by, leaving the parade on Broadway, no doubt. The man told Joshua to watch his language in front of the women and children.

Harry slid the knife out of sight and put a restraining hand on Joshua's shoulder. "Walk with me," he said quietly.

They headed toward the McIlhaney house where Harry set the knife on the cutting board next to the dish towel, only moments before the front door opened and the family returned.

"Ma'am," Joshua said, his voice still a little shaky, "this is my friend Harry Weaver. He was kind enough to loan me a handkerchief earlier in the day and I asked him to stop by so I could return it." He pulled the white cloth from his pocket and folded it neatly before handing it over.

Mrs. McIlhaney smiled and directed the children to go wash their hands. "I'll have supper ready in an hour," she told Joshua. "Mr. Weaver, you are welcome to join us."

Harry declined politely, but the moment her back was turned he sent Joshua a meaningful look before he left. Joshua went to his room and began a letter to Maddie, putting a bright tone in his words and, frankly, including a few outright fabrications. He could never admit to her that he wasn't farther along in his quest by now.

The dinner hour was a struggle. Joshua's anger boiled just under the surface. Each time he tried to follow the conversation or respond to a question, his mind went back to the sight of his cash disappearing at that gaming table. He finally thanked his landlady and pleaded tiredness so he could be alone in his room.

He didn't know how, but he would find a way to get that money back.

Chapter 12

Drake came up behind me, smelling of eucalyptus shampoo, and planted a kiss on the top of my head. I was at the kitchen table, still batting zero with the sketchy information I was able to provide to the missing-person websites.

"So, do I win the bet with Barney?" I asked, giving my husband a sideways glance.

"Depends. Did either of you bet that the emergency at Cabin Three would consist of Junior forgetting his backpack, the one with the spare batteries to some video game he couldn't live without?"

I felt my gaze go toward the ceiling. "Seriously?"

"The backpack was where he had stashed it, under the seat." He opened the refrigerator door. "What do you say we go out, maybe find a pizza or something?"

Well, he didn't have to ask twice. I closed my computer and picked up my jacket before the fridge light went out. We walked toward the bustle on Broadway.

"And, it was lucky that I carried a spare satellite phone with me. The father had actually called his office in New York and asked them to ship more batteries for the kid— with no clue what address they could use. He must have stayed on the call quite awhile because the phone was more than half depleted. He sputtered a bit when I told him there would be a charge for the extra flight."

I could well imagine. People don't have a clue.

"And the nanny and the mother?" I asked as we stepped inside Gino's Pizza. More than one person had told us it was the best in town. It must have been true—there was one empty table and the air smelled of yeasty crust and Italian spices.

"I didn't see the wife," he said, holding my chair out for me. "The nanny was trying to get the kids organized and equipped to try their hand at panning some gold from the creek. She seemed more enthused about it than they did."

He stared at the menu for a minute after we ordered drinks. "So, you looked pretty busy when I came in. Making any progress?"

We ordered a large pizza and I filled him in on my conversation with Ron and my hour's worth of fruitless web searches.

"I understood that the workers hired for the pipeline were all union," he said, taking a sip from his frosty beer mug. "Maybe they would have records."

I had no idea which unions or how we might go about finding those records, but it was as solid a lead as we'd come up with yet. He named a few that might have been represented on that type of job—welders, teamsters, heavy equipment operators. I filed the thought in the back of my mind for now and concentrated instead on putting away as much of the steaming, cheesy pizza as I could manage.

"It's a good thing we have to walk back to the house," I said later. "If I don't work off a little of that meal, I'll never sleep tonight."

He took the box containing the leftovers; we'd barely hit the halfway mark on the huge pie. We strolled a few blocks out of our way, and I have to admit that I felt less stuffed by the time we reached the house. Freckles talked me into another short walk before we finally settled in for the night.

Drake lit a fire and I found myself dozing on the sofa beside him, but when I tried lying in bed the heavy dinner didn't settle well. I pulled on a fleece top with my flannel jammies and fuzzy socks, padded quietly back to the living room and pulled out the box of old letters.

I hadn't really taken everything out of the box yet, had only started with a stack of bound envelopes postmarked from Alaska. There was a second stack, these with feminine handwriting and a San Francisco return address, addressed simply to Joshua Farmer, Skagway, Alaska. I flipped through the postmarks and opened one.

June 28, 1898
Dearest Husband,

We are well although our little Isabelle misses her father, as do I. She is walking now, very confident in her steps until she takes a tumble. It is quite amusing to watch her as she works at the problem and tries again. Mother and Father are enjoying our company, I believe, although it feels odd to be sleeping in my childhood bedroom.

What wonderful news you sent! I am so pleased that you were successful in acquiring the necessary equipment for your journey. And I am much relieved that you will have two traveling companions. The trail must be terribly lonely and frightful with no companionship. Your news has eased my mind. I do hope that you will be able to find a way to send letters to me during the journey. Are there civilized outposts along the way? I live beside the windows, watching for the postman on his rounds.

I envision a time in only a few months when you will return to us. My daily prayers are directed toward this outcome.

Your faithful and loving wife,
Maddie McDowell Farmer

After falling asleep in the chair and dragging myself to bed sometime in the wee hours, I did somehow manage a decent night's sleep. I woke to the sounds of Drake puttering in the kitchen, and came out to discover that he had not only taken care of the dog's needs but he was whisking eggs in a bowl in preparation for omelets. I didn't have the heart to tell him that a slice of plain toast was more in order after that huge dinner but since I couldn't be rude about it, I managed to put away a plateful of fluffy eggs with a healthy scattering of vegetables sautéed into them.

My phone rang as I was clearing the table. Mina.

"I just filed my assignment for the week," she said, "so I'm hoping we can get together and toss around some ideas about the case. Maybe over breakfast?"

I nearly groaned but told her I could probably manage a cup of tea while she ate. We agreed to meet at Tootie's Place in twenty minutes. Despite being stuffed to the gills I had to admit that the kitchen scents were heavenly and Mina's bear claw pastry looked good enough to risk clogging an artery for. I forced myself not to stare at it.

"Sorry I was tied up with my other story," she said after taking an enviably huge bite of the pastry. "Were you able to find anything that might help us?"

I filled her in on Ron's recommendations and my efforts to ferret out some names. "We just don't have enough details to really get anything from most databases. But Drake suggested that we follow the angle that our victim might have been a union worker. He says all the pipeline labor was union."

"That's a good idea. I wonder which one."

I felt a little hopeless there, with absolutely no experience along those lines.

"I know where we might find out," Mina said, mumbling around another bite of cinnamon filling. "Wilbur's got a brother who has mentioned working on the pipeline. Maybe he'll talk to us."

That's how we found ourselves, at ten o'clock, arriving at the home of Don Clayton. The place was a neat little frame house, only two blocks from the one Drake and I were renting from Mina's mother.

Mr. Clayton greeted us at the door, making sure we noticed the dahlias blooming near the front porch. His white hair glowed in the bright sunlight and his blue eyes were punctuated by rays of squint-wrinkles.

"The wife loved gardening more than anything," he said with a hint of sadness. "I've tried to keep all her best plants alive."

"I guess Wilbur told you why we were asking about your work on the pipeline," I began, once we'd settled onto nearby wooden chairs.

"Something about the unions?" His wrinkles deepened a little.

"We're actually trying to find out the identity of a man who died nearby, sometime in the 1970s. The pipeline came to mind because it brought so many new people to the state, and my husband said all the labor for the job was unionized."

"That's right," Don said. "It's how I came here, myself. I was a welder back in Oklahoma, heard about the work here. Gosh, the pay was good. If you could avoid gambling away your money or blowing it on a vacation to Hawaii you could put away a lot of savings. That's what I did. Saved nearly every penny for three years, invested it in mutual funds."

"I bet the work was pretty exciting," I said.

"Nah, not really. Long hours, bad weather. But we got paid even on weathered-out days, so that was good. Rest of the time I was welding pipe, same as in Tulsa. Besides us, there were Teamsters—lots of 'em. Anything to do with transportation and supply, they handled it. Then there was the Operators, heavy equipment guys. And laborers— bunch of those, too. Good food, though, especially in the beginning. I guess it got a little too expensive to bring in prime rib and lobster after awhile. Pretty soon we started getting camp food that cooks turned out by the gallons and boxed lunches."

"Big crews?" Mina asked.

"Oh, you wouldn't believe it. 1975, there was 28,000 men on the job. Mostly men—some women, but not many. We lived in these camps set up all along the way. Like big old dorms. There was fights and gambling and, even though it was against the rules, a fair amount of drinking took place." He chuckled. "We were given this little booklet of rules, but you know all those were broken pretty regularly."

It was hard to imagine the enormity of the job and the problems that could crop up with that many different personalities working alongside each other. But I wanted to steer Don to our present-day situation.

"The unions—I assume they keep records on all the members," I said. "Do you suppose they would know if any of the workers didn't return home at the end of the project?"

"Records, yeah. There are those. But I can tell you offhand that some guys didn't return home. Thirty-two men died during the work. Some just stayed, like a buddy of mine did. It was what gave me the idea to do it too. Well, and the fact that my brother loved all the stories I'd told him so he'd already settled here in Skagway. Wilbur and that newspaper, inseparable."

I wondered aloud who we would contact to find out about the others—anyone who wasn't confirmed dead but didn't show up back in the lower forty-eight. But Don didn't really know. He'd retired more than ten years ago and he'd only witnessed union workings from the laborer side of it. We thanked him for his time, then Mina and I set off again.

"Well, surely we can get the information we need," I told Mina as we walked toward her mother's house, where she'd promised to pick up an extra loaf of bread from Berta's morning of baking. "We just need to figure out who to ask."

We parted company at Berta's, where Mina went inside and I continued around the block to our little rental. When in doubt about where to find information, I usually just turn to my brother. If he hasn't encountered it in nearly twenty years as a private investigator, he probably knows someone who has. I called his cell number.

"How many hours do you want me to devote to this?" he asked after I explained the mission. "I can make a few calls but we're talking about records that go back a long way. It could run into time and expenses if I have to fly somewhere and then spend hours going through archives with someone."

He had a point. No one was paying for this investigation and Ron's time could best be used on real, paying jobs.

"How about calling around, let's say a max of two hours of your time, just to see if we're even entitled to the information. If it hits a dead end I'll tell the police chief here and see if he wants to keep going."

"It would save some time for me if you can at least locate basic information, such as which local unions sent workers."

I remembered the types of workers Don Clayton had mentioned. "Start with the welders from Tulsa, Oklahoma. I'll be looking up others and I'll call you back."

At least it felt as if we were doing something. By the time I had researched a few others, Ron had received the word from Tulsa that they would not release any personal information about members without a warrant.

"So, that's that?" I asked.

"Looks like. I can't imagine the others will give me any different answer. Looks like time for your police chief to step in. The case is in his jurisdiction."

True. But I pretty much knew how that request would go. Branson had already put the cave-guy's death on the back burner because of other, more pressing matters.

"Give me the names and phone numbers of those on your list," I told Ron. "The least I can do is present it to Branson and see if he'll try talking to them."

I wrote down what he told me but the more I thought about it, the more this felt like a dead end. Here we were, on an inlet that sat a long way from the pipeline itself or any of the boomtowns of the time—Anchorage, Fairbanks or Valdez. There was no real proof that our dead man had worked the pipeline or had ever been to one of those cities. Our only connection was the tenuous evidence that our victim had died in the 1970s. I sat at the table for awhile, tapping my fingernails and trying to come up with another line of thinking.

We had a set of bones; we had some items of clothing. I wasn't sure whether Chief Branson's forensic team had gathered anything else from that cave but I'd been nearby and didn't recall them talking about it. The whole exploration had become a bit muddled when the second skeleton turned up. I decided to give Branson a call.

Chapter 13

Joshua's feet became uncovered as the quilt bunched up around his shoulders. He rolled over for at least the twentieth time since he had blown out the candle. His ill-fated faro game kept replaying through his mind, the way he had won so many hands until, finally, he had bet everything. The fact that Soapy Smith had stood there with a benevolent smile on his face as the dealer scooped up all the cards and all the cash. His blundering attempt at taking back his money, only to be faced down and laughed at. With a mild oath he sat up in bed and jerked at the quilt, struggling to rearrange it.

At the window, dawn was already showing. It was probably only three o'clock but he knew he would never fall asleep now. He tiptoed downstairs in his socks, then put on his boots and went outside. The streets were empty and the air chilly.

He walked briskly, passing the Red Onion, where he saw a group of card players through the window. All-night games were not uncommon here, he'd discovered. Four blocks farther along, he spotted Smith's Parlor but the door was closed and the windows dark. He wondered if Soapy lived on the premises.

A tiny attic room rose like a chimney above the front door. He stared at it from a distance. The space might hold a narrow bed, but he couldn't envision a wealthy man like Smith living there. More likely it would be for a guard, someone to keep an eye on the liquor and any cash on hand. A single window in the turret faced the street. If the place was guarded, the man would see Joshua long before he could gain entrance.

He strolled by, passing the fire station's closed double doors and pretending to simply be out for some air while gathering information about Smith's place. There was a glass window in the upper half of the door and a wide window beside that, but all were heavily curtained and he couldn't see any way inside that could not be easily seen from the little tower-room above. He walked on.

In the next block there was an alley behind the row of buildings on Holly Street. So there *might* be access to Smith's place ... but just then a man approached and Joshua didn't want to be recognized. He stared ahead and kept walking.

In a town where daylight hours ran from four in the morning to nearly midnight, and men were always coming and going—on their way to the gold fields or returning—it would be difficult to choose a time when there would be no risk of being caught. He needed more information on Soapy's movements. He headed back to the Red Onion in hopes of finding breakfast and coffee.

The corner card game had disbanded by the time Joshua walked in. A young lad was sweeping the wooden floor, creating a dust cloud from yesterday's tracked-in dried mud. When Joshua asked about food, the boy nodded toward a table in a corner where he'd already swept.

"I'll get Rosa for you."

Joshua ordered bacon and eggs, and the young woman rushed away, probably to cook them herself. While he sipped coffee from a heavy ceramic mug, another man walked in and tipped his hat. He took a seat at an adjoining table.

"Been in town long?" he asked. It was the standard question between any two strangers who started a conversation.

"Few days," Joshua said. That was the standard reply, too. If you'd been around longer than a week or two, it was practically an admission of failure if you hadn't already hit the trail for the gold fields.

"Me too." He gave a name but Joshua didn't bother to remember it. That's the way it was in boom towns; few considered themselves permanent residents. Everyone was here for one thing: to make a fortune and leave. He would probably never see this person again, just like all the others. The man accepted coffee from Rosa and she bustled back to the kitchen to throw more bacon into the pan.

"Man, I got into a heck of a card game last night. Did pretty well." He rubbed at tired-looking eyes.

Jealousy jabbed at Joshua. "So you'll be heading up the trail soon, then?"

"I figure one more night like the last—yeah, I'll be ready."

"Well, don't go to Jeff Smith's Parlor. The man's a crook and so is everyone in his place." Joshua couldn't help himself; his voice rose, the words tumbled out and he felt his anger returning with fresh vigor. "I get my hands on him, I'll ..."

Rosa arrived with his breakfast and sent a nervous glance his way.

The other man had opened the newspaper he'd carried in with him. Joshua ignored him and wolfed down his own breakfast. He had better things to do than listen to some fellow brag about his successes. You got enough of that in this town anyway. He plunked a quarter down on the table and walked outside.

The streets were busier now as businesses began to open. He cut over to Runnalls Street and made his way back toward Holly. Somehow, he would find an opportunity to get inside the small gambling saloon and get his money. It would be an added bonus if he could catch Soapy Smith alone and beat the tar out of him, teach the scoundrel a lesson.

For three days he watched and waited. The routine at Jeff Smith's Parlor varied little; someone would arrive mid-morning and open the doors, gamers would come and go all day and well into the evening. Soapy himself came and went, but never alone. A minimum of three men walked with him every time. Joshua followed a few times, but Soapy was always in a crowd—conducting business with the town's muckety-mucks, checking on his various business enterprises. Joshua was amazed at how far the man's reach extended.

On the fourth day he sensed something different in the air. After several sleepless nights, Joshua had allowed himself the luxury of sleeping past sunrise and staying in to eat with Mrs. McIlhaney's family and ask if she would mind doing his laundry, so it was nearing ten o'clock before he set eyes on Soapy's parlor. He took up one of the several posts he'd been using, places where he could observe Smith's actions unseen.

Some type of game was in progress in the narrow space between Smith's place and the adjoining building. A man who looked as if he might have just come off the White Pass Trail laid a coin on their makeshift table and the dealer—one of Soapy's men—worked the cards. Three-card monte. An easy game to lose, Joshua thought as he watched in fascination.

The stampeder protested, voices were raised. Triplett, the dealer, placated the gambler and there was another brief exchange of cash. The man seemed to be out of money but the others were allowing him to get deeper in debt. He heard one voice say, "You have the dust."

Gold dust. Men just back from the fields always carried it.

"Let's see it," one of the others said.

The gambler and one of the other men left but were back within a few minutes. The new man unrolled a pouch and Joshua could practically smell the greed surrounding him. Suddenly, one of Soapy's men grabbed the pouch, tossed it to the card dealer and shouted "Run!" The dealer took off while the other two held the gambler. Joshua's heart nearly stopped. This was all too close to home for him.

The gambler jerked away from the others and gave chase, but the card dealer had vanished. He looked both ways and spotted Joshua.

"Sir! I've been robbed. Where can I find an officer of the law?"

"I ..." he stammered, considering quickly. The only deputy he could think of was soundly under Soapy Smith's control.

But the man had rushed off. Joshua ducked around the corner to take up watch from another angle, in case Smith's men had seen him. They rushed into the parlor and a few minutes later Soapy and several others came out. Their eyes scanned the street. The victim was gone but Joshua could tell that Soapy was up to something. He followed at a distance.

On Broadway, he caught whispers and murmurs as he watched Soapy chat with people, denying that anyone had been robbed. Joshua wanted to stand up and proclaim the injustice from the rooftops, but the looks of Soapy's men intimidated him. He hung back.

"Mr. Stewart lost his money in a fair game," Soapy insisted to the owner of the hardware store, where Joshua stood pretending to admire merchandise in the window. "There's been no robbery."

The merchant lowered his voice. "... disavow the men who did this. Save yourself, man, and let them take full blame."

"We'll see," said Soapy. "Perhaps, if the man makes no roar in the newspapers. We might see what can be done for him."

Joshua turned his back as the party of con men passed him. Up the street, he heard raised voices. The man named Stewart was shouting about the injustice of the loss and the fact that the law was doing nothing to stop Smith's men from robbing anyone they chose. Joshua approached and blurted out his story.

"It's true! Listen to this man. The men blatantly took his

pouch. They did the same to me a few days ago. A rigged card game and all my money was gone in one afternoon!"

Several in the crowd looked sympathetic; some were openly hostile—Soapy's men, no doubt; no one seemed shocked. A tap came on his shoulder as Joshua turned, intent on marching up the street and forcing the sheriff to listen to him.

"Son, let's go." It was Harry Weaver. "It's not smart to be talking this way."

Harry took his elbow and steered him down a side street.

"What are you doing?" Joshua demanded. "It's my chance to be heard if I join together with this other man. I watched as they blatantly took his money!"

"I'm not saying it isn't true," Harry said. "Just that it will be taken care of, but not in this way. The sheriff is in league with Smith. He will never pursue justice for the victims. But there are others who will."

"Who?" It came out more as a demand than a question.

"There's a committee—The Hundred and One. Some call them vigilantes and they may be, but they are working to stop this lawlessness. They are meeting right now, as we speak."

Joshua didn't know what to say. A committee was probably a good thing, but would he really get his money back?

Harry began to move. "Let this lie," he said. "I'll buy you a cup of coffee."

They went into the nearest tavern and Harry ordered, but Joshua's mind wouldn't slow down. He pictured Soapy bragging about what a good citizen he was and pretending regret that the unfortunate man had not been lucky at cards.

His teeth ground together and it was all he could do to take a sip of the coffee, which burned its way down his gullet.

"… an ultimatum," a man was saying as a pair of newcomers walked in the door. "Says he'll return the gold by four o'clock this afternoon."

Joshua's ears perked up. Maybe …

"District Commissioner Sehlbrede is on the way. He'll sort this out. Meanwhile, Joshua—" Harry looked up to be sure his young friend was paying attention.

"Don't cross Soapy's path. He may act like a mild and friendly man, but he's dangerous."

Joshua let the words fly right past him. He intended to keep an eye on the situation and make it known that he, too, had been swindled by Soapy Smith.

As if he'd read Joshua's mind, Harry spoke up: "You are only one of hundreds, son. File your complaint, but don't let your livelihood hinge on the result. It may take months for this to be completely resolved."

Months. Joshua didn't have that long. He had money to live on for a week.

They finished their coffee and Harry excused himself to go to the post office. He was still monitoring the comings and goings of men from the gold fields, confident that his quarry, Jessie Durant the bank robber, would show up soon. To that end he constantly monitored the most-frequented places in town.

Joshua felt a bit at loose ends. He couldn't imagine sitting in his room at Mrs. McIlhaney's house, listening to her children at play, or being caught up in conversation with the woman as she cleaned house or prepared dinner. He had written to Maddie yesterday but thought better of posting it. Her most recent letter to him expressed excitement on his behalf that he was on the way to the Klondike. When Gariston and Connell offered him a place on their team, he had foolishly written his wife in such a way that it sounded as if he were already on the way. Now, he had to pretend to be gone for several months before he could communicate with her again.

Of course, once he received his money back from the Smith gang he would find other partners and set out immediately. It was just the waiting—he chafed at the knowledge that he was already three months behind schedule.

He ambled back to one of his posts with a view of Smith's parlor. A group of men was standing about, but he heard no laughter or music. Conversations appeared intense. Joshua backed into the afternoon shadows between two buildings to remain unseen. As the hours passed, his legs felt tired and he slid to the ground with his back against the rough wood siding.

"Commissioner called a six o'clock meeting," a voice said. It was so nearby, Joshua started. He must have dozed off.

"Will Soapy attend?" said a second male voice.

"He's on the way there now."

Joshua carefully plucked his watch from his pocket. It was nearly six-thirty. He felt hungry and wondered if Mrs. McIlhaney had saved any food for him. A small commotion across the street erupted.

"What happened?" he heard someone shout out to Soapy.

"I gave that commissioner what-for," the slight man in the tan hat said. "Told him if he wants to call me a thief then he can do so! I walked out of there." He had a glow about him. "Drinks on the house!" he shouted.

The gathering of men pushed their way in. Joshua debated going inside to see what would happen, but this was unfriendly territory and the situation was clearly heating up. He crossed the road and edged near the open door. Men stood shoulder-to-shoulder in the small bar, raising glasses and laughing at everything Smith said. When he bragged about outwitting the feeble law enforcement in this town, a cheer arose.

Two more men in well-cut suits approached and Joshua ducked between Smith's parlor and another building, into the same small alley where he'd watched the man called Stewart this morning, when the pouch of gold had been stolen. The gathering grew noisier as drinks were consumed. Technically, Alaska was a dry state but as with some of the other laws around here, that one clearly had little enforcement.

Harry had told him the commissioner and this vigilante committee had a lot of power here. A showdown of some kind seemed inevitable and Joshua felt tension run through him like an electrical current.

No longer able to stand still, he walked toward his rooming house. Broadway was quieter than normal, as were Holly and Runnalls Streets. At the waterfront, some six blocks away, he could see a gathering of people but couldn't determine their mood. He looked at Mrs. McIlhaney's place but couldn't bring himself to stay in isolation there. Whatever happened out here on the streets, knowing the outcome was more important than staying safe. He hurried forward on Broadway, as far as Second Avenue, where a man wearing a deputy's badge cautioned him to turn around.

A genuine lawman, or one of Soapy's conspirators? He

had no idea who to trust but he took the advice. He turned the corner, watched at a distance for awhile, then walked up Runnalls, cutting over at Holly just in time to see a portly man push his way into Smith's place. He was carrying a slip of paper.

Joshua had no way to know what the note said but moments later Soapy Smith emerged from the parlor, stuffing the paper into his pocket and carrying a Winchester .44-40 repeating rifle. Smith took a few unsteady steps then hefted the rifle to his right shoulder, barrel pointing skyward, strode confidently into the middle of Runnalls Street and headed toward the wharves. Six or seven men hurried to keep up with him. Joshua let the flow of people from the bar ease before he turned and followed. It looked as if Soapy Smith's legendary nerve was very real.

Merging with the crowd Joshua kept his eye on the bobbing barrel of that rifle. Ahead, he caught occasional curse words from Smith.

"Ain't never seen him quite this mad," said a man nearby. Another, to whom the remark had been addressed, only nodded.

Halfway between Second Avenue and First, Joshua saw that Soapy had stopped and turned to the thugs who had come out of the bar with him. He must have told them to wait. He walked on alone, out onto the twenty-foot-wide swath of the Juneau Pier. The rifle wasn't up on his shoulder anymore.

Several men had apparently been assigned to guard the entrance to the pier; someone in the crowd around Joshua muttered that the committee meeting was taking place, at that moment, in the large building at the end. Two men approached Soapy, and whatever he said to them made them scatter. As another man came forward, Joshua caught the glint of a gun. Soapy raised the rifle and suddenly there was a scuffle, with the two men only inches apart, and two shots sounding simultaneously. The guard reacted, apparently hit, but he held his ground well enough to get off three more shots.

Soapy Smith fell to the wharf.

"He's dead!" came shouts. "Jeff Smith's dead!"

The other man fell back, wounded. Others rushed to his aid and word spread quickly through the crowd. It was Frank Reid, a bartender who had become the town surveyor. People rushed to rig up a stretcher and carry Reid away.

Joshua watched as the wounded man passed right by him, his face white in contrast with the blood on his clothing. Soapy Smith's followers seemed to have dispersed. The con man's body lay on the wooden planks, ignored.

Chapter 14

I woke up at daylight with one of those eyes-wide-open flashes of insight. The pockets! Last night I had sorted laundry, reaching into every pocket in our clothing so as not to miss a ballpoint pen or vital slip of paper that shouldn't go through the wash cycle. It never fails that I'll find a few things.

So, whether our cave-guy had been wandering the woods and happened to get lost at the moment marauders bushwhacked and stabbed him, or if he'd been tracked there intentionally, there was the likelihood he had not gone up there with empty pockets. I already knew he had no ID but hadn't asked what else he'd carried with him. A little obsessive, yes, but you never know what might turn out to be a clue.

I waited until a decent hour—eight o'clock—to call the

police station and speak with Chief Branson. He sounded like a man who'd not had his coffee yet but he agreed to let me stop by and see whatever personal possessions the crime lab had returned with the skeletal remains.

"We'll be burying the older remains this afternoon at four," the chief said as he offered me a seat in his office. "In case you'd like to come. Normally, when it's an old case like this and there are no next of kin, I just send as many of our officers as it takes to lower the coffin into the ground."

I felt a stab of regret for the poor set of bones that had been so completely abandoned. "I'll come. Maybe Mina would like to be there too." And if Drake and Kerby weren't busy, I supposed we could come with a small group to pay respects.

"Invite them all. The more the merrier, I suppose," he said. "Meanwhile this is what we got back from the lab on the more recent John Doe."

He pointed to a cardboard file box with the lid off. Inside were a collection of plastic bags, sealed with bright tape, and an attached form that anyone opening a bag had to sign and date.

"I can't let you open them," Branson said. "Chain of custody—*if* this thing should ever go anywhere. But you can see the items clearly enough through the plastic."

His phone rang and he put the caller on hold long enough to escort me to an adjoining room where he set the evidence box on a conference table. Through a wide window I saw him go back to his desk and pick up the phone. I turned my attention to the contents of the box.

Someone had shaken out the loose dust and crusty dirt that had covered the denim pants and polyester shirt, although that didn't mean the clothing had been washed.

Folded to display the front, the brightly patterned shirt showed its grisly collection of rips and bloodstains. I found myself repulsed and fascinated at the same time. Setting that bag aside and seeing nothing unusual about the pair of blue jeans, I turned to the small pouches that contained personal effects.

It felt strange to look into a life that seemed modern but was pre-electronics. No cell phone, no pager, no PDA, no earbuds or music player. The low-tech possessions consisted of such ordinary things: a plastic comb, a pack of gum, a few coins. So weird to see that the wrapper on a package of sugarless chewing gum had survived decades in a cave far better than the flesh of the man.

Notably missing were a wallet and keys. Surely this person wouldn't have taken the time to pick up his comb but leave his more important things behind. It seemed logical, then, that the killer had taken anything that might identify the body. I said as much to Chief Branson when he walked in a few minutes later.

"I agree. We searched pretty far into that cave and there was nothing else associated with him. Odds are that the wallet was stripped and the pieces dumped in trash bins somewhere."

"Do you think the motive might have been robbery? Maybe this man was carrying a lot of cash."

He shrugged. "It's certainly possible. No way to know now."

I spotted one final zipped bag, no bigger than one used for a sandwich. I plucked it from the box and saw that it contained a pale yellow slip of paper.

"What's this?"

Branson gave me a patient stare. "Paper. Can't read

anything on it, though. Well, nothing important."

I pressed it flat and held it under the light. Very faint gray lines indicated that a note might have been written in pencil. But water had gotten to the paper at some point and I could only make out a couple of non-consecutive letters. Branson was right; the writing wouldn't tell us anything.

"Was this inside a pocket?"

He shook his head. "On the ground, under the body. He might have had the note in his hand when he fell."

"So the killer probably didn't see it, didn't know to take it." I mused aloud. "Do you know if the lab ran any special tests to try to bring out the writing and make it more visible?"

He sighed. "We have limited enough resources for the *new* cases. The crime lab is way understaffed and it practically takes an act of Congress to get the okay on testing and equipment we *really* need."

"In other words, no."

"Right. I thought about it, but I need to hold my chips for the times I have to cash in on something ... else."

Something, or someone, important. His meaning was clear and although it didn't seem fair, few things in this world really are. Everything was a matter of judicious allocation of time and money. He didn't expect to catch either of these poor old skeletons' killers and could only see a waste of time in looking. I got that. I also felt a surge of determination, some sense of doing right at least for the more recent man, not to mention his family, who may have been living in worry and grief for a very long time.

I asked if it would be all right to take pictures and he nodded. I snapped away with my phone camera, getting an image of each item before placing all the bags back into the box. The chief had been called back to his desk so I gave a little wave and showed myself out.

Driving to the airport I thought about the note under the body. Logic would dictate that it had to be relevant to his being at that location. Directions, perhaps? Maybe even the name of someone he was supposed to meet. Considering that he was hardly dressed for cave exploration or mining, it was hard to think of a logical reason for him to be there unless he had planned to meet someone. But who?

Figuring that out was beginning to feel like a monumental task; thousands of people came and went from this area every year, brought in by cruise ships, tour buses and job opportunities. And those thousands usually scattered to the far corners of the earth after their visits; I could see myself traipsing off to some distant region before this was all over. Without the identity of the man, we had an impossible assignment ahead of us.

I dialed Mina's number and told her about the burial this afternoon, suggesting that it would add to her story if she was there. In truth, I just didn't want to be the only one standing at the graveside. I pulled into a parking slot and saw that both Kerby's and Drake's helicopters were sitting on the pad.

Inside, the guys were drinking coffee and staring at the wall map.

"Hey, you," I said to Drake. "I brought your truck back. Anything going on this morning?"

"Not much. You were sure out the door early."

I told him about the sudden opportunity to look at the evidence. "Chief Branson says they are burying the gold-rush man this afternoon. I thought I'd go. I mean, it won't be a real funeral or anything, but the poor man ... all alone even now. Want to join me?"

Drake knows how I am about funerals and saw through my desperate plea for support. "I'll pick you up at the house and we can go together," he said.

"Kerby? I'm sure anyone can attend."

He seemed on the verge of saying no, but changed his mind. "Sure. As long as we don't get a flight, I suppose I could come."

"Bring Lillian too. If she's not busy." I said it before it dawned on me that the mayor is probably always busy. But even if it was just Drake, Kerby, me and Mina, at least that would seem like some bit of care for poor old John Doe.

Clouds had begun to form over the mountaintops, bringing a whiff of dampness. Weather always seemed to be a factor here; I hoped Drake wouldn't end up flying. Pushing through crowds of tourists, I cut away from Broadway and walked up State. I managed to while away a few hours doing exciting stuff such as sending out monthly statements to our clients on behalf of RJP Investigations.

By four o'clock those clouds had closed in, giving the small gold rush cemetery just outside of town along the Skagway River the sort of dismal feeling that prevails on such occasions in Victorian novels. Mina brought her mother along, and the two of them stood near the foot of the grave. Drake, Kerby and I had crowded into the front seat of his small pickup truck. Other than the police officers who were simply here to do their jobs, we were the only mourners.

The graves were set out somewhat helter-skelter over the uneven ground, with tree roots intertwined around headstones that tended to lean with the slope of the land. A decent spot had been selected for our unknown stampeder near a prominent obelisk marker. Chief Branson said a few words, something that sounded canned, as if it was a short chapter in the handbook of odd police duties.

I had tucked two umbrellas into my shoulder bag and by the time Branson gave the order to his two men to let down the ropes bearing the plain pine coffin, I felt the smack of a few raindrops. The men quickly filled the hole with dirt and we scurried to our vehicles as the rain began pelting down in earnest.

"Let's go somewhere for a toast," Mina suggested. "Make it a short, informal wake or something."

A toddy of some sort sounded good to me, and we told her we would meet her at the Red Onion. She and Berta ducked quickly into their car.

A blur of motion caught my attention as a tan Escalade skidded to a stop beside us.

"Lillian, I thought you'd forgotten," Kerby called out.

The mayor gave a sideways glance toward Mina's car. "Earl had car trouble and I had to go pick him up."

Peering under the edge of my umbrella I could see Lillian's brother sitting like a lump of discontent in the passenger seat.

"Everyone's going to the Red Onion for a bit. Want to go along?" Kerby asked.

He stood halfway between our vehicle and his wife's, waiting for her answer to tell him which ride he would accept. At her nod, he opened the back door and climbed inside. I noticed that Earl's mood seemed to brighten considerably at the prospect of a drink.

My own mood lifted a bit, too, once we'd drifted toward

a corner of the famed bar with glasses in hand. Mina offered a few words about cave-guy, a wish for the repose of his remains and peace for any unknown family he might have out there somewhere in the world. No mention of an award-winning story for herself, at least not until the two of us had managed to snag a small table.

Drake and Kerby had walked off to one side, talking helicopter stuff as usual. Earl had spotted someone he knew at the bar and planted himself on a stool. Lillian stood near them, studiously avoiding direct conversation with Berta. I couldn't imagine what old rift existed there. When a friendship had suffered that bad an injury, it seemed that either you patched things up or you moved on and avoided the person entirely. Maybe avoidance wasn't completely possible in a town this small.

Berta didn't seem to care; she had spotted a gaggle of friends seated at the opposite end of the bar and had greeted them with hugs and exclamations. Perhaps it was her way of showing Lillian that no matter how important she might be, she wasn't affecting Berta's own ability to thrive. Someone turned the music up and several of the women were bouncing on their barstools to the beat.

"So," Mina said to me. "Tell me what you learned when you talked with the chief this morning."

I described the items from the box, keeping my voice as low as possible.

"The note was the interesting thing. I wish I could say that they tested it and a bunch of hidden writing showed up, but that didn't happen. I suppose it was probably his directions to the area. I've flown over it a bunch of times now, and there is a trail that runs on the ridge just above where we were—maybe a hundred yards to the cave entrance. You'd have to know what you were looking for to spot the cave, but the distance isn't all that far. There's a parking area for the trailhead; usually a few cars are up there."

"So ... where did this guy's car go?" she asked. "I mean, he couldn't have walked all the way from town, so he drove to the trailhead, walked to the cave ... then what?"

I did a mental head-slap. I'd homed in on the missing wallet and the fact that he carried no keys. Then I'd become distracted by too many other things and had forgotten to ask whether Branson's department would have records of an abandoned car from that long ago.

Lillian had finished working the room and walked over to take the extra chair at our table.

"Maybe you would know the answer to this," I said to her. "Would the police department keep traffic records from a long time ago? Something like an abandoned vehicle?"

She shifted in her seat and glanced down at her drink before answering. "I suppose they file those things somewhere, but I have no idea how long they would keep traffic reports."

The way she emphasized *traffic*, as if I'd asked about old road kill, made me realize that probably was very low on their totem pole.

"I suppose that would be fairly low priority," I admitted. "Even today, much less all those years ago, before computerized records and all."

"How long ago?" she asked.

"Close to forty years, I would guess."

"Does this have to do with that body in the cave?"

"Actually, yes." I told her about Mina making the connection. "If there was a record of the man's abandoned car being found at the parking area ..."

"I'm sure the car would have been sold from the impound lot ages ago. There's no possible way the borough could keep every old vehicle we ever found." She said it with such authority that I didn't even bother to ask whether there would be a record of the ownership of said vehicles.

"I wonder if the state DMV keeps old records," Mina mused. "If we just knew what kind of car, the year ... something more." She pulled out a pen and scratched herself a note.

The group at the bar had disbanded and Berta edged her way through the rest of the crowd, coming toward her daughter. Lillian worked it so that she stepped away from the table with her back toward the other woman. She approached Earl and said something to him, then to Kerby, and the three of them left the bar. Apparently, when Lillian was ready to move on, the family moved on.

Drake, finding himself abandoned in the middle of the room, walked over to join us. While Mina talked about ways to find out cave-guy's identity through some kind of media blitz, my husband sent out various secret signals that meant he was hungry. I suggested that we order something here, and soon we had a huge plate of chicken wings and halibut nachos sitting in front of us. Berta, on her third drink now, laughed at my question about the nature of the feud with Lillian.

"A man. Of course." She chuckled at the memory.

Mina looked as if she wanted to stick her fingers in her ears and say la-la-la-la for the next ten minutes.

Berta leaned toward the center of the table, one forearm planted under her ample bosom. "A little background on Lillian Allen—she's actually been married a few more times than she lets on, and she was quite the wild little thing in our younger days. Don't let that prim-and-proper 'I only shop from the designer catalogs' attitude fool you. She and Earl come from everyday, common Alaska stock, born and raised here in Skagway, right back to her grandfather. Hell, maybe even farther back than that. The only reason she can put on that east coast, superior attitude is because husband number two came from New York and she lived there the whole three years she was married to him."

Mina piped up. "She's right. Even though I was a kid I remember people talking about her when she came back, saying how different she was."

"So ... what's the part about the feud?" I prompted.

"Oh, that. Lillian swore up and down that if I hadn't stolen him away, she would have been the one married to Archie Gengler."

"Daddy?" Mina's eyes were wide.

Berta started to say more but there was a shuffle next to our table as the police chief slid into the remaining empty chair.

"Sam?" Berta said, scooting her chair to make a little more space.

Branson looked at me. "Well, I've got a whole new wrinkle in that case you want to investigate. I hadn't asked them to do it—guess the crime lab guys got my instructions mixed up—but they ran a comparison on the DNA from the two sets of bones in the cave."

He paused a moment to be sure he had our attention. He did.

"Those two men share enough markers ... they're related."

Chapter 15

Joshua followed the small crowd behind Frank Reid's stretcher, as they walked slowly through the streets to the doctor's house. The wounded man was borne inside, while the doctor's wife insisted that all but the two stretcher bearers remain outside. She shook her finger as she admonished them to stay clear of her flowers.

"Can you believe it? Soapy Smith, gone for good."

"For well and good," said another man. "I only hope that the rest of his men will leave town too. We're well rid of all that lot."

The two men who had carried the stretcher came back out, their faces grim. One raised his hands and spoke softly to those gathered around.

"He's in a lot of pain. Doc's doing all he can. Says if Frank isn't better by morning he'll put him in the hospital."

The crowd grew quiet. The situation was serious, then. None but the gravely ill went to a hospital. The men began to disperse and Joshua trailed along. For a brief moment he debated going once again to Smith's parlor to see if he could retrieve his lost money. But when he passed it, a half-dozen of Soapy's henchmen were gathered near the door. A couple had foul expressions but most merely seemed stunned.

At the corner of Holly and Broadway Joshua caught sight of a wagon bearing a man-shaped lump covered with a blanket. It stopped in front of Ed Peoples' undertaking parlor. An officious-looking man jumped down and Joshua heard him telling the undertaker that he was ordering an autopsy.

"We'll know with a certainty which gun the fatal shot came from," he declared.

Around him, a murmur arose. "... wasn't Reid at all ..." "at least three different guns" "ambush, that's what it was" "Murphy's the one who got 'im—I saw that clear as day."

The rumors flew and the discussion traveled toward the bars. Joshua thought about going into one of the lively places to hear the rest of the story, perhaps to be treated to a free beer. But in the end he realized that all he'd wanted was to get his money back and with the new vigilante committee in charge it would be days before the whole situation got sorted out. He felt a heavy cloak of weariness settle over him as he trudged to his rooming house.

The next morning he awoke, hearing an unusual timbre to the voices out on the street below. Something was going on beyond the normal bustle of horses, wagons and miners. Joshua put his clothes on, ran a comb through his hair and slipped out without stopping at the kitchen to exchange pleasantries with his landlady.

A newsboy stood near Mrs. McIlhaney's front stoop, waving a stack of newspapers and calling out the headline: "Soapy Smith's Last Bluff!"

Joshua hesitated only a second before handing over his coins. He scanned the front-page article. "Shot Through the Heart by Frank Reid," read the subheading, and "Armed With a Winchester He Endeavors to Intimidate a Large Meeting of Indignant Citizens on the Juneau Wharf" gave the gist of the encounter last evening. Frank Reid was hailed as a hero, helping to rid the town of the criminal element which had intimidated the population for so long. Joshua felt a stab of jealousy. *He* could have become the local hero, if only he'd gotten to Soapy Smith first.

He fumed as he marched toward the Red Onion. Why hadn't he been more forceful? Why hadn't he obtained a weapon and rushed the con man, right out on the street? The article said Frank Reid was now in Bishop Rowe Hospital and there was strong hope for his recovery. Joshua pictured the man sitting up in bed, telling all who gathered around that he really hadn't been afraid as he stared down the barrel of Smith's gun. Later, there would be celebrations and Joshua himself could have been at the center of them all.

He took an empty chair and read the rest of the article as he sipped a mug of coffee. Smith had lain dead on the wharf for some hours. Charles Augustus Sehlbrede, the recently appointed U.S. commissioner for the district, appointed a coroner's jury and ordered an autopsy. The local jail was reported nearly full of members of Soapy's gang and bands of armed citizens were rounding up more. No wonder the atmosphere felt electrified this morning.

Beside the article on Smith's death was another, touting the amount of gold coming out of the Klondike, claiming that the bank and various hotel safes were stuffed with the golden dust and yellow nuggets. Another wave of bitterness shot through him.

"Good morning."

The voice, so nearby, startled Joshua and he sloshed his coffee. He looked up to see Harry Weaver standing beside him.

"You don't look nearly as happy as everyone else in town this morning," his friend said, taking a seat at the small table.

Joshua shrugged. He started to ask whether there was a possibility of getting his money from Smith's Parlor, now that the boss was dead and the others were being rounded up, but Harry was speaking of another subject.

"I have a lead on my suspect," he said. "Rumor says he's been loitering among that band of reporters who have their camp up the road. I'm heading that direction right after breakfast."

Harry tapped the folded newspaper that Joshua had dropped. "Klondike gold, indeed," he said. "You ever wonder why everyone in this city isn't dressed in the finest attire and buying rounds for all at the bars?"

"Some are," Joshua replied.

"A few, those who are complete fools with their money." Harry signaled the one waitress to bring him some food. "You notice, though, that the ones who aren't showing off their money are heading quietly for the next steamer out of the inlet."

He gave Joshua an intent look. "There are no fortunes

up there, friend. The big strikes happened, all right, but they happened a year ago, two years ago. It's been picked clean."

Joshua felt as if his chair had been kicked out from under him.

"If you haven't found a job or started a business here yet, I'd suggest that you go back to San Francisco and ask for your old job back. You'll be farther ahead than if you stay around here."

"But—"

"Come with me, Joshua. Come to that journalism camp and I'll show you. Those men who write these stories— they're not writing from the gold fields at all. They're right up the road, making up whatever sounds good enough to sell newspapers. They wire their stories back to the big cities down south and men continue to dream and travel all this way. For nothing."

Joshua's ears rang with the implications. So, even if he did manage to get his money back from Smith's Parlor and buy his supplies, he still wouldn't find gold when he got to the Klondike?

Harry's food arrived but Joshua shook his head at Rosa's query whether he also wanted something. He could barely afford the coffee. He excused himself, telling Harry he would see him around before he walked out to the street.

His mind spun. If he sold the few provisions he'd acquired—to some poor rube fresh off the boat—he could get home to Maddie and Isabelle. But he would arrive home destitute. He couldn't face his wife in that condition.

How could Harry's assertion be true? He saw men with big smiles, men who bought rounds of drinks and frequented the gambling tables—he *knew* big fortunes existed. The news reporters probably talked to these men as they were heading back from the gold fields, their pockets filled. That's where they picked up the optimistic stories. He turned back toward the Red Onion, reaching the door just as Harry emerged.

"I'll go with you," he said in a rush. "To that place you described with the reporters."

"Liarsville," Harry said. "Sure. I've rented a horse and carriage for the day. Let's go."

Joshua had a moment's uncertainty. They called this place Liarsville? Harry was walking quickly toward the blacksmith's shop and Joshua dropped his negative thoughts and caught up. Thirty minutes later they were riding up the narrow road that led northeast out of Skagway, Harry's confident hands on the reins.

The encampment was nearly a small town in itself. A wooden building housed a small store where food and tobacco were sold, according to the crudely painted sign above the door. A few dozen canvas tents stood around a central open area, and Joshua caught a glimpse inside one, where a man sat on an upturned barrel with a small typewriting machine on his lap. A wooden bunk with a thin mattress and a valise with clothing spilling out of it fairly well filled the space. The man didn't acknowledge their passage as he chewed the end of a cigar and punched the keys on the machine.

The open area boasted a large fire pit ringed with stones and men sat around on split logs that they'd pushed near to use as benches. A woman in a shabby ruffled dress ducked out of one tent and went into another. For a fleeting instant Joshua thought of his infant daughter and prayed that she would never know such a life as this.

"I'm posing as an editor from an east coast newspaper,"

Harry murmured as they descended the carriage. "Wander about, if you wish, but don't talk about what I'm doing. With luck, I'll catch my quarry and if you help watch him on the way back to the pier I'm authorized to pay you a little something."

Without another word he walked toward the wooden building. Joshua edged near the fire. Tall trees blocked nearly all the sunlight, giving the little makeshift village a damp, chilly air. Two men in dusty suits, sitting on the log seats, nodded toward him. Joshua remained standing, holding his hands toward the warmth.

"Well, that's this week's story. Soon as I get to town, I'll telegraph it to my editor," said a man who approached, pulling his jacket on over an untidy shirt and suspenders. He was the one who'd been typing away in his tent.

"What'd you say this time?" asked one of the campfire group, shifting to his left to get out of the drifting smoke.

"Same as usual," said the newcomer. "I toned it down a little from last week, when it was supposedly a quarter million in gold. This week it's only a hundred thousand."

He sat down and pulled a fresh cigar from his pocket, sprawling his legs toward the flames and letting his shoulders relax.

One of the other men let out a hoot. "Surprised those back in the offices don't question a thing. You know good and well that last stampeder only had about a hundred in dust on him."

"Hundred dollars, hundred thousand ... what's a few extra zeros?" The reporter laughed out loud.

Joshua eyed the men. So Harry was right—the news stories were completely fabricated. He caught them staring and lowered his gaze to the ground.

"What's your story, stranger?" one of them asked.

He looked up to see that all three had their eyes on him. He shrugged. "No particular story. Haven't been able to get outfitted yet, is all. A few friends of mine went, though. Two guys named Connell and Gariston. Earlier, there was one called Mick Thespen."

One of the reporters' expression brightened. "Thespen. I'm fairly certain he was the one who came through here couple of days ago."

"Yeah, the fellow with a hundred that he wished was a hundred thousand!" All three men laughed raucously.

Joshua forced a faint smile, nodding, feeling embarrassed that the men he'd wanted to travel with were now the brunt of this crude humor. He let his gaze travel through the camp. Harry had come out of the store and was heading toward the fire. Joshua remembered what he'd said, averted his eyes.

"Afternoon," Harry said to the three reporters. He edged in close and took one of the benches. "Harry Weaver, *Fairfax News-Gazette*."

The others offered introductions; when it came Joshua's turn he merely gave his name.

"My publisher knows a man who said he was coming out to the Klondike. Wants me to write up his personal story," Harry said. "A Jessie Durant. Any of you seen him come through here?"

"Name doesn't ring a bell," the man at Joshua's left said.

Harry gave a description but Joshua noticed he didn't pull out the Wanted sheet he'd been carrying.

One of the reporters spoke up. "I did see that one. A limp and a scar on his left cheek, you said?"

Harry nodded.

"And a western hat. He came through, maybe two, three days ago."

"Is he still around?"

The man pursed his lips. "I don't think so. Lots of stampeders come and go through here, very few stay around. They all want to get to the city and spend that money."

Another laugh rippled through the gathering.

"You're sure he left?" Harry asked.

"As much as you're ever sure of anything around here," the man answered.

Harry stood. "Mr. Farmer, I can offer you a lift back to Skagway if you want it."

Joshua pretended to consider. "Thank you, sir. I will accept it."

The reporter in the suspenders stood as well. "Might I trouble you to drop this at the telegraph office when you get there?" He pulled two sheets of paper from his jacket, the story about the false gold claims.

Harry took the pages and the two of them walked back to the rented carriage. During the ride back, Harry seemed preoccupied, probably wondering which direction his quarry had taken now.

Joshua didn't mind the lack of conversation. His mind replayed the talk back there at the campfire. Was nothing in this territory real? Was everything he'd ever heard about the gold rush and the vast fortunes a falsehood?

He thought about the man who had left a few weeks ago. If he had come back already, even with just a hundred dollars, it was likely more than Joshua would find on his own, especially if he had to lay out the money for food and supplies first. His brow pulled into a knot as he contemplated the unfairness of it all.

Aside from Harry Weaver, he hadn't met an honest man here yet; from the miners to the reporters to the gangsters and con men, everyone was out to cheat. His anger flared again; he was tired of being the one who repeatedly got swindled.

Then the idea struck. What if he simply took what he needed?

Maddie's face appeared in his mind. She would be mortified to know he was thinking this way. He edged his eyes toward Harry, another who would be ashamed of him. But Harry had other concerns right now. And what Maddie didn't know wouldn't hurt her.

Chapter 16

There was a good two minutes of silence at the table as Branson's words settled upon us. I finally remembered to chew the rest of my chicken. Mina sat with a wing-bone clasped in her fingers. Then the questions began.

"Related." I said. "But how——?"

"You said the two deaths must have happened more than seventy years apart," Mina said to the chief. "What could possibly be the relationship?"

It was pretty close to the same question I'd been trying to formulate.

Chief Branson shrugged. "The lab guy told me it wasn't a direct line, say, father to son, or two siblings. That's obvious anyway. But it's a connection, nevertheless."

"So, now you have a new angle," I told him.

"Let's say that *you* have a new angle." He glanced back and forth between Mina and me.

"But—"

"The case is still impossibly old," he said, "and I don't have any more manpower than I did last week. Minutes after we left the burial this afternoon, I had to send one guy out to a traffic accident and another to check out some lady who tried to steal a puppy from the sled-dog excursion guy. Guess she thought she could sneak it into her suitcase on the cruise ship. Eventually, I might get to these two sets of bones, but this is June and things won't slow down here until at least October when those ships quit for the season."

"Even then," Mina said to me, "it's not as if Skagway doesn't have anything for the police to do on a regular basis."

"Thank you," said Branson. He pushed his chair back. "Meanwhile, you ladies have at it. Investigate to your heart's content. Just be sure you don't taint any actual evidence you might find, and report to me if you learn anything of value."

He started to walk away then turned back. Leaning over the table he said, "A news story might be one way to start the ball rolling—figure out how to word it so it jogs someone's memory. Just a thought."

We watched him leave the bar.

"I like it," Mina said. "I can see my lead ... something about 'Missing a Few Skeletons From Your Closet?'"

Drake laughed out loud, which only encouraged her.

"Or, 'Brothers Bones Bring Bereavement ... something' Oh, I can't think of the right word for closure, but I'll figure it out."

We stayed long enough to polish off the platter of appetizers while Mina brainstormed her story idea aloud and Berta and I threw in occasional ideas. Drake pleaded tiredness, but I suspected that he simply lost interest. He said he would walk home and feed the dog her dinner, that

I should stay as long as I wanted.

It didn't take long, though, for the ideas to run out. Mina seemed distracted as she jotted notes, clearly wanting to get to her computer and start writing up a draft of her story. Berta's verve had dissipated, most likely because she'd enjoyed a couple of drinks with her friends in addition to the ones she'd consumed here at our table. I offered her a ride home, which she accepted, and so it was that Gold Rush Guy's wake broke up early in the evening.

Back at our little rental house I downed a large glass of water to dilute my more-than-usual quantity of wine, then Freckles talked Drake and me into taking her for a lengthy walk in the fading daylight. Drake found a ball game on TV and I curled into a corner of the sofa, the dog resting contentedly at my feet and the floral-papered box of old letters on my lap.

So far, it seemed that I fell asleep each evening before I'd finished reading one or two of them—not that the prose wasn't interesting—mainly I suppose because I was still adapting to the new work and location. Plus my mind kept being distracted by current events.

I had learned that a man named Joshua Farmer came to Skagway to search for gold, but although he didn't want to admit it to his wife back home in San Francisco, the undertone hinted that for whatever reason he'd been unable to actually start up the White Pass Trail. He had mentioned meeting some men and planning to join them for the long trek. Occasionally, he referred to something the wife, Maddie, had said in one of her letters so I turned now to those.

Written in a beautiful copperplate hand that I couldn't

even aspire to on my best days, the words seemed overly formal for communications between husband and wife but I supposed those were the times. I thought of the quick text messages Drake and I often use with each other. If they should be found a hundred years into the future, no one would have any idea of the depth of our feelings for each other. Maybe ours was not so different from the more reserved times of which I was currently reading.

July 10, 1898

Dearest Husband,

You might not have the opportunity to read this missive for months, I realize as I write it. You are now on the trail to the Klondike! It is astonishing to me, beyond contemplation, to think of you so far away and in such wild conditions. The newspapers continue to be filled with utterly fantastic tales of the region and I imagine you there, in the midst of it. It is with hope that I pray someone will be able to get this letter to you soon, if only for you to hear my voice in your head as you endure the hardships of the trail, for I have no doubt that this is not an easy path you have taken, my brave husband.

You mentioned your new friend, Harry Weaver. How fascinating that he is a detective! I would imagine it to be interesting and yet somewhat dangerous work. May I say that I am pleased that you did not say you wanted to take up that profession yourself. Much more reassuring that you intend to finish your adventure in Alaska in short order and come back home to us.

Isabelle continues to grow and change daily. I fear that you will not recognize her when you return. She walks quite steadily on her sturdy legs, toddling from room to room. And she tries to say words! Twice I would vow that I heard her say Ma-ma. I show her your photograph and coach her that this is Pa-pa. By the time you arrive I am determined that she will say it directly to you.

I must close now, in order to mail this letter before the post office closes. My apologies for the brevity of today's news.

Anxiously awaiting your return,

Your loving wife,

Maddie

I set the wife's letter aside and reached for the stack from her husband, the gold rush stampeder. There was only one more.

My dearest,

It is with great joy—oh, forgive me but I cannot be so formal—I have found gold! I shall be catching the next steamer for San Francisco. Buy yourself a new gown—we are going to celebrate!

J

The note was so much shorter than all preceding it that I flipped the page over and looked inside the envelope to be sure I hadn't missed something more. But really, I supposed, what more was there to say? The man had realized his dream of finding gold in the Klondike and was on his way home. Happy ending.

I felt mildly let down, wishing I knew how the story turned out. Did Joshua treat his wife to more than a new dress? How much gold did he find? Did the family gain a better lifestyle, or like so many modern lottery winners did they squander it in a short time? There were still a few envelopes with the wife's handwritten addresses. I picked up the next one from her.

The television clicked off before I had opened the envelope and Drake leaned across the sofa, reaching for me with a gleam in his eye. I dropped the letter back into the box and gave myself over to the more pleasurable real-time moment.

* * *

A couple of days passed in a blur: I made flights to bring departing customers in from their adventure trips (many with little vials of gold dust in their proud hands); I delivered cleaning crews to the cabins, then I took the next incoming groups out to begin their own adventures. Usually, I flew our JetRanger while Drake and Kerby alternated flying his A-Star, but sometimes it was the other way around. I felt that I was gaining some proficiency in the French-built machine, although I was still most comfortable with our familiar one. I had just landed at the heliport when I spotted Mina, rushing toward me.

"Hey, what's up?" I asked, pulling off my headset and letting the rotor blades wind down.

Her eyes were wide, her breathing quick. "My story was picked up by the wire services—look!"

She held out a tablet computer with a news page on it. I wasn't displeased to see that she'd skipped the alliterative Brothers' Bones headline and used a play on the idea of Missing Skeletons.

"Wow, congratulations! So, is there a Pulitzer in this for you?" I threw the tease out there while I finished the last couple of steps to shut down the helicopter.

"I don't know, but guess what?"

"Somebody knew who they were?"

Her expression drooped a little.

"Sorry. It really was a wild guess."

"Actually, yes. Leads are coming in from all over, people calling Chief Branson. He called to tell me so I could run a follow-up story if any of the leads pan out."

Kerby Allen walked up before I stepped down to the tarmac.

"Leads on what?" he asked.

"Mina's news story." I caught a warning glance from her. Oops. She probably wanted to keep it quiet so her next piece would actually be news. "But you probably wanted to talk business," I said to Kerby as I climbed down and secured the door.

"Just wanted to let you know that I've got Drake booked for a flight in the morning but you're free. So far. Bookings are coming in every day, though, so I'll keep you posted."

"Sounds good." I hoped my tone conveyed proper enthusiasm but not so much that he would hang around to eavesdrop. He headed back toward the FBO office.

"So, tell me about the calls ... ?" I walked beside Mina toward the parking lot.

"Branson is asking anyone who thinks they might be related to go to their local police and submit a DNA sample. The lab can compare them and if any are a match, we're on the way to solving this. Wouldn't it be exciting if my story was the direct connection?"

"It would," I agreed. I tried to imagine what direction this might take. Perhaps someone who remembered '70s-guy going away would now discover that there was an even older ancestor in the picture.

"Did your story mention that both men were murdered?"

"No. I really wanted to tell that part of it, but the Chief felt it might keep someone from coming forward. You know, a family that might feel its reputation would be tarnished or something."

There was also the real possibility that they would get more false leads. People in today's world have little if any shame about things that weren't talked about a generation ago. Dirty linen is the stuff of popular television nowadays.

Mina and I parted ways at her car. She said she was heading to Branson's office to see if there was anything new to report, while I had to fill out my logbooks and wait for Drake. I should have asked Kerby what time he was due in, but I could find that out now.

Inside, Kerby sat behind his desk talking with someone on the phone, so I went into the conference room and logged my flight time into the aircraft log and my personal one. Through the open doorway I could hear radio chatter, Drake's voice saying he was on final approach, the dispatcher's reply.

Within a minute I heard the A-Star, and a minute after that I saw him hover into position and set the craft down on the helipad. Chuey walked out to greet the passengers and escort them to the building. I gave him a quick smile and wondered if he and Mina were becoming less serious; she hadn't mentioned him in several days.

Even in private aviation, it seems that everything takes longer than you wish it would. It was thirty minutes later that Drake walked into the building, after shutting down his aircraft and giving it a little once-over inspection. He carried the logbook inside and muttered something about the JetRanger being due for an oil change, so he disappeared again to give Chuey the news. My cell phone rang before he returned.

"We found her!" It was Mina's voice.

"Her?"

"A woman whose DNA tested as a sibling match for cave-guy."

"Wow—he had a sister."

"Yep. I just left Branson's office where he was on the phone with her. Her name is Katherine Ratcliff and she says her brother's name was Michael. He was thirty years old when he came to Alaska and she says he never returned."

A hundred questions went through my mind. Was Katherine the only relative or had Michael been married, had children? Where was he from originally, and what had brought him here? And, most importantly, who had killed him?

"Ms. Ratcliff is flying up from Seattle day after tomorrow," she said.

"So, does this mean Chief Branson will be taking over the murder investigation again?"

"I don't know. He didn't say that to me, but it might depend on how hard the family pushes to have answers. I do know the phones were ringing off the hook there at the station."

I pictured Branson, not easily flustered but perhaps feeling a little overwhelmed. It occurred to me that I might be able to find some information on my own, something to bring in the way of help. I said goodbye to Mina and immediately dialed my brother.

Drake meandered in, was hailed by Kerby, and the two of them stepped outside the conference room to discuss the next day's schedule.

I spent a few minutes reminding Ron of our previous conversation about finding background information on someone long missing, and told him I now had a name. He questioned me on a few other details, but I was sadly lacking in real information. I told him I would talk with the police chief here and could probably get back to him in a couple of days.

Kerby gave me a long look as I emerged to join them.

"Hey," I said. "Sorry, that took longer than expected. So, do I have a flight tomorrow morning?"

I probably should have called Ron later, giving priority to the business I'd been hired to do here.

"Nope. Drake's got the morning covered," Kerby said. "I have a possible VIP. The assistant is supposed to get back to me within the hour. But I can take that one."

Not surprising. Drake had once told me that at every company he'd ever worked, the boss always seemed willing to step up and take extra flights whenever a celebrity showed up. I wondered for a moment who it might be, but then decided I didn't really care.

Kerby's desk phone rang and he dashed for it, while I filled Drake in on the latest about cave-guy's long-lost sister and her imminent arrival.

Chapter 17

Joshua stared at the front of Smith's Parlor. The windows and door had been boarded up since Soapy's funeral ten days ago, by most accounts a paltry affair with only eight people in attendance and the con man's body relegated to a rocky, undesirable section of the cemetery. Apparently, no one else planned to take over the once-lucrative gambling hall. Harry had told him this was because twenty-six of Soapy's men had been rounded up and arrested. Any others were undoubtedly lying low and avoiding the vigilantes.

The drone of voices from State Street had deepened as the citizens gathered. Joshua hurried the half block west and saw two horse-drawn wagons in front of Union Church. Close to a thousand people filled the street. Men, women and children crowded near the door, although only a fraction of them would ever fit inside. The town's mood had been somber since the news yesterday that Frank Reid had succumbed to his wounds.

"The poor man," said a female voice beside him. "Can you imagine, Mr. Farmer? Him lying there in agony these twelve days since the shooting? That's what they're saying. It was awful for poor Mr. Reid."

Mrs. McIlhaney dabbed her eyes with a spotless white handkerchief. Her children stood at her side, craning their necks toward the open church door.

Joshua nodded. He'd envisioned being the hero who shot Soapy Smith; he didn't quite picture it ending this way.

A hush rippled almost tangibly through the crowd as six men carried the flag-draped coffin out and placed it in one of the wagons. Women followed, their arms laden with flowers from the church, and placed them around the coffin. Reid's closest friends climbed into the second wagon and in a matter of minutes many in the streets who had brought their own carriages fell in behind.

At a greeting from a woman a few yards away, Mrs. McIlhaney turned away from Joshua and he meandered closer to the two wagons.

"I'm taking my rented carriage out to the cemetery," Harry Weaver said when he walked up. "I figure in a large gathering like this there's a chance I'll spot Durant. You may ride along with me, if you would like."

Joshua nodded absently, imagining the body of Reid inside that coffin. The first wagon began to move slowly, at parade pace, along the street. From the sidewalks, people watched, men removing their hats and women waving handkerchiefs—all bidding farewell to Frank Reid.

Harry nudged Joshua's arm and the two made their way to the blacksmith's shop where the carriage waited with the horse already in its traces. Harry guided their ride to the north edge of town and pulled aside, allowing the two wagons and the other conveyances to pass. A string of people, probably more than a hundred, trailed along on horseback and on foot. He showed Joshua the photograph of the bank robber, Jessie Durant, once more.

"Advise me if you see him," he said.

But Joshua's attention was riveted by another familiar face.

Mick Thespen, the man who'd started up the White Pass Trail shortly after Joshua arrived. So, he had come back, and better off than he'd left by the look of it. The man wore a satisfied expression and a slight smile, despite the somber nature of today's occasion. Joshua took in the clean suit of clothes, complete with a silk necktie and gold nugget tiepin. He watched as Mick passed within a few yards, apparently not recognizing him. The small knot of resentment he'd felt toward the hero-worship of Frank Reid coalesced into a gut-sized lump when he saw the man with whom he could have made his fortune, traveling now in style—and without him.

"There, on the large gelding," Harry whispered. "It's Durant." He let the man pass by, on the far side of the crowd, then he snapped the reins and guided the carriage into position to follow at a distance.

The cemetery was slightly more than a mile from town, situated near the Skagway River in a wooded area. Those on horseback and in carriages pulled aside and tied their mounts before walking toward the hole in the ground where Frank Reid would rest. Someone had chosen the best plot for Reid, on a high spot with majestic trees behind. In contrast, the freshly covered mound that marked Soapy

Smith's final repose was in a rocky section of the cemetery, where barely a foot of earth covered the grave and a plain white-painted wooden board gave the barest of details on five lines of black lettering: Jefferson/R. Smith/Age 38/ Died July 8/1898.

Harry handed the reins to Joshua and leaped down from his seat, ducking into the crowd to keep his bank robber in sight. Joshua tied the reins to a slender tree trunk and scanned the crowd, spotting Mick Thespen's neat bowler above the heads of others. He held back for a moment, considering. The recent trip to Liarsville had continued to nag at him.

A preacher stood beside the open grave, directing pallbearers to lower the casket, raising his hand heavenward as he offered a final prayer. Joshua subtly edged his way toward Thespen. When the man turned, he spoke up.

"Mick? Mick Thespen?" He held out his hand.

Mick looked puzzled for a moment.

"Joshua Farmer. We met at the Red Onion, the night before you left for the Klondike."

Vague recognition dawned.

"It appears you've done well for yourself. I'm happy to see a man achieve success." He clapped Mick on the shoulder, smiling broadly. "Connell and Gariston left shortly after you—did you see them out there, by chance?"

With the other two names, Thespen finally placed the conversation. He gave Joshua a warm smile.

"That I did. Gariston stayed, but Connell found a lucky place and panned some decent nuggets. He'll be arriving in Skagway this afternoon and I offered to take him out for a celebratory drink. Say, would you care to join us?"

Joshua accepted but before Mick had walked out of

sight began to doubt himself. He would be expected to pay for his share, he felt sure, and his cash was depleted. He could perhaps sell another of his mining tools and come up with enough. He squared his shoulders and walked through the crowd.

A ripple of disturbance caught his attention near the edge of the cemetery. He spotted Harry and hurried that direction.

"Joshua! Pull the pair of handcuffs from my back pocket," Harry said, struggling a bit as he held both arms of the man he'd come to capture. Despite Durant's limp, the man was strong.

Two men stepped forward the minute Harry said he was a Pinkerton detective. They helped subdue the prisoner while Harry fastened the rigid metal cuffs onto Durant's wrists. Joshua and Harry gripped his biceps and guided him toward the carriage.

"I'll restrain him but I surely could use your help in making certain he doesn't cause any trouble on the way back to town," Harry told Joshua.

He positioned Jessie Durant in the center of the carriage's long seat and looped a length of chain through the handcuffs and around a metal bar near their feet, securing it in place with a padlock that he drew from the satchel he'd brought along. He pulled a pistol from a holster under his jacket.

"Joshua, please drive."

The ride back to town felt endless. The bank robber kept eyeing Joshua, as if he would be only too happy to push him out and take over the reins. Twice, Harry nudged the man with the barrel of the gun.

"Drive straight to the police station, Joshua. Durant,

you're waiting in a holding cell until I arrange for your trip back to face justice in Washington."

But they found the police station empty, closed up. Harry tried the door while Joshua stood beside the carriage with the reins in hand.

"They must have all gone to the funeral," Harry said, "those who weren't arrested last week for taking part in Soapy Smith's shenanigans. Let's go to the wharves. The *Queen* is in port. I'll see what I can arrange."

They took up their positions once again and Joshua steered down to First Avenue where the steamship was, indeed, moored at the Juneau Wharf, the same where the shootout had taken place. Harry jumped down from the carriage, leaving Joshua in charge of both the reins and the pistol.

Durant growled at him, low in his throat, and laughed aloud when Joshua flinched.

Scoundrel.

Harry reappeared within ten minutes.

"Good news. She sails at five o'clock and they have a secure bin below decks where I can lock this one away. I've had them telegraph my office in Seattle to expect us and to meet the ship with law enforcement aplenty."

Joshua started to hand over the pistol, unsure what to do next.

"If you can stay around a few more minutes ..." Harry glanced over his shoulder and saw that two burly crewman from the ship were approaching. "The Pinkerton Detective Agency has something for you. But first, I need to see to this."

With the sailors at hand, Harry opened the padlock and the three of them muscled the prisoner down from the carriage and started toward the gangway to the hold of the ship. Joshua ran his hand down the horse's neck, his thoughts going a hundred directions as he watched the bustle surrounding the busy harbor.

Harry had said the officials at the other end of the line would meet 'us.' That meant he was leaving. Joshua felt a small premonition of loneliness. He would miss his friend, the only man he'd met here who seemed a hundred percent genuine. He blinked hard when he saw Harry walk down the gangway and come toward him.

"This is the official reward for assistance," Harry said, holding out some folded bank notes. "I'm sorry it isn't more, but I have added a little extra because I'll ask that you return the carriage for me. I need to stay here and be sure no one mistakenly opens that storage space."

"So, it's goodbye then."

Harry nodded. "Unless I can talk you into coming along. We've talked about this before, friend. You know my advice: leave the gold behind and get home. There might even be a starting position available at the San Francisco office of Pinkerton's. I would be happy to give a recommendation."

Joshua stared at the money in his hand. "I don't have the—"

"I could advance you enough for your ticket. It's not a problem."

"I— I'm not sure."

Harry busied himself holstering the pistol Joshua had handed him. "Fair enough. Think about it. My offer stands until she sails at five o'clock. I've booked a cabin for myself but it's a double and you are welcome to the second bunk. Be here by four-thirty if you want it."

Joshua felt torn. Maddie would love for him to be home.

He would love to see her again, and soon. But something about this town and the lure up in the Canadian Rockies pulled at him.

"I shall return the carriage," he said. "And you might see me later."

Harry patted his shoulder. "I hope so. If not, I wish you luck. It's been nice knowing you."

Despite their words, the goodbye felt permanent. Joshua climbed into the carriage and took the reins.

Leaving the blacksmith's an hour later, he felt a hand on his shoulder.

"Still want that drink?" It was Mick Thespen.

With money burning a hole in his pocket, Joshua tipped his hat and fell into step beside the other man.

"Alastair says he'll meet us at The Board of Trade." Mick talked nonstop as they walked. "He told me he came back with over a thousand, after only two weeks! I did better than that myself, but it took me darn near the whole season."

Joshua soaked up the news, including the fact that the saloon at The Board of Trade was reputed to be one of the nicer ones in town. At gold rush prices, his twenty dollars probably wouldn't buy much. He would have to pace himself.

They walked into the neatly painted building with its wide windows across the front. Alistair Connell sat midway back in the large room, at a four-place table, and it was apparent that he'd begun drinking earlier in the day.

"Josh, old man, good to see you again!" he exclaimed, exhaling the scent of Scotch whiskey.

Joshua held out his hand, smiling despite the fact that he never allowed anyone the familiarity of shortening his name.

Mick pulled two chairs out and plopped himself into one of them. A woman in an extremely low-cut gown came over.

"I'm Bitsy," she said. "Would you gentlemen like to buy a lady a drink?"

Mick and Alastair gestured for the woman to take the empty chair, and she signaled the bartender to bring over a bottle.

Joshua felt his eyes grow wider. "How much will—?"

Mick interrupted Joshua's question, leaning toward him. "Never mind. I'm buying." He patted his side.

The bartender carried over a tray with a whiskey bottle and three empty glasses.

"Ain't you having none, sweetheart?" Alistair asked after the man walked away.

"Silly Joe, he forgot a glass for me!" She was out of her chair and scampering up to the bar before any of the men could move.

Mick poured a generous two fingers into each of the glasses, and Bitsy returned with a glass already filled for herself.

"Here's to all of your success in the beautiful Klondike!" Bitsy said, raising her glass. "Drink up, boys."

Alistair tipped back his glass and drained it. Mick took a more restrained drink from his; Joshua only sipped.

Bitsy gave Alistair a wink. "Looks like this one needs a refill," she said, reaching for the bottle.

Connell didn't flinch as he downed the second glass, and Mick finished off his first one. With each refill, the laughter grew louder, the tales of their exploits on the trail more outrageous. Joshua eyed them carefully. The more they drank, the less careful they would be. He excused himself to use the outhouse and stepped to the back of the saloon.

Beside the back door a man stood, leaning one shoulder against the wall of the narrow hallway, eyeing the festive atmosphere in the bar.

"Hope you're one of the rich ones," he said as Joshua walked past him.

He paused. "What do you mean?"

"She's a percentage woman," the man said. "Every woman here is."

"A what?"

"You never met one? Well, the deal is that they'll get you to buy 'em drinks. Except you notice she don't fill her own glass from the same bottle? The bartender always fills hers. She's drinking weak tea. But you're buying whiskey, usually the most expensive one in the house. Bartender gives her a percentage of all the sales for your table. And if someone wants a little female company later in the evening, she'll be happy to do that too. After you're too drunk to care about the price."

"Why are you telling me this?"

"Hell, I don't work here. I just keep an eye out for the innocent ones, and you look like you just came in off the boat."

Joshua felt himself bristle. He walked out the back door without another word and pushed open the door of the crudely built latrine. Did he really have such a gullible look about him? First the town merchants, then Soapy Smith, now a woman named Bitsy—all out to take advantage. Even Thespen and Connell had gone off to seek their fortunes without including him—were they any more entitled to the riches in their pockets than he? The unaccustomed liquor raced through his veins and his thoughts turned dark. He finished his business, buttoned his pants and stamped back inside.

At the table, the whiskey bottle was empty. Bitsy drained her glass and stood, offering to go to the bar and get another.

"To our new friend Bitsy!" Alastair slurred. "May we spend even more hours in her lovely company."

Joshua thought of the man near the door. He raised his glass.

"To Bitsy. And to all the other lovelies in our fair city." A solid gulp of the whiskey burned its way down his throat, emptying his glass. "We can't spend all our energy in one place, can we now?"

He turned to Mick. "How about if we visit a few other places in town first?"

Mick seemed surprised but he stood up, and since all the others were standing Alistair did, as well. Only Bitsy seemed a little taken aback.

"I'll ask the bartender for your check," she offered.

"What's this about?" Mick said under his breath.

"Just wanted to see what some of the other saloons are like," Joshua said with a shrug.

Outside, the evening air had a crisp bite to it. Music drifted from a different establishment each time a door opened, creating a disjointed jangle of sound.

"Where to?" Mick asked. "Clancy's, The Red Onion, one of the hotels?"

Alistair wove a little unsteadily as they began to walk.

"I hear interesting music this way," Joshua said, turning into an alley a half-block from where they'd started. "Let's find it."

Ten feet into the narrow alley, the path disappeared into blackness. Joshua turned abruptly and Alistair ran into him, tripping and landing face-first in a muddy puddle. The water splashed over Joshua's trousers legs and he let out an exclamation. Mick began to laugh, bending down to assist his friend, and the white of his neck showed in a faint gleam under the half moon.

A slender, vulnerable band of white.

Joshua didn't allow himself to think—he raised his arm and sliced downward with the bladelike edge of his hand, a quick chop. Mick fell, unconscious, on top of Alastair who hadn't made a sound since his own fall.

Quickly, working as quietly as possible, he rolled Mick over and felt the man's pockets. The bulk of a leather purse revealed itself and Joshua plucked it from inside Mick's silk-lined jacket. He jammed it into his own trouser pocket and shoved the limp man aside.

Alistair's face was covered in mud when Joshua rolled him over. He couldn't tell if the unconscious man was breathing or not. At the moment he didn't care. He rooted through pockets—pants, jacket, vest—finally coming upon a clutch of bills wedged into a silver money clip.

Voices sounded at the far end of the alley. Like a cat, Joshua leaped over the two prone men and fled the way he had come, back onto Holly street. He caught sight of the boarded up, dead-eyed windows of Smith's Parlor. What he had just done, was it any different from what he'd witnessed here when the card dealer stole a man's pouch of gold? He shoved the thought aside and made his way as casually as possible back to his rooming house, his heart thumping audibly.

Chapter 18

It had been decided that Chief Branson would meet Katherine Ratcliff at the airport and talk with her at the station before bringing Mina and me into it. I found myself re-dusting the furniture and actually cleaning the refrigerator as I waited impatiently for his call. The station was only a few blocks' walk, but still, I found myself eager to learn how it would all turn out. When the phone rang at eleven-thirty, I jumped.

I'm not sure what I expected of our missing man's sister, but I found myself surprised to be facing an elderly woman. Katherine stood up when I entered the room and I greeted her a little breathlessly—granted, I had speed-walked all the way from our place. She had a puffy cap of short, white hair and a gently lined face that attested to an indoor lifestyle and the mild, humid climate of the Pacific Northwest—as opposed to the leathery look of outdoorsy women in the dry Southwest. She may have once been about my height but stooped shoulders and an uncertain posture had taken away some inches. She wore a pantsuit of pale blue with a flowered blouse in the same tones, and I noted that the blue almost perfectly matched her eyes. It startled me to realize that, had my mother lived, she would be close to this same stage of life.

"Charlie, I'm pleased to meet you," Katherine said. "Chief Branson tells me you are a private detective. That's exciting. I'm glad you will be working on our case."

I felt pretty certain that I hadn't mentioned my quasi-detective status to the chief. Mina must have told him. Either that or he'd run a background check on me. In either case, I didn't bother to correct the misconception with Ms. Ratcliff.

Branson glanced over my shoulder. "And here is Mina Gengler, the reporter whose story brought you here."

Katherine and I turned to see Mina edging her way between desks in the squad room, approaching the chief's office with a mixture of excitement and fluster on her face.

"Sorry I'm running late," she said. She handed Chief Branson a stack of message slips. "People have been calling the newspaper, too. Wilbur thought you should have these."

Once her hand was free she extended it to Katherine and introduced herself. I got the feeling that she, too, was a little disconcerted to realize that our cave guy would now be an old man if he were alive today.

"Maybe we can find a quiet place to talk," I suggested. The perpetually ringing telephones and conversation between two officers at their desks didn't provide a very conducive setting.

"You may use my office," Branson said, "or there's a room with table and chairs that we alternate using as a conference room and interrogation space."

"We might take our guest to lunch," Mina suggested, and since that seemed like a far better way to put Katherine at ease, I seconded the idea.

Then came the decision about where and how to get there, which led me to wonder how able-bodied our witness was, but she surprised me by taking the lead toward the station's front door. We walked two blocks to a teahouse Mina knew, a place far enough off the main drag to be largely undiscovered by tourists. The three of us settled at a table near the window and ordered salads before getting down to business.

"I brought a photo of my brother," Katherine said, opening the clasp of her boxy purse and plucking out a single picture. "It was taken a year or two before he left. At the time, we filed missing person reports and posted flyers wherever we could think to do it."

She handed me the photo and I placed it on the table between Mina and myself, so we could both study it. It was an informal shot of a blond man with long sideburns and hair that touched the collar of his tan leisure suit. He had a wide smile as he leaned against a concrete barrier of some sort, with the Golden Gate Bridge in the background.

"I took this—I distinctly remember that, although I can't recall many other details of the day. I was married at the time and I'm not sure why my husband wasn't there. Or maybe he was. I've forgotten the exact circumstances. The marriage went badly and I changed back to my maiden name when I divorced. That's a whole other story, the marriage, and not a good one. Anyway, I pursued my degree and ended up teaching high school English for close to forty years. I'm sure those kids thought I was such a fossil by then."

She chuckled, and conversation waned as the waitress brought our lunches.

"Do you have any idea why your brother came to Alaska?" I asked, once we'd finished such details as passing the pepper and taking first bites of our salads.

Katherine shook her head. "I've been thinking about that ever since I responded to your news story. It doesn't make much sense."

"What was Michael's life like at that time? What was he doing?"

"We grew up in Seattle. It's where our parents had lived their whole lives. Well, he was six years younger than I, still in junior high school when I left home, so we really traveled in different worlds. I was accepted at an east coast college, met my future husband, married him and settled near Boston. Aside from letters and occasional phone calls home—remember, there were no cell phones in those days and long distance calls were still pretty costly—well, I got the barest details from Mother but rarely saw them more than once every year or two.

"As I mentioned, it wasn't until my husband and I split up that I moved back to the west coast. By then Michael had finished school and was working for a private equity company."

I started to ask the name of it, but she went on. "Long out of business now. They had folded by the time we started looking for Michael in 1975."

"Maybe he came here looking for another job," Mina suggested.

"I don't think so. Mother was getting fairly frail by then,

Dad had passed away a couple of years before—they were not young parents, even when I was born—and Michael continued to live at home to take care of her. She believed that he'd merely gone on a vacation; she insisted it was a trip to Portland, Oregon. Then again, her mind was getting fuzzy by that time. She also told me that he had taken a real interest in family history. It's possible that the trip was related to that, but I can't think how. I've never heard of any relatives in Oregon, much less in Alaska."

"I imagine genealogy research was a very different process in those days, before the Internet and all the ancestry websites that have sprung up," I mused.

"I suppose. As I said, Michael and I really didn't have a lot of contact during those years. Even when I moved back to Seattle I immediately became involved in earning a living for myself, commuting to Tacoma for my teaching job."

"So, neither you nor Michael ever married or had children?"

"No. I'm afraid I'm the end of the line for our branch of the Ratcliff family."

"What about his friends?" Mina asked. "I suppose you—"

"Oh, yes. We contacted everyone we could think of, although there weren't many. You have to understand that Michael was something of a loner. He was a studious boy in school, never went out for sports, not that I'm aware of. Aside from a couple of boys from childhood, he didn't seem to pal around much with anyone in particular. We tried tracking his co-workers but, as I mentioned, the company was defunct and many of the young, go-getter employees spread across the country as they found other jobs."

"In the process of your previous search, was there any

evidence at all? Anything that would give us a clue why he came to Skagway, who he might have been meeting here?"

Katherine shook her head slowly. "Nothing. Of course, we had no reason to believe this was his destination. Had we known I suppose we could have checked with some of the ships or airlines to see if he'd bought a return ticket or something. I chided my mother for going to all the trouble we did to find him. At the time I really thought he was hiding out to avoid me."

Liquid pools formed in her eyes. "Michael and I had our differences and I have to admit to being furious with him at the time he left. He'd taken some money—not important now. My regret is that Mother died, not knowing."

She wrapped her napkin around an index finger and dabbed at each eye. "He's my only relative—*was* my only relative. I suppose it can't matter to anyone but me now, but I really would like to know what happened."

Well, we sort of knew *what* happened, just not why or who did it. And my first thought was that there could very well be a killer out there who believed he'd gotten away with Michael's murder. I wasn't sure how much Chief Branson had told Katherine but figured I'd better get it all out there.

"The police chief ... did he tell you the cause of Michael's death?" I tried to keep my voice gentle.

She nodded, two quick little bobs. "That he was stabbed, yes. And that he was found in a cave or mineshaft, or some such place."

"Yes, that's true. I saw the place where he was found. And did the chief mention a second set of remains?"

Her eyebrows pulled together in a narrow white wave. "He did say something ... I guess part of that slipped by me when I heard how Michael had been killed." Her voice broke slightly on that final word.

I took a deep breath. "There was an even older set of bones in the same cave. When the crime lab tested them, it revealed that those remains and Michael's were related. It's why they wanted your DNA before asking you to come here to claim your brother."

"What are you saying?"

"It means that you are also related in some way to the older person."

She pushed her plate away. "I ... I don't know how that could be."

"We don't either," Mina told her softly. "But it's what we plan to find out."

I used my salad as an excuse not to talk for a few minutes, to mull over what we'd learned. Katherine seemed stunned. Mina had received a text message and was busily typing a response. I tried to think of ways to get any information whatsoever on a dead body from more than a hundred years ago.

"Katherine, do you own an old family bible or anything like that?"

She shook her head. "If there was one sometime in years past, I don't have it now."

"You said that Michael had become interested in family history. What about his notes, anything he might have compiled in his search?"

"I've never come across it. But, when I cleaned his room—after Mother's death I had to clear things out and sell the house—I did save a few boxes of his possessions. Since we'd never located him, I had no way to know what might be important. At the time I was thinking in terms of what he would want when he came home. There was a time, a few years ago, that I discarded a lot of it. You know, thinking he would never care about clothes from ages ago. I just don't remember what I threw out and what I might have kept. Oh, lord, I might have thrown all of it out. I don't remember."

I reached out and squeezed her hand.

"Don't stress over it right now," I said, "but when you get home it would be very helpful if you could look for those boxes. Go through them and let me know what's there."

I wrote down my cell number and Mina's and watched her put the slip of paper into her purse. Now if only she could keep a clear enough head that she would remember to do it.

Mina dropped a credit card on the small tray that held our check. "Business expense," she said.

Normally, in our investigation business, these types of things would be passed along to the client, but in this case maybe we needed to see how it worked out.

Katherine remained preoccupied as we walked her back to the police station. Luckily, Chief Branson took over once we went inside and took seats in his office.

"Ms. Ratcliff, I've made arrangements for your flight back," he said. "The remains are securely packaged and will be delivered to the airport tomorrow for your flight. I'm speaking of Michael's remains. The older gentleman was buried in the local gold rush cemetery shortly after our lab finished the identification work. Both cases remain open with my department, although you must understand that the older man's killer will likely never be determined. That might be true for your brother's murderer as well. I can't make any guarantees."

Katherine nodded, her countenance more stoic than mine would have been.

"Now that we know of the familial relationship, we can have the older remains exhumed," he said. "It won't happen today but I could have them shipped ..."

"No, that's all right," she said. "I think it's appropriate that he remain in the gold rush cemetery."

"I've made a reservation for you at the Golden North Hotel tonight and I can give you a lift to the airport in the morning."

I have to say, I was most impressed with the chief's bedside manner. Cops come in all personalities and many are very caring people, but not all of them would take it this far with a crime victim's relative.

"I can give you a ride to the hotel," Mina said, eyeing the suitcase in the corner of the chief's office, one that would be a little iffy for a seventy-something woman to pull down the uneven sidewalks of the side streets here.

Katherine spent a few minutes giving Chief Branson some additional contact information while I carried the large bag out to Mina's car which sat in the gravel lot in front of the small station.

"Remind her about looking through Michael's papers when she gets home," I said. "I have a feeling there's going to be some important clue in something he left behind."

"Will do. What's our next step, then? Wait to hear from her or keep working on it from this end."

"I'm going to talk to my brother again and check some more online databases. Not sure where that might lead, but at least we now have his name and a little bit of history. Call me tomorrow and we'll take it from there."

Chief Branson and Katherine Ratcliff walked out, and

I waited until she was settled in the car and Mina had pulled away before I started walking toward home. Little did I know that my next contact with my detecting buddy would come in the middle of the night when she called in tears, practically incoherent, to say that someone had delivered a dead cat to her doorstep with a note made from cut-out magazine letters tied around its neck: LEAVE THIS BUSINESS ALONE!

Chapter 19

"Mr. Farmer—is that you?" came Mrs. McIlhaney's voice from the parlor. "You've missed supper but there are some biscuits left if you'd— My goodness, what happened to your trousers?"

He froze, halfway up the stairs. Damn the luck—she'd spotted the mud, despite the dim light from the single lamp burning on the hallway table. He didn't dare walk down and speak with her; she would smell the liquor on his breath and she had strict rules about boarders being in a drunken state in her home. He felt like an errant child and cringed at the notion that he could be asked to turn out his pockets, revealing the stolen money.

"A wagon, I'm afraid. I was standing too close to a large puddle."

"Well, get them off and I shall clean them for you in the morning."

She returned to her needlework and he quickly locked himself in his room. His heart pounded as he dropped the leather pouch and the thick clip of cash onto his bed.

What have I done?

Alistair Connell might be dead—heaven forbid, both men might be. He'd given Mick Thespen a hard whack to the neck. He could be charged as a murderer. If they were not dead, the situation would not be much better—they would track him down to get their money back. Joshua had clearly been seen with the pair in the Board of Trade Bar and the law could come knocking at the door shortly. Mrs. McIlhaney liked him, he felt sure, but she would never harbor a criminal. He began jamming his possessions into his valise.

He pictured the *Queen*, sitting at the pier. Harry and his prisoner had gotten aboard, and Harry had offered Joshua the extra bunk in his cabin. He could race down there, tell Harry he'd changed his mind about going ...

But the *Queen* had sailed at five o'clock, he realized. A lump settled at the pit of his stomach. There wouldn't be another outbound steamer for days, perhaps even a week. He would have to hide somewhere until then, perhaps out at Liarsville, the camp full of journalists. He could find an unoccupied tent ...

The stack of provisions he'd accumulated for the Trail lay in front of the dresser. He picked through them, deciding what might be of use. At this point he wouldn't need spare changes of clothing as much as he should have food. The large bags of flour and sugar would only be useless weight. He had two chocolate bars and some dried fruit, which he tossed into the valise. What was he thinking? He stopped moving about and forced himself to calm down.

Skagway was teeming with people, an easy place to remain anonymous, he told himself. He had money; as long as he stayed away from familiar haunts and moved to different lodgings, he could surely keep out of sight for a few more days. He sat on the bed and counted the money.

His heart pounded as he eyed the pile of bank notes. Connell's cash was more than Joshua had ever made in a year. And the gold in Mick's pouch—he was amazed at the amount of it, surely the total came to tens of thousands of dollars. Cash and gold, beautifully unidentifiable. He carefully transferred the anonymous riches to his own money belt.

Maddie. Their lives would be transformed by his new fortune; although this amount of money wouldn't make him a wealthy man, it would provide the basis for a new start. He pulled out paper and pen and sat down to write, then he paused. What to say?

He could never admit what he'd done. Besides, why tell the truth about his Alaska adventure? No one else did, it seemed. Corruption among officials and businessmen, lawlessness practically everywhere, and the press blatantly printing whatever they wanted to as the truth, no matter what the facts were. Joshua had been shamelessly cheated and now he had turned the tables. Would his wife rather hear about those things, or would it be better to simply say that he had found his fortune? He penned a few quick words and sealed the envelope.

Downstairs, he could hear Mrs. McIlhaney's voice. His pulse quickened—had someone come to the door? He blew out the candle and peered out his small window. The street below was never quiet, but at the moment he couldn't see evidence of any activity at the door of this home. He edged to the door and opened it a tiny bit. The landlady's words were unintelligible but her tone was soothing; she was probably speaking to the children, convincing them to get ready for bed. He softly closed the door and stretched out on the bed.

Sleep was impossible. His thoughts roiled. He couldn't leave the house until he knew the family downstairs was asleep. Even then, he might be heard sneaking away into the night. And where would he go? Other rooming houses were usually full, and no respectable woman would admit him this late. Besides, many of them knew Mrs. McIlhaney—word would get back and the gossip would start.

A hotel was a possibility, but there again, questions about his arrival in town so late at night. And hotels were the first place the law would come looking. Make that the second place—if Mick and Alistair reported the theft, or came looking on their own, they knew where he lived. His nerves tingled; he must get out of this house at the earliest opportunity.

He slipped out of bed and padded across the room in his socks, cringing when one of the floorboards creaked. Below, the household had become quiet.

Back to the question of what provisions to take. He couldn't very well walk around town with more than his smallest valise, not without weighing himself down. For the time being, checking into a hotel or rooming house would attract too much attention. He would pack what he needed for the voyage to San Francisco into his suitcase and hide it somewhere, perhaps beneath the stack of wooden crates he'd noticed in the yard behind the house.

Carrying a pack of essentials on his back, he would blend in with the population on the streets and look for different places to sleep each night until the next ship was ready to leave port. He dressed in his warmest pants, mackinaw and boots and waited for morning.

Clouds hung low over the mountaintops when Joshua reached the street after moving softly through the house and closing the front door as quietly as possible. He swiftly covered a few blocks, heading toward the mail office with his letter to Maddie in hand. Depositing it in the box for outbound mail, he realized that he might very well be on the same boat as the letter and that his wife would receive himself and his written account of the news at the same time. He smiled at the thought of her joyful expression when she realized their money worries were over.

"Collection for a grave marker for Frank Reid," a man called out, holding a tin can out to passersby. "Donate to the fund!"

Joshua shoved his hand into a pocket and came out with two dollars, which he stuffed into the container. A magnanimous gesture toward the man who'd taken the glory for killing Soapy Smith—or a small token to assuage his own guilt? He shoved those thoughts aside and walked on.

The smell of fried meat wafted from the door of a hotel restaurant and he paused to stare in the windows. The place glowed with light from overhead kerosene lamps—too much light. He would too easily be seen from the street. He made his way around back and hesitated beside the open door. A cook spotted him.

"Down on your luck, mister?" The grizzled man eyed a bucket of garbage and fished out two biscuits and an undercooked strip of bacon. He stepped to the doorway and extended his hand. "Here, take these. Go on, take 'em.

I just tossed 'em in there a minute ago."

Joshua wanted to protest, but his stomach growled and he couldn't honestly think of a place in town where he would feel confident about sitting down at a table in a brightly lit room and ordering from a waiter. He lowered his gaze and took the food.

Humiliation washed over him. The first time in his life that he could have bought the finest food on the menu, without regard for the cost, and he was afraid to do it. His stomach growled again and he wolfed down the first biscuit. The bacon and second biscuit followed. Hunger appeased, he slunk out of the alley and tried once more to think of a safe place to go.

Sticking to the side roads, Joshua watched vigilantly for lawmen but the early morning streets were fairly quiet. He worked his way toward The Board of Trade saloon where last night's trouble began. No music came from the establishment but a few hardy souls could be seen inside, a table of card players and a lone man talking to the bartender. Joshua turned his back and quickly walked a half block before realizing that his quick pace could easily draw attention at an hour when most men had only just awakened or were stumbling home from a night of drinking and whoring.

An alleyway opened to his right and he realized it was the place, the scene of his crime. A cautious peek into the shadows revealed no bodies on the ground and he found himself releasing a long breath. They weren't dead after all.

Or, if they were, someone had discovered them and taken the bodies away. Either way this wasn't good news. The law could be hunting him for murder, or Connell and Thespen could be after him for their money.

He hurried off in the opposite direction.

A newsboy called out from outside the offices of the *Skagway News*. Joshua pulled the brim of his hat lower and approached, handing over the correct change for a copy of the morning edition. He tucked it under his arm and walked a few blocks before finding an empty bench in front of a hardware store to sit.

The front page stories covered another lucrative find in the gold fields, which Joshua could easily imagine coming straight out of a typewriting machine in Liarsville, and an amusing piece about dance hall girls by a columnist calling himself The Stroller. Surely the discovery of two dead men would rate front-page coverage, and it was not there. He scanned the inside pages but saw nothing about the theft of a sizeable amount of money.

He should have felt reassured but he didn't. Eventually, Mick and Alistair would surely report the theft and the lawmen weren't turning a blind eye anymore like they did in Soapy's day. He felt a renewed urgency to get out of Skagway. He hurried toward the docks.

A clerk with uncombed red hair and granules of sleep sand at the corners of his eyes looked up as Joshua approached the ticket counter.

"The *Portland* docks tomorrow," the young man said, after yawning hugely. "She'll be in port five days before sailing again to Seattle then on to San Francisco. Takes that long to offload cargo and such."

"So there's nothing leaving in the next day or two?"

"Oh, sure. The ferry sails to Dyea this afternoon. Now I know that one will go, for a fact. The sheriff was just here and he's wanting to get over there today. Tracking some criminal, he says."

A sheriff—no, the risk would be too great. And for what? To get fewer than five miles up the Taiya Inlet from here.

"Thank you," Joshua said. "I will have to think about it."

He walked away, hoping his reaction to the news about the sheriff on board the Dyea ferry had not been remarkable. With luck, the sleepy clerk would not remember him.

A steady rain began to fall; within minutes it was dripping from the brim of his wide hat. He thought of his soft bed at Mrs. McIlhaney's, the spare clothes and fire in front of which to dry himself. However, that would be the first place they would come looking for him—he dare not chance it.

He walked the entire length of the town—nine blocks—mainly to keep awake and to force his limbs to move. Behind a house on Runnalls, he found a three-sided shed full of musty tarps and broken-handled tools. No signs of activity showed in the house, so he ducked into the shed and dropped to the bare ground in a corner, pulling one of the smelly tarps over himself. His thoughts grew blurred and his eyelids felt heavy. Soon, he slept.

A sharp sound jolted him awake. The rain had stopped beating its staccato pattern on the tin roof and he could hear voices.

"Toss 'em in there," a man was saying.

"Everything?" said a second male voice, younger.

"Yep. All of it. One of these days I'll get around to repairing this stuff. I can always sell it as long as these rubes keep coming along with their gold fever."

Joshua edged the tarp aside and caught a glimpse of a man in overalls talking to a teenaged boy, the two of them standing beside a small cart loaded with more of the same broken tools that already nearly filled the shed. The older man walked away and the young one picked up an axe with half a handle. He hefted it back, ready to toss it. Joshua flung the tarp back.

"Wait! Don't throw it yet."

The young man nearly dropped the deadly axe head on his own foot.

"What in the devil—"

"Look, I only needed some sleep. I shall go now, and I won't come back. Please don't tell your boss."

"He's my father."

"Just please don't tell him you found me here. I don't want trouble."

The kid shrugged. "Fine." He glanced toward the house. "Better get out before Ma starts supper. She'll see you out that kitchen window."

Joshua leaped up and dashed out through the narrow doorway, realizing only after he'd traveled three blocks that he'd left his pack behind.

The sun dipped lower in the sky, making the point that the days were getting shorter. He patted his waist and pockets and felt the reassuring lumps of the cash and gold. Thank the lord he hadn't put those into the pack. At least he had money. But what was he to do with it? He couldn't think of a single hotelier or boarding house matron he could trust with his secret. Except perhaps Mrs. McIlhaney.

Maybe if he pleaded, if he paid extra. All he needed was for her to let him stay out of sight. He could say there'd been some trouble, without actually admitting he'd broken the law. She would never condone that.

Broadway Street was crowded now in the early evening.

Joshua felt refreshed. He must have gotten six or seven hours of much-needed sleep. He pulled his mackinaw tighter against the chilly air and his hat brim low enough to obscure his eyes from casual view. His jaw was rimmed with stubble; perhaps this would be a good time to let his beard grow. Any scrap of disguise could help.

He walked through the crowds on the board sidewalk, the opposite side of the street from the boarding house. Its neat white paint with blue trim showed brightly in comparison to the plain, unpainted wooden structures around it. His attic room window faced the street and while he watched, an unseen hand drew the curtain aside then let it drop into place again. Joshua froze.

A momentary gap in the flow of pedestrians revealed the front door of the house. Alistair Connell stood on the front stoop, talking with Mrs. McIlhaney. Mick and the sheriff must be upstairs, searching his room. They'd come looking for him, telling the story from their own viewpoint, how Joshua had gotten them drunk and robbed them in an alleyway.

His last place of refuge was lost to him.

Connell's head turned toward him, but Joshua had ducked into the doorway of an outfitter's shop. He counted to five, then casually strolled to the corner of Bond Street and turned to face the mountain.

Walking, with no particular destination, no goal other than to find a place where he could vanish until next Thursday, he saw a path. It followed a small stream, leading up the mountain and away from town. He took it.

This wasn't the same one the men took to access the White Pass Trail, so he should be able to remain out of sight. He'd heard of some small lakes out this way; perhaps camping out under the stars for a few nights would be a pleasant option. He would have to decide shortly, though. Night would come soon.

Joshua had covered a half mile on the narrow path, pushing aside branches of bushes loaded with reddish berries, when he heard the sound. Steady footsteps that almost precisely matched his own. He stopped, they stopped. He resumed, quickening his pace. The other steps sped up and there was a mild oath as a branch whipped the pursuer with a whoosh. Joshua's heart raced. Connell must have seen him, back there at the rooming house. One or both of them were surely behind him.

He could barely see the trail now and his boot stubbed against a stone the size of his two fists. He picked it up and stepped off the trail to wait.

Chapter 20

I took a deep breath and went into the bathroom, hoping Drake's sleep wouldn't be completely ruined. I asked Mina to repeat what she'd just said. She choked at the description of the poor, deceased kitty; I told her I was more interested in the note.

"Have you touched it?"

"Yuk, no!"

"I meant the note. The police may be able to get fingerprints from the paper."

"My doorbell rang, like twelve times, so I put on my robe and went to see. Through the peephole, I couldn't see anyone so I opened the door just a crack. And there it was. I switched on my porch light to be sure ... then I just slammed the door."

"Call the police. They can take the cat, I'm sure, but be

sure to tell the officers to give the note to Chief Branson."

Over the phone I could hear her blowing her nose.

"You didn't see anyone running away or driving off from your house?"

"No," she admitted. "I'm sorry. I'm not making a very good detective, am I?"

"It's okay. You were shaken up. Anyone would react the same."

"What if they come back?"

I doubted they would. This was a first warning, and I suspected the note-writer would wait now to see if Mina had taken his threat seriously.

"After the police leave, why don't you go spend the rest of the night at your mom's? You'll feel safer there."

She agreed.

I edged my way back to the bedroom and managed to smack my toe on the corner of the nightstand, which clattered as the lamp tipped over. I gave out a little pain-curse and grabbed for the lamp, and naturally with all this Drake woke up. So much for my attempts at consideration. He pulled me on top of him and one thing led to another ... and by the time he was contentedly snoring away once more, I was really wide awake.

I wrapped up in my robe and went to the kitchen, thinking in terms of hot cocoa. Across the way, I could see lights on at Berta's and two indistinct shapes moving about in her kitchen. Clearly, they weren't getting any sleep either. I turned off the kettle and made my way across the grassy expanse of the two back yards.

When I tapped at Berta's back door I heard a tiny shriek, so I called out. Berta pulled back the curtain and I waved.

"Sorry, didn't mean to scare you. I saw the lights."

Two cups of tea sat on the laminate kitchen table, one of them untouched, which I guessed was because Mina would not sit still. She paced the width of the small room three times before I got inside.

"Poor little Georgie Girl," she said. Her eyelids were puffy and red.

"When the police came, Mina recognized the cat," Berta said. "It was a stray that she'd begun feeding. She'd planned to adopt it."

"I never was sure whether it was male or female, so the name went from George to Georgie Girl," Mina said with a sniffle.

"I'm so sorry." I thought of our year-old pup and how Drake had taken her in because she was about to be abandoned.

"There's the note," she said. "I know, I didn't follow instructions but when I went to cut the string off Georgie's neck I guess I got so upset ... I tossed the note out of the way and then the officer came and he just seemed eager to get the job over with. He barely took the details. He offered to take the kitty away but I told him she—he—should be buried nearby. So he got busy digging a hole near my garden and we both forgot about the note." She picked up a baggie. "I did remember to put it in plastic."

I took the little parcel and looked at both sides. As she'd told me, someone had gone to the trouble of cutting out magazine and newspaper letters to form the short sentence: *Leave this business alone!* They were glued to a piece of cardstock with a round hole punched in one corner. Through the hole the perpetrator had threaded a double strand of rough twine. There were a few dark cat hairs stuck in the twine, attesting to the fact that it had been tied pretty tightly.

A big-city crime lab could probably run analysis of the glue and the card and the letters and the string and come up with a profile and sources for the materials. But a veiled threat and a dead cat probably wouldn't warrant the use of those sorts of resources. Still, we would give Chief Branson the note and the story and insist that he keep it as evidence until we knew exactly what it was about.

"Just to be sure," I said to Mina, "are there any other stories you've worked on recently that might bring someone to do this?"

"You know what the 'police beat' around here consists of. Sure, I suppose some guy could take exception to my coverage of the grand opening at the new auto parts store, but *seriously*? There's the little Police Blotter column that lists traffic citations and drunk-and-disorderly calls, but no one is mentioned by name. This has to refer to the cave-guy story."

She was right, of course.

"So, all that's been printed in the paper so far was a plea for anyone knowing about the disappearance of an unknown man ... yada, yada ..."

She nodded.

"His name and the visit by his sister ...?"

"Not yet. I was planning to run a follow-up this week, saying that a relative had been located and that the investigation continues."

"But very few people know about Katherine yet, right?"

She nodded.

"Okay, so it has to be someone who knows there's been new information to follow up on. And that's a limited list."

"Right."

"Let's think about this." I asked Berta for a pen and

something to write on. "Who knows anything at all about it?"

"Well, everyone in the police department," Mina began. "Probably some other city officials. I mean, all the offices are pretty well connected."

I jotted down the chief's name and the other officers who'd been present when Katherine came in. Mayor, fire chief, head of street sweeping ... but none of those seemed like serious candidates.

"What about anyone who might have overheard us talking?" I asked.

"Well, we took Katherine to lunch, so I suppose the owner of the tea house and the girl who waited on us."

"Hardly seems likely that one of them would go so far as to kill—to do this. Unless they have a grudge against you anyway?"

"I know the restaurant owner by name, barely, and I think the girl working there is new. I've never seen her before. That wouldn't be unusual during the summer months."

"When you first learned about Katherine, where were you?"

"At the news office. So, there's Wilbur and Betty who answers phones, and Gilda who does advertising layouts. Only Wilbur was there when I talked to Katherine, but I suppose he could have mentioned it to anyone."

"And we were at the airport when you came to tell me about it, so that includes Drake and Kerby and Chuey. Have you talked about this case much with Chuey? Just asking ... about everyone." I didn't want to cast aspersions on her new boyfriend.

She shook her head. "He knew I was excited about my original piece getting picked up by the wire services, but I really haven't seen him much in the last week or so."

The wire services. That pretty much opened up the list of who knew Mina's connection with the cave-guy to the rest of the world. I felt a little overwhelmed as I wrote R-O-W on the list. I scratched it off. We had to be reasonable about this.

If there was one certainty about any of this, it was that the person who wanted to threaten Mina away from the case was someone who could easily find out where she lived and who knew that killing her cat would come as a blow to her. They wanted the threat to stick, and most likely they wanted to be around to see if she backed off the investigation. It was someone local.

"We have to look at motive," I said. It's what my brother and his homicide detective buddy always do. "If 'this business' refers to solving the murder of Michael Ratcliff, who wants you to stop? It has to be the killer."

That was a little sobering, the knowledge that someone who committed a murder forty years ago was still around, perhaps just watching and waiting.

With that unsettling thought I left the two of them and returned home where I tried to sleep, with no success at all. By six o'clock I estimated that I'd probably dozed for a whole thirty minutes so I gave up and went into the kitchen to make the biggest breakfast I could think of: scrambled eggs with green chile and cheese, plus toast. Drake, being the real cook in our family, could have done much better but he was still in the land of post-coital slumber. He finally came out of the bedroom when the scent of roasted green chile could not be ignored.

"Mm, hey," he said, flashing me a sexy smile. "You read my mind."

I had a feeling I'd read more than one thing on his mind. I set plates on the table and offered the quick explanation of why my slippers were sitting by the back door, soggy with dew and covered with grass stains.

"Let me know if I can help," he said, slathering his toast with a good half-inch of strawberry jam.

"For now I think I'll try to dig up some leads online. Mina's going to hold her follow-up story, if Wilbur is agreeable. Poor thing, she was pretty upset about the cat."

He ate quickly and went to shower, saying that Kerby had scheduled his first flight for nine o'clock. I estimated that it was not an unreasonable hour to call my brother in Albuquerque, so I dialed the office.

Sally Bertrand, our part-time receptionist, sounded chipper, considering that I could hear her six-month-old son fussing in the background. She filled me in on such interesting facts as little Ross's morning intake of oatmeal before switching me over to Ron.

"I don't know what to suggest," he said, after congratulating me on our discovery of the dead man's identity and location of a relative. "You'll have to go pretty far back in time and there weren't computer databases then. The police consider a case cold a few weeks after the fact."

"I can't remember that we've ever been brought into a case as old as this one."

"The basics should be the same. Find out who knew him and who had reason to kill him."

He made it sound so simple. But who in Skagway knew a man who'd somehow ended up here from Seattle, when even his own sister hadn't a clue why he'd come. On a wild hope, I passed along Michael's full name and work history in case Ron had any spare time to help search. I hung up, knowing how rare his free time was these days, deciding I needed to proceed full-speed ahead on my own.

I spent the morning puttering around in websites that Ron had told me about before, hoping that I might stumble upon something, but by noon I still had absolutely zero. Those boxes Katherine had mentioned that once belonged to Michael were probably our only hope. Since the lady was now homeward bound on a plane, I couldn't very well start pressuring her for at least a day or two. I drummed my fingers on the table, wondering what to try next.

I thought about dropping in on Mina at the news office, mainly to have someone with whom to hash over all the random thoughts that were nagging at me, but my phone rang and Kerby informed me that I had a flight. I chafed at the change of direction but decided it might be for the best. Taking a break from bones, cats and creepy threats could do me good.

Boxes and bags waited near the A-Star when I arrived at the helipad. Chuey approached, carrying a box that rattled with the sound of wine bottles.

"Resupply for the group at Cabin Two," he said. "Looks like they're planning to have a great time during their second week."

The case held a dozen bottles, so I had to agree with his assessment. We opened the cargo compartment and began stacking cartons containing eggs, bread, milk, cereal and fresh produce. I asked him to place the wine on the floor of the passenger cabin, a spot nearer to the craft's center of gravity and somewhat more stable than the back. We had finished the loading when Kerby walked up.

"I hope I didn't pull you off something important," he said to me.

I knew he was fishing for information on Mina's story. Half the town probably knew that Katherine Ratcliff had come and gone yesterday.

"Nothing that can't wait," I said. "Unless you know anything about a guy named Michael Ratcliff who might have hung around town a little in 1975."

"Too far back for me. I came to Alaska to work for a tour company out of Fairbanks, met Lillian there and the rest is history. First time I set foot in Skagway was ten years ago when she and I returned from our honeymoon."

"Oh, yeah? Where'd you go?" After our own wedding we'd gone to a ski area, where Drake worked to ferry skiers to the back country. Upside was that we'd managed a three-month honeymoon out of the deal.

"Maui. I flew tours there for two years, stayed in touch with some folks and got us a deal on a seaside condo."

Drake had flown on Kauai for a long time, yet the two never met during that time. It only showed how, even in the relatively small world of commercial helicoptering, you couldn't possibly know everyone.

Kerby helped me complete the preflight and then handed me a few pieces of mail for the clients. I climbed in and started the turbine engine. Twenty-five minutes later I had Cabin Two in sight. Two adults and four kids came rushing out, obviously eager to see a new face after a week together in close quarters—either that or they couldn't wait to break into that wine.

The husband, a Mr. Smith (although, truthfully, they were all beginning to blend into generic Smiths by now), helped unload the supplies. When he instructed the kids to carry boxes to the cabin's kitchen, a scramble ensued over the one containing the frosted chocolate cereal. I handed over their mail, checked the batteries on their satellite phone, and asked whether they needed anything else.

The missus had already applied the corkscrew to the first bottle of wine; she gave a vacant nod.

"Look what I found." One of the little girls, who had stayed out of the cereal fray, proudly showed me a glass vial with two decent-sized gold nuggets.

The father spoke up. "I weighed them for her. She's got close to a thousand dollars worth there."

"Wow—good for you!" I said.

The kid beamed. I doubted Kerby had seeded the area with anything that valuable, and it was reassuring to know that the customers really did have a chance at finding something worth some real money.

I waved goodbye and cautioned them about standing back while I pulled pitch and headed back toward the airport. Seeing those nuggets reminded me again about the older of the two skeletons we'd found, most likely a gold rusher. So many stories floated around, lots of them about vast fortunes; I wondered how much, in today's terms, the average man ever really found. Which led my thoughts around to the box of letters I'd been reading. Maybe by the time I finished them I would know the answer to that question.

The heliport came into sight as I cleared the last of the rugged peaks to the east of town and I, as always, felt a rush of relief at seeing Drake's ship already there. I made a neat landing and started my shut-down procedure, pulling my cell phone from my pocket while I waited for the turbine to cool down. I had missed two calls, one from Mina and one from Katherine Ratcliff.

Katherine's message was brief but informative. "Charlie,

something kept nagging at me on the flight home. I need to tell you about it."

Chapter 21

Katherine answered quickly, sounding a little out of breath.

"I'm so glad you called right away," she said. "I've just been up to the attic and verified what I thought. It's here."

"Can you back up a little? I didn't get—"

"Oh, sorry. Didn't I say in my message? It's an old trunk. I had forgotten all about it but I do still have it. It's a rather quaint antique, I suppose—leather-covered with brass fittings and thick leather handles that have since rotted through. It was among the things at my grandmother's house when she died."

I tamped down my impatience to know where this was going.

"Michael laid claim to it the minute he saw it. That was the thing that sparked his interest in family history, I believe."

"Have you looked inside?"

"Oh yes. There are some yellowed baby clothes, including a christening gown that my father wore. There's an old sepia photograph of him."

"I'm thinking more along the lines of something that would have brought Michael to Alaska."

"There are some books. I haven't had time to really look through them yet."

This didn't seem to be exactly a hot lead, but I suggested that she look everything over and give me a call if she discovered any references to Alaska. She promised to do that, although I could tell she was tired from the trip. I didn't expect to hear back from her anytime soon.

"Gonna spend the night here?" Drake said, opening my door and giving me a grin.

I was still belted into my harness. I held up my phone. "Sorry, something I needed to address."

"I'm done here and I can offer you a lovely Alaskan crab dinner and a ride home, if you'd like to finish your paperwork and call it a day." He held up a box with two wriggling live crabs in it.

Nothing I could imagine sounded better than that. Thirty minutes later we'd settled at home where I was happy to turn over the task of boiling a huge pot of water to my kitchen-capable hubby. I only wanted a shower.

In the middle of suds and shampoo I remembered that I had not returned Mina's call but I got distracted when Drake shouted that dinner was being served in five minutes. I rinsed and toweled off and showed up in the kitchen wearing sweats and wet hair, just in time to microwave a stick of butter into golden oblivion. The ripping, cracking and shredding of crab legs went by in a kind of blur.

By the time we adjourned to the sofa Drake was ready for television but I couldn't concentrate on the scientific program with way too many unfamiliar concepts. I dialed Mina's number but when it went immediately to voice mail I remembered Chuey saying something about their having a date tonight. I spotted the floral box of letters and picked it up.

On my previous foray into the past, I'd come to the end of Joshua Farmer's letters. The only thing to do now was to see what his wife might have written once he'd told her of his gold strike and announced that he was on the way home.

Dearest Husband,

I am near frantic with worry. It has been a month since your letter saying you were on the way home and yet there is no sign of you. I have called in at the steamship line almost daily and I fear they are becoming impatient with my presence. There seems no record of your purchase of a ticket. But as no ships have been lost at sea, I can only assume that something has delayed your return journey.

Please forgive my wifely worries, but do find a moment to send a line or two and reassure me that you are all right.

Your loving wife,
Maddie

By postmark dates, the next letter was even shorter.

Dearest Joshua,

I have sent telegrams to the offices of the law in Skagway and in Fraser, Canada, hoping for some word of your whereabouts. Neither of them has provided me with any substantial answer, merely stating that thousands of men are on the trail and they cannot possibly know how to find any certain individual.

Please, please, contact me, even if it is to say that you have changed your mind about coming home. I only want to assure myself that you are safe.

Your wife,
Maddie

How awful, I thought. In those times the poor woman must have felt hopeless. Today, we have cell phones, radios, GPS and the Internet, and yet I know first-hand how frightening it is whenever Drake goes out on a job and I don't hear anything for a day or two. Maddie Farmer's situation would have driven me crazy.

I picked up the next letter, realizing only after I had extracted the thin sheet of paper that this one was not addressed to Joshua Farmer.

September 30, 1898
Mr. Harry Weaver
c/o The Pinkerton Detective Agency
Seattle, Washington

Dear Mr. Weaver,

I do not know if you are familiar with my name, as I am with yours. My husband Joshua Farmer mentioned you on more than one occasion in his letters home from Skagway, Alaska.

I am writing today to beg your assistance. Joshua wrote to me almost two months ago, saying that he was leaving Alaska after a successful trip into the Klondike. I assumed he would arrive in San Francisco within two or three weeks, but to date he has not appeared here. Understandably, I am nearly beside myself.

I would like to engage your firm to look for him and report to me.

I contact you directly because of your connection to him, but please be assured that I am not expecting preferential treatment. I shall acquire the money to pay, if you will advise me as to the rates and procedure. Unfortunately, I am woefully ignorant about such matters.

I look forward to hearing from you at your earliest convenience.

Yours very truly,

Maddie McDowell Farmer

I reread the letter twice. Had Joshua Farmer mentioned that Harry Weaver was a Pinkerton detective in his letters?

The next letter in the stack was written in an unfamiliar hand, addressed to Maddie Farmer. I opened it to discover it came from the detective.

October 12, 1898

Dear Mrs. Farmer,

I am indeed acquainted with your husband, Joshua, and am very sorry to hear that he has not arrived safely in San Francisco. I was unaware of his successful gold strike, but perhaps that is because my Pinkerton duties took me to other locations while Joshua remained occupied in Skagway.

I will be most happy to make some inquiries on your behalf. Do not worry yourself about payment arrangements. It would be my pleasure to pursue this on my own time, for now. If agency involvement is warranted, I shall apprise you of the status and we can discuss a plan.

I shall remain in contact,

Harry Weaver

A gap of two months went by before the next postmark. I opened the letter from Mr. Weaver.

December 20, 1898

Dear Mrs. Farmer,

I regret that my efforts have not brought better results. At this point, I have completely exhausted leads that might take us to Joshua. During a trip to Skagway, I interviewed his former landlady, Mrs. McIlhaney, who remembered him well. She informed me that your husband left many of his belongings behind when he departed, without a word of farewell. She stored the items—an assortment of clothing, some gold panning equipment and a few tools—I looked through them but found no indication of his plans. If you would like to have these personal items, please advise Mrs. Eulaila McIlhaney, Broadway Street, Skagway, Alaska, and enclose twenty dollars for the shipping. She will hold them a few more weeks and then discard them.

I also spoke with a series of tavern keepers and local merchants, with even less result. There are, I fear, too many faces and too few connections to accurately place yet another stampeder in this melee of humanity. I must say, though, that I have wandered the streets of the city and posted myself at likely places where I might see him, and have had no success.

My employer has, today, summoned me to another assignment and I must travel to Chicago. Depending upon the duration of my duties in that case, I may possibly have free time in the coming spring months to return to Skagway, but I hesitate to promise that it would be a fruitful trip. At the present time, the winter winds blow bitterly here in the north, and I hold little hope for anyone who attempts to travel to the gold fields now.

I pray that your husband returns, safe and unharmed. If that is the case, please write to me in care of the Pinkerton Agency and let me know the good news. I was fond of Joshua and always wished him well.

With kindest regards,

Harry Weaver

I set the letter back in the box, the last of the correspondence. How many adventurers met a similar fate? I had not taken time to visit the museum yet, but I imagined history would show that many, many of them never returned home.

Drake's TV show was ending and I felt my eyelids drooping, the result of our big dinner and the previous night's sketchy sleep. We turned out the lamps.

My sleep was restful until the first time I rolled over. That act awakened me just enough to get my mind churning, rummaging through names. Something in Harry Weaver's final letter had stayed with me, the name of the landlady. There were other names, too, ones I'd come across as I'd begun to read the letters in the first few days after our arrival here.

In the meantime, several of those names had become familiar.

Chapter 22

My early awakening had provided enough time to go back and reread all the letters in the box, which only opened up far more questions than they answered. Once the sun had fully hit the streets and warmed the air, I took the opportunity to go for a nice, brisk walk with Freckles and think it over.

While Mina and Chief Branson were giving the majority of their attention to Michael Ratcliff, the more recent of the two murders, a seed of suspicion made me wonder about the older one. The time frame was about right—what if there was a tie between someone named in the letters and the skeleton that dated back to the gold rush era?

We passed Berta's house, where curtains were still drawn and nothing indicated she was up yet. So many of the names in the letters seemed familiar to me that I'd written them all down and I wanted to run them past either Berta or Mina. An online directory search showed that several of those original families still resided here in Skagway—among those I had met already were McIlhaney, Thespen and Connell. On the off chance, I had also looked up Farmer but didn't find any.

Maddie Farmer's last letter still haunted me—the desperately worried wife who never received satisfactory answers about her husband's whereabouts. Joshua Farmer had come to Skagway full of hopes and the dream of becoming rich. By late summer he had claimed to find gold and said he was on the way home. But he never arrived. Perhaps Joshua had lied to his wife about the gold. It wouldn't be the first time a man away from home had met another woman and simply abandoned the family back home. The desertion scenario didn't feel right though; the letters between the two of them were frequent and loving. If there had been anyone named Farmer here today, I would have loved to quiz them.

I spent the rest of the walk trying to decide where to go next for information. The minute I walked into the living room, the answer was staring at me from the front page of this week's newspaper. A headline about the historical society's annual fundraiser caught my attention. What better place to gain some additional information?

Drake had left me a note: *Got a nine o'clock flight. See you for lunch?*

I speed dialed his cell phone and told him I would meet him at Zack's Place at noon, to let me know if his plans changed. Then I left Freckles happily crunching down a doggie cookie and headed toward the Skagway Museum.

A man of about seventy sat behind the information

desk, wearing a green jacket, a bow tie, and a pleasant expression. I briefly outlined the fact that I had come into possession of some letters from the gold rush period and wondered if there was a way to find out what had become of the writer. He reached under the desk and pulled out a few pages.

"This is a list of people buried in the Gold Rush Cemetery," he said. "Of course, the person had to be in town at the time of his death. If the man you're looking for died along the trail, he was probably buried on the spot

"Now here's the other main cemetery, the one on the Dyea road, the Pioneer Cemetery."

I quickly scanned the names, which were thoughtfully presented in alphabetical order, but didn't see any that tied to those in the letters.

"This man, Joshua Farmer, would have arrived about April of 1898," I told the docent. "I have letters he wrote home to his wife, saying he was gathering his gear for the trail. Later, he says he's leaving for the Klondike, then in July he wrote that he'd found gold and was going back home to San Francisco."

The docent gave me a hard stare. "Three months? I think your man may have been fibbing to the wife. Most of the men spent a good year on that trail. The Canadian authorities required that they bring supplies for a journey that long, so's they wouldn't get up there and starve to death on Canadian soil."

"So, you're saying there's no way he could have gone to the gold fields and back in the time he says he did?"

"Let's just say I would be real surprised." He shrugged and the skepticism was clear on his face. "The Chilkoot Trail was shorter, but you see there was a bad avalanche that spring. Lot of men killed, lot of danger. The Chilkoot was closed for awhile but it wasn't necessarily a lot faster anyway because it was so much steeper. You want to see the evidence, the displays inside are pretty amazing."

I purchased an admission. He was right about the incredible story that unfolded with the displays of supplies, tools and gambling equipment that had been preserved, and I gained a whole lot better image of what life must have been like in the old days. I could not imagine trudging through snow on those high peaks, wearing leather boots and carrying a pack that weighed more than I did, having to cover the distance dozens of times to move the required two thousand pounds of gear. And after the arduous hike a man had to construct himself a boat and float down the river to reach the site of the gold discoveries. Still, regarding Joshua Farmer, I didn't find my answers.

"Miss?" The same man was at the desk when I exited. "I thought of one more thing. A lot of men went missing during those years and their families tried to find them. The official records were either sketchy or non-existent, but there's a woman here in town who compiled a list of the inquiries, whatever she could get her hands on. It's not a fancy list, and we couldn't figure out a way to turn it into a museum display, but you could call her if you like."

I took the slip of paper he handed me and thanked him. Maddie Farmer's inquiries were already known to me, through her letters with the Pinkerton detective, but you never knew what else might turn up. I sat outside on a low stone wall and dialed the number for Gertrude Manicot.

Ten minutes later, after explaining how I'd gotten her number, I was on the way to her house, which turned out to be a cozy wood frame structure with a huge blooming

Sitka mountain-ash tree outside. Since speaking to the docent at the museum, I couldn't help but wonder about Joshua Farmer's final letter to his wife. If there wasn't time to actually find gold in the Yukon, maybe he had come by his riches in an illicit manner and didn't want to admit as much to Maddie. There had been hints of his gambling and names of several men with whom he'd become acquainted. Before I had time to piece any of those ideas together, Gertrude's door opened.

"Hello, you're the gal who just called." Gertrude Manicot (just call me Gert—everyone does) had little-old-lady features and lumberjack clothing. Heavy wrinkling indicated a lifetime of smoking, and she was due for a visit to the colorist judging by the inch-wide strip of white at the part-line in her dark hair.

"Yes. The man at the museum ..." Darn, I'd forgotten to get his name.

"That would be Stewart."

"Thank you. He mentioned that you kept some records of missing miners?"

"More like a little catalog of people who've called looking for someone. You'd be surprised—folks still contact me now and then to see if they can find out whether their great-great-grandpa was on the gold rush. Some of 'em love genealogy, others just think there might be a family fortune up here in Alaska."

She had stepped aside and ushered me into a small living room jammed to the rafters. Overstuffed armchairs and two couches were sized too large for the space, and they had been shoved into a tight grouping around a coffee table, the kind with two overflowing ashtrays. This allowed room for a pot-bellied woodstove in one corner. Shelves of VHS tapes and lopsided books filled the longest wall, while four or five unsealed cardboard cartons revealed office supplies such as scissors and marking pens, bargain-sized packs of double-A batteries, lengths of wire and cable that looked as if they belonged to a stereo system. She could have wired two more homes with the materials she had here.

"Come on in," she said in her gravelly voice. "Sorry, I didn't have time to tidy up."

In the past ten years. I edged my way toward the deep chair she indicated.

"Now, let me just find my database," she mumbled, her gaze darting around the room.

The database turned out to be a shoebox, and when she lifted the lid I saw two tightly packed rows of white index cards.

"Everybody seems to think you need a computer these days. Internet and all that stuff," she said. "Not me. My mother started with a box of scrap papers from the old postmaster's attic. She came up with this system, and then I just added entries for every letter and phone call we ever received. I can find what I need, right here."

I suppressed the inclination to look around the cluttered room, trying to meet her gaze and give a nod instead.

"Now, what did you say the name was?"

"Joshua Farmer is the man who wrote the letters home, saying he'd found gold and was on his way back."

Gert began flipping through the cards, no easy task given how tightly they were jammed into the box. I caught sight of a clock on one of the shelves that indicated it was a quarter of twelve. Yikes—the morning had gotten away from me and I would be late meeting Drake for lunch.

"I need to make a call," I said. "If you don't mind?"

Gert nodded and kept flipping. I speed-dialed Drake's phone.

"Hon, I'm really sorry," he said. "I meant to call you fifteen minutes ago. Kerby booked me on another flight."

"Do you need me there, to take some of them or anything?"

"Don't think so. He would have called you." The turbine engine spun up in the background. "Go ahead and eat without me. I'll grab something."

"Ah-ha! Told you!" Gertrude's exclamation came just as I clicked off the call. She waved a white card in the air. "Farmer, Joshua."

I got out my little notebook, ready to copy the information. She didn't hand it over, but began reading from it.

"Contact: Letter. Date: 1947. Interested party: Isabelle Farmer. Relationship: daughter."

I scribbled. "That's it?"

"In the Notes section Mother put down that the woman said he'd come to Skagway to get to the Klondike. Last contact with family: July, 1898."

Isabelle. The infant daughter who had been mentioned in Joshua's and Maddie's letters to each other. By 1947 she would have been about fifty years old.

Gert set the card beside her on the couch and flipped through a few more, near the spot where she'd marked her place with an index finger.

"Nope. Looks like that's the only one."

"Could I make a copy of it?" I asked. "I'd be happy to run to the library and then bring the card right back."

"No need. I don't like these cards to leave the house." She set the box aside, walked to the shelving and picked up a stack of videos. Placing them on the floor, she revealed a small, inexpensive printer. "This thing's made me about a million copies already. I'll just do you one right now."

"Did you keep the actual letters these family members sent?" I suspected a request letter would be a little more rich in details than what Gert could fit on an index card.

"Oh, yes. Certainly."

"It would help me to read Isabelle Farmer's correspondence, if I could also get a copy of that."

The machine lit up and made a series of jerky little noises.

"Well, I don't quite have all those as neat as the things in this room. Give me a day or two. I'll find it."

With little hope that the letter would ever turn up, I gave Gert my card and held out a ten dollar bill. She brushed it away but accepted a dollar to cover the paper and ink for her printer.

"I'll call you," she said as I walked outside and breathed fresh air.

With no lunch plans after all, I decided to catch up with Mina. She sounded a little harried on the phone—something about Wilbur pushing a deadline—but said we could chat as she ran an errand for him. When I told her where I was she said, "Gotcha" and a moment later a horn tooted behind me.

"How's that for service?" she said, powering down the passenger window of an unfamiliar white sedan, herself at the wheel. "Hop in."

"So this is Wilbur's car?"

"Right. Here we are on deadline and it's suddenly going to be an emergency if the car doesn't get washed today."

She made a couple of turns.

"With Wilbur, it doesn't matter what job in the office you are hired to do, you do whatever he wants done at the moment. I don't mind, really. It breaks up the routine and, really, I'm getting paid either way."

She pulled up to one of those drive-through outfits, where she pressed a few buttons and inserted some cash at the electronic voice's request. As we cruised into the contraption, she turned to me.

"So, what's up?"

"I may be on the brink of finding out how our two cave skeletons are related." I told her about my visit to Gertrude Manicot. "The letters I found in the garage of our rental house were between a man and wife during the gold rush. They had an infant daughter named Isabelle and a woman named Isabelle Farmer inquired about her father, a missing gold rusher, a bunch of years later."

"He might be the man in the cave?"

"He might. Or, he might be our killer."

Mina digested that information while a spray arm traveled across the top of the car, splattering gloppy suds onto it, encasing us in a cocoon of soapy seclusion.

I went back over the general content of the letters, telling what I'd learned about Joshua Farmer's activities when he came to Skagway—the gambling, the feelings of resentment, the desperation as he ran out of money and needed to get home.

"A lot of what I'm saying involves reading between the lines," I said. "He tried to paint a good picture for his wife, but there's just something ... I'm not sure what, exactly, that sounds, off. He didn't come prepared to make the journey to the Klondike. He didn't have much of a plan, doesn't mention any job skills to earn the money he needed. He claims he was cheated at cards. Every setback was always someone else's fault."

"So, we have to wonder," she said as clear water blasted the car, "did he ever intend to prospect for gold or did he come here as a thief who intended all along to take someone else's treasure?"

"Maybe that. Maybe he started out with good intentions, became desperate, resorted to violence at the end. The skull in the cave was pretty thoroughly bashed in."

"And, according to Chief Branson, there was nothing of value found among the clothing or possessions, right?"

"Exactly. So, if the man who walked up that trail toward the cave had money or gold, it was taken."

An obnoxious buzzer came on, cuing Mina that the wash was done and we'd better get out. She put the sedan in gear and guided it toward the exit door.

"What's our next step then?" she asked, as she paused at the street for a few other vehicles to go by.

"I've been thinking about that. We know the two skeletons are related. We know the identity of the younger man, Michael Ratcliff. If we can prove that the Ratcliffs and Farmers are related, we can be pretty sure the older man is Joshua Farmer. If not, then there is someone else in Skagway's history who died a violent death in that cave."

"And someone who killed him."

Chapter 23

I rode along with Mina to drop her editor's car back at the news office.

"The layout is going to eat up my afternoon but it goes to the printer at four o'clock," she said. "If you want to get together after that, we could do some more research."

I felt a little impatient at the delay, but there were things I could do and I always like working on my own anyway. We said goodbye at the sidewalk. From this central location in town I was now free to go anywhere I wanted. My stomach reminded me about the skipped lunch so I stopped for a deli sandwich and found a bench in the sunshine where I could sit and eat it.

My first thought was to ask more questions of Katherine Ratcliff so I dialed the number she'd given me.

"You must be a busy lady," she said. "Still working on my brother's case?"

"On both of them, really. Remember the second set of bones that were found in the same location? Well, I've been asking around, trying to find out that man's identity. An inquiry was made a long time ago, a woman named Isabelle Farmer asking about her father, Joshua Farmer. Do either of those names mean anything to you? Are they connected to the Ratcliffs at all?"

A few seconds went by. I could almost hear her thoughts bouncing around.

"My father's name was Charles Ratcliff, and I'm fairly certain his mother's first name was Isabelle. Our family lived in Seattle and Grandma was in San Francisco, and we had little contact. I don't remember her well. She lived to her seventies. I had married and moved east and was unable to attend her funeral."

"But you're pretty sure she was Isabelle?"

"It sounds very familiar but don't ask me to swear to it in court." She chuckled a little.

Once again I asked her to call me if she found any new information, then hung up. This sure seemed like slow going. I wadded up my sandwich wrapper and tossed it in a trash barrel at the edge of the park.

I spent the time as I walked home thinking of possible scenarios. If Michael Ratcliff had discovered that he was related to Isabelle and Joshua, he might have decided to come here to continue the search that his grandmother had initiated in the 1940s. How did either of them know that Skagway was the place to look, though?

Then it hit me. The letters.

The very letters I'd been reading must have been in Isabelle's possession. If she had stored them in the old trunk and Michael the history buff went through it and came upon them ... that could very well be the thing that spurred him to research his family's history. That made sense. The name Isabelle had been used in the letters between Joshua and Maddie, and maybe Michael snapped to the connection a lot quicker than Katherine did just now.

Was there something in the letters that I'd missed, something that would lead a great-grandson on this journey? Or was I trying to make too much of it? Perhaps it was simple curiosity on Michael's part, nothing more. It felt as if there were too many gaps in the story.

I stopped at the market on the way and picked up fresh greens and vegetables to make a big salad for tonight's dinner. Next to the tomatoes I spotted Berta.

"Hey Charlie, how's it going?" She lit up with her usual smile, all signs of having dealt with Mina's cat tragedy gone now.

"That box of letters I told you I found in the garage at the rental … If they aren't yours, do you have any idea how they got there?"

"Some previous tenant, I imagine," she said. "I've owned that house for thirty years and rented it out every single summer."

I nodded. "Have all the tenants been summer workers, like us, or did you ever rent long-term to a local?"

She looked a little impatient at the questions, trying to focus on choosing tomatoes instead.

"I don't know, Charlie. I don't hardly remember any of them. It's a whole new set of faces every year, and really, you and Drake are the only couple I've ever conversed with much."

I apologized for being such a pain and thanked her even though she'd really given me nothing, but as I checked out and started the walk home, the line of questions did begin to spark an idea. At the house I set my grocery bag into the fridge and went out to unlock the garage. If a tenant—specifically, if one of them in pre-Berta times—had left the box of letters, he may have very well left something else, something that connected the dots about how and why Michael Ratcliff came to Skagway and what the connection was with Joshua Farmer.

I shoved one of the big garage doors aside and looked around for a light switch. Finding none, I went back to the house for a flashlight, chafing at the delay. I must be getting hormonal—everything today made me impatient. I shined the light in a general arc around the space, settling on the shelf where I'd found the box. I started in on the stacks of dusty boxes that filled it.

The first box contained light fixtures and another had an assortment of plumbing parts, all old, all appearing to be taken off and discarded when a newer replacement was installed. My guess was that before Berta a man had owned this place, the kind of guy who never threw away anything. When she bought the place as a rental, she must have concentrated on making the house comfortable; she'd pretty much admitted that she didn't care about the garage. Next to the spot where I'd found the floral-printed box sat a carton bristling with wires; I set it on the floor and aimed my light at the back of the shelf. Jammed up against the wall, behind the box I'd just removed, were two leather-bound books and a cheap notebook with a rusted spiral binding. On tiptoe, I could barely reach them.

I pulled the three items out and gave them a closer look by flashlight. The leather-covered books were of good quality and a thumb-through showed feminine writing.

The spiral looked like the kind of thing I used to carry to sophomore English. The handwriting had a strong slant to the neat, block print that filled quite a few pages. I spotted the name Isabelle and my heart began to beat a little quicker. Finally—on the right track. I hoped.

I blew off a cloud of dust and carried them into the house.

In the living room, Freckles lay on her belly, front paws and nose aimed toward the door where I had departed without her. I knelt, rubbed her ears and reassured her I really hadn't left forever, and she sniffed the books until the dust went up her nose and she let go with a huge sneeze. I found a cloth and tried to clean up the books a bit so I wouldn't end up doing the same.

The two of us settled on the sofa and I turned on a lamp. The smaller of the leather-bound books had a pink cover and the dated entries began in 1917.

Isabelle referred to her mother and a man named Franklin, how they had invited a young man to dinner and blatantly hinted that he would be a wonderful husband for her.

I could only think, what might be the matter with him, aside from possible flat feet or bad eyesight? With the war on, surely he would have been called up if he were eligible. I knew in very short order that David Ratcliff's penchant for undue flattery and the habit of stroking his thin mustache before responding to a question would annoy me to no end.

I understand, truly, why Mother and Frank want to see me marry. I am a burden in their household. I am not his child and he has been most patient with me as it is. And little Frankie has so many health needs. But a quick marriage to someone I care nothing about—the thought makes my heart heavy.

So Maddie Farmer had remarried at some point after Joshua failed to return home and she had a son with the second husband. I wondered if the laws were the same then, a years-long waiting period before a person could be legally declared dead. Surely, women of that time who had no careers or money of their own would need financial support right away. I skimmed through the pink book, knowing that Isabelle did indeed eventually marry a Ratcliff. The entries spoke of her wedding and her sorrow at leaving her family in San Francisco when, during her pregnancy, David's work required a move to Seattle.

A son! David Junior has my complexion and hair color, I am pleased to note. I imagine—from the one photograph Mother saved—that he will look very much like my father. I think of him often now, my father who probably died in the search for gold. A tiny part of me holds hope, though, a hope that he might someday come back, to find me and meet his grandson. Perhaps when finances permit, one day I shall undertake to locate him.

Meanwhile, a baby is such a joy and requires such a commitment of time. I often allow my housework to accumulate while I sit and rock my little one and sing to him. David is, at times, not happy about this. I have come to learn that we take our happiness where we can find it—little Davey is my delight now.

The entries continued in this vein, revealing cracks in the marriage without overtly saying so, the words of a young mother who doted completely on her son. As far as I could tell, this baby was their only child. I skimmed to the end and picked up the other book, this one bound in brown—the neat handwriting now had a jagged edge to it. The entries began in 1939. As with the first one, this seemed more a journal of her life's important times, rather than a daily diary. Scanning quickly through, I got the news that little Davey grew up and married (a grasping, clutching war bride from England) and shortly after his return from combat they had a son, Michael. At last, a name I knew.

Setting that one aside, I looked more closely at the spiral notebook.

It didn't have a "This book belongs to:" label or anything, but after reading the first few lines, I felt fairly certain these were Michael Ratcliff's notes and that it might very well contain the clues as to what had happened to him, with whom he met.

Being a bottom-line sort of gal, I'm surprised I didn't choose to read it first.

Chapter 24

The masculine hand revealed sketchy notes, written as a linear recitation of facts he had learned, more so than the journal-style entries his grandmother had made.

Isabelle Ratcliff – Father, Joshua Farmer

Manifest from USS Portland – Joshua Farmer, passenger arrival in Skagway, Alaska on May 12, 1898

* * *

Michael Ratcliff slammed down the phone receiver and stared out his second-story window toward the park across the street, paying no attention to the lush spring greenery outside. *Dammit, Candy, I'm not proposing to you just because my thirtieth birthday is coming up.* Why was it that a girl would be all hot and fun, up to a point? Then she's starting with the little hints about marriage, and pretty soon she's withholding her favors until she sees a damn ring. He stared at the phone; he could call her back, give in and make the reservation at that place she wanted to go. He reached for the instrument but yanked his hand back when it rang.

She'd given in first, called him. It had to mean that she regretted her tearful ultimatum; that's the way it always went with her. *Okay, sweetie, let's see what you have to say.* He picked it up with a gruff hello that masked the smile on his lips.

"Vince wants the money by Friday, Mikey-boy, and if he don't get it ... well, you don't want to know."

The male voice threw him for a split second. Then his gut went watery. No way he, or anyone he knew, could come up with the thirty grand. He held his breath.

"Just remember this, kid. Vince don't make loans to *dead*-beats." A dial tone buzzed in his ear.

The unsubtle emphasis shot a bolt of fear through his body. He dropped the phone and ran for the bathroom. His bowels emptied—twice—before he had a coherent thought. Were the goons calling from Vegas, or were they somewhere here in Seattle? They could be right outside his building. He ventured from the bathroom and edged the bedroom curtain aside enough to see the street below. A black car sat at the curb, a wisp of exhaust coming from its tailpipe.

He had to get out of here.

His sister was the last person in the world he wanted to call—stuffy Katherine, with her tight little conservative haircut, her east coast clothing and her preachy ways—but he had no one else. Candy would take him in, in a minute, but she couldn't keep her mouth shut. It wouldn't take a full day before she was blabbing to one of the other beauticians or one of those gossipy old ladies in the shop with their hair in rollers, yakking away under those hideous dome-like dryers, telling them how Michael had moved in with her and how they'd be getting married real soon.

His boss wouldn't welcome him. Randy had chewed him out Monday morning when Michael asked for an advance on his paycheck—like a hundred dollars would even *begin* to satisfy the men from Vegas. Randy was the kind of supervisor who just wanted you to show up for work, put in eight hours riveting bolts into airframe bodies, go away at the end of the day and not get in his face about anything at all.

And his friends weren't being all that friendly these days. He'd already tapped everybody he knew, borrowing a little cash here and there to stay just beyond the clutches of those dangerous men. Hiding out at a buddy's house wasn't an option.

He ran his fingers through his curled hair—courtesy of Candy, after hours at her shop—and agonized over what to do. It was going to have to be Katherine's place. He would have to listen to her woes over the breakup of her marriage to Mr. Snob from Connecticut.

He stewed over it as he jammed clothes into a backpack. What did she think, anyway? She'd married the guy because he was successful and dressed all classy, then whined when he smacked her around now and then. Just because she had a degree in English something-or-other, did she think a guy from the country club set wouldn't look down on regular working-class people from the west coast?

Back in the tiny bathroom he opened the medicine cabinet, grabbing essentials and tossing them into the pack. He couldn't walk out of here looking like a guy who was traveling. He stared at his face in the mirror for a long minute. The curly hair, being new, might help as a disguise. His sideburns were just the way he liked them, trimmed right at the edge of his jawline, full and fluffy along his narrow cheeks. He chewed at his lip a minute and picked up his razor.

"Hate to do it, man," he said to his image as the facial hair went away.

He flinched at the result. His face looked like a damn cue ball, all round and geeky. *Hey, men are out there who want to break your kneecaps*, he reminded himself. *Buck up and do what it takes.*

He looked around the apartment. The bold-patterned polyester shirt was too noticeable. He took it off and folded it neatly into his pack, choosing a plain white one from the back of the closet. As he buttoned it, he looked around for accessories. Some pens for the pocket, an old pair of dark-rimmed glasses he used to wear in school. Hopelessly out of date now; for sure no one had seen him wear them. He put them on and practiced walking around the room without his usual swagger. Meek and mild, he reminded himself, trying to look like one of those guys you saw around the university, the ones who studied how to build electronic devices they claimed would change the world. Yeah, right.

Katherine's new place was probably only four or five bus stops away; he hadn't actually been there yet but she'd given him the address when she called to say she was moving back to the city. He could easily walk it but that car was still at the curb and he didn't want to be on the streets in his own neighborhood any more than necessary. He checked the pack to be sure he had what he wanted, then sat down to wait.

An hour passed before he saw the car pull away. When it made a left turn at the corner, he slipped out and made his way down the set of concrete steps to the street level, then ducked through the breezeway to the back of the building. He'd sold his car six months ago, to pay off his previous trip to Vegas. Too bad. With a tank of gas he could be nearly anywhere now.

One of Katherine's warnings flashed through his head. "Michael, you can't spend every cent you earn. You need to start saving."

He brushed it off. Saving for what? So he could marry Candy and buy a stupid suburban house somewhere and afford to drink enough to get angry and start hitting his wife the way his sister's husband had done? Screw that.

From the shadow of the breezeway he scanned the parking lot. No black car. Few cars at all; everyone who lived here was at work right now. He should be, too, but what better way to track a guy than when he had predictable movements? He would stay at Katherine's only long enough to come up with something better, maybe look at getting a job somewhere really far away, like Albuquerque.

He liked that. New Mexico was practically next door to Nevada, wasn't it? Or maybe not really. Maybe he should just move to Nevada, get a job in a casino. It would be like a kid working in a donut shop. He pictured Vince's face. Nah, there had to be a better place than Nevada. He would give it some thought, he decided as he walked to the next block and slumped on a bench at the bus stop.

Katherine's apartment was sure a lot nicer than his, Michael noticed as he approached the building. A lobby where you had to either have a key to the locked front door or get someone to buzz you in. He found the button for her apartment and pressed it, wishing belatedly that he'd called ahead to be sure she would be here. What if she'd already found work and was gone all day? He glanced warily up and down the street.

"Yes? Who is it?" came the familiar voice.

"Hey, sis. Me, Michael."

A moment of silence, then the buzzer sounded. He entered a lobby where a row of mailboxes filled the wall on the left and a fake potted plant and striped upholstered bench on the right made it look as if this was where you might leisurely kick back to read your mail. He pressed the elevator button for the fourth floor and stuffed the glasses and pocketful of pens into his backpack.

Katherine's greeting seemed stiff. No huge surprise; everything about his older sister had always seemed rigid to him. She eyed his curly hairstyle and one corner of her mouth tilted upward.

Don't get judgmental on me. He suppressed the thought with one of his charmer smiles and accepted her compliment on the white shirt and pressed slacks.

"You look like you're going out for a job interview," she said. "What's up?"

He immediately resented the hopeful tone in her voice. "No interview. I've got vacation days saved up and just thought I'd spend a little time with you, maybe take a quick trip somewhere. We haven't seen much of each other recently."

She accepted it at face value and offered him some tea. He'd rather have a beer but decided not to push his luck until he was sure she would let him stay.

"Really nice place you got here," he said, following her to the kitchen where she poured from a tall pitcher and then added ice cubes to glasses.

"I'll buy something permanent once the divorce is final," she said. It was hard to tell whether she was happy or sad about that. "And I'll finish my teaching certificate and find work. Every city needs teachers."

She always thought that way, many steps ahead, in everything she did. He put a bright smile on his face and nodded as if he agreed with everything she said.

Back in the living room he noticed stacks of boxes against one wall. Among the cardboard was a small trunk with brass fittings and a couple of really old lamps that might be antiques. Maybe even worth something.

"What's all this?" he asked.

"Grandma's things. I closed up Mother's house this week and had to do something with all the clutter from her attic. I could rent a storage unit but then it would just be one more place to let things accumulate. I'll go through it all and probably donate anything usable to charity. I don't necessarily want to haul it all to my new place and store it there either."

"The little trunk is kinda cool," he said.

"I glanced into it. It has a bunch of old letters and diaries. Apparently our great-grandfather was one of the men who got gold fever and went up to Alaska during the gold rush. That's what Mother told me. Grandma, at one point, tried to find him—her father, this was—but Mother never knew how it turned out. I don't know what I'll do with it all, not yet."

Michael had lifted the lid of the trunk and pulled out the letters. No gold bars under the paperwork. Damn. He looked at the fancy writing on the envelopes. Maybe the old man had written home to say what he'd done with his gold, or the two diaries might reveal what his grandmother had learned. He barely remembered the old woman; when he was a kid they had visited her a time or two in San Francisco but he only remembered riding the cable cars.

"Look, I've got an appointment," Katherine was saying, "at the university ... I really need to get going. You can take the letters with you if you want."

Now-or-never time. "I was kind of thinking of staying with you a day or so. Get the chance to visit and catch up on things. I could do something with these boxes while you're doing your appointment."

Hesitation flickered over her face. "Okay, fine."

She shrugged into a jacket that matched her skirt and picked up her purse.

"I should be back by five. I suppose we could go out, grab some dinner someplace after that."

"Sounds good, sis." He worked on the charmer smile again. "It's great to see you again."

The moment the door clicked shut behind her, Michael emptied the little trunk completely and examined the sides and bottom for hidden compartments that might conceal some gold. At today's gold prices, it wouldn't take much to get him out of his current spot. A bit more than that and he could be set for life.

He realized that no one had exactly said that their great-grandfather had actually found any gold in Alaska. Michael rummaged through his sister's kitchen cabinets where he found a bottle of cognac and poured himself a decent share of it. Then he settled onto her creamy beige sofa with the drink and the letters.

It didn't take long to figure out that most of them were sappy stuff, written in really old-fashioned language, between a husband and wife. God, he could almost hear Candy waxing all poetic over this and wanting to talk to him that way. He skimmed through most of them, noting with some pride as he read between the lines, that his great-grandfather had also been a gambling man. The old man would be proud of Mike for the plan that was taking shape in his head.

Michael opened the last one that had a Skagway postmark. *I've found gold!* The words jumped off the page at him.

Oh, man. Oh, man. This was great! Joshua Farmer was clearly brilliant. He'd managed to get hold of a big stash of gold without having to do a whole lot of work and risk his life out there in freezing-ass weather; he'd thrown the wife off the scent by saying he was coming home, then he'd skipped out somewhere. Or maybe he'd just stayed in Alaska and paraded around like a rich guy.

He came to a letter addressed to a Harry Weaver at the Pinkerton Detective Agency. He'd heard about them in a movie one time. Uh-oh, the wife was tracking Joshua, trying to find him and his gold.

Other letters, however, revealed that the detective and the wife had never found him. *Good going, Gramps!*

Michael let the cognac burn a nice, fiery path down his throat and settle into cozy warmth in his belly as he thought about this new information. Joshua Farmer must have hidden out, possibly even hiding the gold somewhere, just in case the detective found him. It had to be a lot of gold—a lot!—to sustain him the rest of his life. Maybe his grandfather also had some of Katherine's traits—saving money, building his startup capital into a vast fortune.

Mike could go there, find it, claim it. He could repay Vince. Hell, men like Vince wouldn't go to Alaska—it was too damn cold, compared to Vegas. He could stay there and be free of Vince, once and for all!

He found a spiral notebook in Katherine's desk and helped himself to a pen, too. He looked up a travel agent in the phone book and spent an hour discussing ways to get to Skagway. By the time Katherine returned, he had a reservation for tomorrow. A ticket would be waiting for him at the airport ticketing counter.

"Hey, sis, you look chipper. I take it the appointment went pretty good?"

"It did. I'm enrolled in some fall semester classes and it shouldn't take long to get my qualifications updated." She dropped her purse at the end of the sofa. "Let me freshen up and we'll head out for dinner."

He heard the bathroom door click shut. It took two seconds to get his fingers into the purse and extract her wallet. It contained a hundred dollars cash and one credit card. Too round a number; she would notice if any of it was missing. He snapped the clasp shut again and dropped it back into the purse before she came back.

"You know, Michael, you should consider going back to school. It would take a couple of years but with a degree you could find a better job, bring in more, start saving for your future."

She meant a wife, house and kids. He knew it. With smile in place, he let her precede him out the door. But she brought up the subject again at the restaurant, where they'd decided to order a large pizza. There was only so long he could let her go on, thinking she was convincing him about her way of doing things.

"You know, sis, I've really developed an interest in our family history. I'm thinking of tracing our genealogy."

"Really? I didn't know you ever cared for history."

"Oh, yeah, it's been a long-term interest of mine." He prayed that she wouldn't quiz him too closely on that. "Finding that trunk of Grandma's letters has me real excited." That much was true.

"That's nice," she said. "I'm glad."

"I figure I can keep working at the aircraft factory and work on family history in my spare time. For instance, with my vacation days now I could starting tracking information on the grandparents and great-grandparents mentioned in those letters."

Careful, he reminded himself. He couldn't afford to let out any clues that Alaska was the destination.

"That sounds like fun, actually," she said, wiping her mouth with a napkin. "I have a little time too."

Uh-oh. Cannot let her invite herself along.

"The price of a couple plane tickets would do it," he said. "I could set it all up."

Her expression drooped. "I can't afford that right now. My tuition is due before the weekend and until I get used to what my monthly expenses will be, I better back away from doing any travel."

He forced himself to look sad about this news. "Well, one thing about history—it'll always be there."

They walked back to the apartment, Michael keeping an eye on every car that passed. Katherine handed him a sheet, blanket and pillow and he accepted the couch as his accommodation, but he hardly slept. He dreamt of gold bars and gold nuggets; he tossed on the narrow sofa and pictured himself in plush hotels from now on, living it up. When Katherine got up in the morning he accepted coffee and fretted silently as he kept an eye on the clock. He had two hours to find enough cash to cover his ticket and get himself to the airport.

Chapter 25

Irubbed my face and flinched as the grime from my fingers transferred. The names were becoming a blur, and as I washed up at the kitchen sink I seriously began to question whether there was any benefit to thoroughly reading and piecing together the life stories of these people from the past. Was I becoming so bogged down in their actions in their own day that I was missing the bigger picture?

I brewed a strong cup of tea and stood at the kitchen counter, sipping it and reviewing what facts I knew.

Joshua Farmer came to Skagway during the gold rush. He wrote that he found gold but never made it home.

More than seventy years later, Michael Ratcliff came here, ostensibly on a genealogy search. He had made a list of people to talk to but he, too, never went home. His bones were identified as those found in the cave.

The two sets of bones were related.

Ergo, it made sense that Joshua was the other dead man in the cave.

Okay. That was half the mystery. The rest of it was to learn who had killed each of them. I had to believe there were two killers. If the person who bashed Joshua over the head were a child when he did it, he would be aged eighty or more when he killed Michael. Neither scenario seemed the least bit likely.

So, the two murders were separated by a couple of generations. But there's no way they seemed entirely coincidental. What was the connection?

It wouldn't immediately come to me, and I tried to put myself in Joshua Farmer's position. His letters gave off a certain desperation. Although he didn't spell it out to his wife, I gathered that he was out of money, wanted to be home, couldn't even afford the steamship passage. His friend the detective had offered to help him financially at times—why didn't Joshua accept the help?

Perhaps he'd made Harry Weaver angry over something and the other man struck out. It would have been simple for the detective to cover his own tracks and report no sign of the missing man.

There was also the possibility that, in his desperation, Joshua had stolen someone else's gold. But that didn't quite jell; it would be the other man lying dead in the cave while Joshua took off. As Ron had once told me on another case, the dead guy isn't always the innocent guy.

Then there was the second murder, Michael Ratcliff. Was he an innocent guy who happened into the wrong place? I had been going on that assumption all along.

My phone rang before I could piece together a string of facts about him.

"Finally!" Mina said. "I don't know why paste-up day seems so long. It's always a crazy-house at the paper. Anyway, I'm free now. Want to grab a drink?"

I glanced at my watch and saw that the afternoon had pretty much slipped away.

"Come by here," I suggested. "I've got some wine and there are a bunch of new documents I can show you."

While I pulled out a couple of wine glasses, it hit me that Drake never had checked in with me after his second flight. I felt a tremor of uneasiness go through me. I dialed his phone.

Luckily, he answered on the first ring. "Kerby and I are just shooting the bull," he said.

From his easy tone I gathered that flying was done for the day. I told him that Mina and I were about to have a drink and go over notes I'd been making from the case. I could tell that he was happy to stay out of our way for awhile.

Mina's highlighted hair was pulled up in a clip, where a little fountain of brown-gold strands spurted from the top. Her bangs stuck out at odd angles, as if she'd tried to rip them out in frustration at some point in recent hours. She flopped on our couch and blew out a huge breath.

I'd brought the bottle and glasses to the living room and she eagerly accepted hers the minute I handed it over.

"It's always those last few hours," she said. "If the layout doesn't hit the printer's office by four o'clock we miss our deliveries on Thursday. At least it's better than the old days. We upload the files now. I remember being sent on a race through town to get pasted-up boards to a plane that was revving up to leave for Haines."

She took a couple of generous sips of the wine. "Anyway, not your problem. Enough of the news biz for awhile."

We leaned back in our seats for a few minutes, Mina unwinding, me thinking over everything I'd read and deciding what to ask her first. Finally, I just started at the beginning, with my trip to the museum this morning and ending with my scribbled list of names I'd pulled from the diaries, letters and notebooks.

"I found some of the names in the phone book," I told her. "Several of the families are still here in town."

"Oh yeah, there's a certain pride in declaring how long you've been here. Guess it's that way in places that tend to have a lot of newcomers."

"At least we know why Michael Ratcliff came to Skagway," I said. "His sister said he had developed an interest in family history, so he surely hoped to find out more information about his great-grandfather, Joshua."

"He did a good job, I'd say. Ended up only a few dozen feet away. Sorry, I guess that's not very respectful, being that they were both murdered."

She'd picked up my list and was scanning it.

"You've met some of these folks already, Charlie. Thespens, of course—that's Lillian Allen's family. Jo McIlhaney was at that art gallery party. Barney Connell works for Kerby."

Barney, our customer greeter with the mountain-man appearance? Okay.

"The Smiths have been around forever. They claim some distant relationship to the infamous con man, Soapy Smith, but I'm not sure if that's true. My friend, Zack, he's a Manicot—related to Gertrude that you spoke to. His parents and grandparents and a whole bunch of them have lived here forever."

My mind raced ahead. When Michael Ratcliff arrived and began asking questions about the missing Joshua Farmer, it might have put someone on alert, a guilty party with some old crimes to keep hidden.

I heard Drake's truck pull up in front of the garage. Mina noticed too and said she needed to get going.

"Hey, that historical society fundraiser is tomorrow night," she said. "If you guys don't mind parting with an exorbitant amount for a halibut dinner, it would be a chance to socialize, meet more folks—maybe view them all as suspects." Her eyebrows wiggled at that last part.

I told her I would see if Drake was interested. I wouldn't mind asking a few questions. Friends of the historical society seemed like the ideal crowd to glean information from in this situation.

As it turned out, we both had a number of flights that day, but we still managed to gussie up and be there on time. We snagged seats at a table that included the gang from Gold Trail Adventures: Kerby and Lillian, Chuey and Mina, Barney and his wife. Sissy Connell seemed an exact opposite of the exuberant mountain man—petite and quiet, with over-styled blond hair and long acrylic nails that had tiny blue and yellow Alaska flags on them.

Lillian Allen didn't sit; she was up and working the room in true political fashion. Kerby, Chuey and Drake managed to find business to talk about, despite the fact that they'd just spent all day together. I tried to engage Sissy in conversation but her shyness was nearly painful and it seemed kinder after awhile not to push it. She kept looking around the room and when she spotted her husband at the bar, she excused herself with a tiny smile and went to join him.

"Shall we mingle?" Mina asked. "There are a few things on the silent auction table I wanted to check out."

That seemed far better than staying at the table with the guys. Part of my goal in coming was to chum up with some of these old-time families and see if I could get an angle on our murder cases. I reminded Mina of the names she'd given me earlier and asked that she introduce me to some of them.

Eyeing a beautiful piece of scrimshaw, made into a pendant necklace, Mina edged near a woman who looked somewhat familiar, with a dark brown pixie haircut and strong jawline.

"Hi, Jo," Mina said. After a few seconds of how-are-you chit-chat, she introduced me to Jo McIlhaney.

"Ah, your name is familiar," I said. "I've been reading a series of historic letters and came across a Mrs. McIlhaney who ran a rooming house here during the gold rush."

Jo smiled. "Yes, we've heard all about that. Elizabeth was a great-great something on my father's side. I lose track. My grandparents apparently kept up the tradition—they owned a small hotel here when I was a kid. It's not one anymore. The building became something else and then something else again, until the Park Service took it over as they've done with a lot of the historic buildings here in the borough."

"In the letters I'm reading, she rented a room to a man named Joshua Farmer, who had come to make his fortune."

"Ah, didn't they all? Too bad so few succeeded. Well, at finding gold. A lot of those pioneers stayed on and succeeded in other things. Today, it's a matter of location, location, location, as they say. Having a shop that draws a lot of tourists is the name of the game. Of course, that's difficult nowadays too. The big stores are owned by the cruise lines and they really push hard to get people in those places. I try to steer folks toward the smaller shops, the ones with locally made items rather than that cookie-cutter jewelry and trinkets they can buy on a Mexican cruise or a Caribbean cruise or ... well, anyplace."

As I talked with Jo, Mina was moving along the table of goodies, scribbling bids for the items she wanted. Jo noticed, and wrote a competing bid for the scrimshaw pendant. I edged away, leaving space for the avid ones.

Jo McIlhaney didn't seem like a valid lead for our case. There had been no flicker of recognition at Joshua's name, anyway. I led into the same line of chat with a few others, once Mina introduced me to a Frannie Smith and then to her friend, Zack Manicot. I noticed that Gertrude, who it turned out was his aunt, had stepped outside for a cigarette. None of my nosy questions elicited a flicker of interest until I had circled the room and caught up with Barney and Sissy.

"Riches from the Klondike?" Barney said. "How about riches from ripping each other off?"

His voice grew a little loud—I suspected the heavy glass of amber liquid in his hand had something to do with that. Sissy nudged him but he didn't seem to notice.

"Yeah, my family has stories all right. My great-great grandfather was here then. His story gets told to every kid in our family, how he'd come back from the trail with a big bag of gold. A guy who said he was Alistair's friend knocked him over the head and stole it! That's what friends were good for then."

Sissy tugged at her husband's arm and he quieted. This was a far cry from the jovial man who met flights full of tourists and gave them the hearty spiel about panning for gold in the streams near their cabins.

"I'm going out for a smoke," Barney muttered, walking away.

Sissy gave a tiny smile and an even tinier shrug of her narrow shoulders before following him. I looked toward the bar to see Lillian and her brother Earl with their heads together. She was probably trying to decide if some mayoral damage control was needed, but the sounds of the party had picked up again and no one appeared to be giving the little incident much notice.

"The Connells have always sort of carried a chip," Mina said in my ear. I hadn't even realized she was beside me. "They never had much money—Barney's dad lives out in a really rough cabin where it's all he can do to keep his snow machines running all winter with duct tape and bailing wire. Barney grew up with that and even though he's worked in town his whole adult life, I guess some things run pretty deep."

"He always seemed like a really happy guy." We started ambling back toward our table.

"Basically, I think he is. He and Sissy were high school sweethearts and they seem good together—jolly guy and soft-spoken wife. She's not usually *this* quiet—she's a hairdresser and is really loved by her clients. She just gets a little overwhelmed in crowds that include the important people."

I glanced toward the door where they had exited.

"Alcohol. It changes people, sometimes in a flash."

Lillian Allen walked over to us, her smile unnaturally bright. "Ladies, everyone having a good time?"

"Absolutely," I said. I held back from posing my

questions to Lillian. The blowup from Barney was one skirmish too many for the evening.

The lights blinked twice and a small gong sounded. Voices quieted.

"Dinner is served," Lillian said, loudly enough for most in the room to hear.

We made our way back to our tables. Sissy and Barney didn't come back until the salads had been cleared, but when he sat down he seemed the same friendly man. I wondered if the quiet Sissy was, in reality, a pretty solid force for him.

Kerby and Lillian dominated the dinner conversation, anyway, which gave both Barney and Sissy a chance to keep their thoughts to themselves. I found my own thoughts wandering. It had been one of those weeks with too much input and I was having a hard time sorting through it all.

Chapter 26

Michael let out a long sigh as the stewardess closed the door on the plane. What a morning! He'd managed to find an envelope of cash in Katherine's dresser drawer, scribbled her a note—*Gotta go, sis, thanks for everything, I'll pay you back soon*—while she was in the shower. With a quick glance around the living room, he'd jammed his few possessions, the money and the letters into his backpack and literally run down the four flights of stairs. A taxi came along a block from her apartment and he was on his way!

He buckled his seatbelt on command from the speakers over his head and settled in for the trip to Anchorage. They'd put him in the back of the plane but he didn't mind. It gave him the chance to watch everyone else who came aboard—an assortment of students, some rugged mountain-man types, and a scattering of businessmen—no one who looked like they were fresh out of Vegas.

"You heading up to work on the pipeline?" asked a guy in the seat next to him.

"Huh? No, not really."

"Man, check it out. It's where all the work is these days. Excellent pay." The guy flipped open a magazine. "I hear everything's super expensive though. I figure, what the heck, it's a chance to earn a bundle for a couple years."

Michael nodded, as if he really cared. He didn't intend to get out in some wide-open, windblown tundra, getting dirty and living in a damn camp. He had a family fortune waiting for him; he just had to find it.

The other guy went back to his magazine and Michael pulled out his spiral notebook and his grandmother's diary. With the tray as a work surface he began making notes, paying attention to names—people, hotels, places. It shouldn't be that hard to trace Joshua Farmer's movements, once he was on site in the little boomtown.

A sharp-looking flight attendant came along and offered drinks and sandwiches. He accepted both. Too bad Candy didn't aspire to a job like that—she'd look hot in that uniform. He thought about her. Maybe he should have brought her along; they could have a pretty good time together staying in a hotel and taking walks in the mountains. Candy grew up in Denver; she loved the mountains and the snow.

He had almost phoned her from the airport to say goodbye, but held back. He didn't have enough for a second plane ticket today and who knew how much she might blab about his plans if she knew them. Nah, better to get to Alaska, find the gold, then he could decide whether to stay there or come back to Seattle in style—hell, he really might splurge for a ring if he was in the mood.

He stuffed his paperwork back into the pack when his food arrived. People griped about airline food but he didn't think this was so bad. It was free, anyway. Without breakfast this morning, it tasted pretty good to him. He wolfed it down, handed the dishes back and settled against the window for a nap. Next thing he knew they were telling everybody to buckle up and get ready to land.

Anchorage didn't give much of an impression—the airport was packed with men, few women, laborers heading for the pipeline, he supposed. Mike found the gate for his commuter flight to Skagway, a little dismayed to see that it was going to be one of those little puddle-jumper planes. What the heck, it was a short flight. Mainly, he was tired from the fits-and-starts of sleep he'd gotten in the past twenty-four hours and hoped he would find a hotel room quickly at the other end of the line.

Skagway was a pretty close fit with the image he had formed from his great-grandfather's letters. The muddy streets were gone—thank goodness—paved over now, and there was now electricity. What he was not ready for was the north wind that blasted down the streets and sucked every scrap of warmth through his polyester shirt and pants. He got a shuttle bus to drop him off at the nearest clothing store where he gave far too much for a jacket.

"Wind's supposed to let up tomorrow," the clerk said when Michael asked her to cut the tags off the coat so he could wear it now. "Should get nice after that. Be glad you're here in June. Later on, the mosquitos show up."

Shit, maybe his idea of staying on was dumb. He'd better just find the gold and get the hell back out of here.

He lucked out on a room, taking the clerk's recommendation of a bedroom sublet from some guy who worked for one of the tour companies. It was three blocks off the main drag rather than one of the places all the tourists were eyeing. Even so, once he was in the single room at the back of the house—view of an alley with weird trash cans that had locking lids—he sat on the bed and counted his money.

There wasn't a whole lot left of Katherine's tuition. If he ate toast for breakfast and peanut butter sandwiches for dinner he could get by until the end of the week that he'd paid for. He jammed the bills into his wallet and refused to think about it—that was too much like his sister, planning ahead all the time. He pulled the phone book from the nightstand beside the bed and looked up the names on his list.

Joshua had said his landlady's name was McIlhaney, and Michael found some of those. A few calls netted him the information that one branch of them was running a little hotel here. He wished he'd known that; he was practically family, after all, could have probably gotten a deal on the room.

He dialed the number, asked to speak to the owner and after a little hedging by some idiot young female clerk got through to someone named Bessie McIlhaney. He told his story and got a blank silence for a good half-minute.

"I don't know what I can tell you, son. There was tens of thousands of hopeful stampeders who came through this city in the heyday. Nobody actually kept track of them."

He stammered out a thanks and hung up. Hm. This might not be quite so automatic as he'd thought.

Farther down in his list of notes was a name of someone

his grandmother Isabelle had contacted, back in the 1940s, a Mrs. Manicot. He found a number and dialed that one. To his delight, she invited him over and gave directions to her house.

"You said your grandmother contacted me?" Gertrude Manicot said as she ushered him into a small living room.

The house was average, filled up with big furniture— leather couches that seemed like they would go better in a huge room rather than this little one. The woman was attractive though. She was probably a few years older than him, which was okay—guys said those ladies in their mid-thirties could be pretty hot—wearing tight brown corduroy jeans and a shirt with just the right amount of buttons undone. She had her dark hair in a ponytail and the first thing she did was offer him a cigarette.

She was watching him, waiting for a response to her question.

"Oh. Yeah, I'm doing some genealogy work and came across your name in a letter." He hoped he sounded more coherent than he felt; he'd never gotten that nap he wanted, back at the airport. "I had the impression you'd be a lot older."

That was a stupid thing to say but she took it the right way, laughing and sending him a flirtatious little wink. She indicated one of the couches and he sat down.

"She would have talked to my mother. Her name was Gertrude, which mine is—legally—although I can't stand that. I go by Gert, sometimes Geegee."

He noticed that she sat on the same couch, and not all the way at the end of it, rather than one of the chairs. When she leaned toward the coffee table to flick the ash off her cigarette, an enticing amount of cleavage showed.

"Your last name's the same too," he said. "So, you're not married?"

Again, that laugh. "Nope, not me." She let it go at that and the silence drew out a little too long.

"Ah. Well. The information—"

She stubbed out the cigarette and stood up. "Let's see what we have."

She walked to a shelf beside the woodstove and picked up a shoebox, bringing it back to the couch—where he swore she sat even closer—and opening the lid. The box was stuffed with white index cards and he supposed there was some system to it all. She ran her fingers over the cards—long, tapered fingers, he noticed, done with a polish that Candy would have probably called Orange Flame or something like that. The thought of the girlfriend back home dampened his enthusiasm a little.

"Mother started this filing system," Geegee said. "Made cards for each missing stampeder that someone asked about, so yours would be filed under Farmer."

She pulled out a single card and showed it to him. Neat block lettering, somewhat feminine. Contact: Letter. Date: 1947. Interested party: Isabelle Farmer. Relationship: daughter. A Notes section indicated that the woman said Joshua Farmer had come to Skagway to get to the Klondike. Last contact with family: July, 1898.

Mike copied it all down, although he didn't have a clue what he would do with this. He'd really been hoping to run into someone who actually knew his great-grandfather, someone who knew about Joshua's gold and might have been privy to where he'd hidden it. It occurred to him that any such person would have to be in their nineties by now.

"I hope that's helpful," Geegee said, replacing the card in the box, shifting position as she set the box on the coffee table so that her hip brushed against his leg.

When she turned to look at him, her face was very close to his. Her breath was warm and smelled pleasantly of menthol tobacco and an undertone of some musky perfume.

"Um, yeah." His breathing came rapidly now. "Really helpful."

Chapter 27

Iwoke up a little groggy the next morning. Too many glasses of wine and too much of the rich hors d'oeuvres that seem a part of every fancy gathering. Drake was on the phone with Kerby Allen when I walked into the kitchen, a hand outstretched for my coffee mug.

"Okay, will do," he said. "We got it."

He turned to me with a kiss before pouring me a cup of caffeine.

"We have flights, I gather?"

"We do. Kerby and Lillian are heading for some conference of mayors in Anchorage, so we're to take both ships and resupply Cabins Two and Three."

I gave an absent nod. Shouldn't be too difficult; we could do it early and be back in time for lunch together and then maybe take the afternoon off to just have a little fun.

I voiced that idea and got wholehearted agreement from him. Poor hubby, between the amount of flying we were doing and the hours I'd spent with Mina going through old documents, we'd not had much pure relaxation as a couple.

Since resupply runs didn't carry any particular time schedule, we took our time with showers and stopped at Tootie's for our favorite breakfast before heading to the airport. The JetRanger and the A-Star sat side-by-side on the tarmac. We checked in with the dispatcher and filed flight plans, then verified with Chuey that the supplies for our guests had already been loaded onto each aircraft. He consulted a page on a clipboard.

"JetRanger goes to Cabin Two, A-Star to Cabin Three."

Out on the tarmac again, Drake slipped into his flight jacket. "You have a preference which ship you fly?"

Normally, I took the JetRanger since I was more familiar with it, but it wouldn't hurt me to log more hours in the A-Star. I pointed toward it and he headed for our ship. We each did our customary pre-flight routine, even though Chuey had said that Kerby checked both craft before he left.

"See you in an hour or so," Drake called out as he closed the door.

Ever the gentleman, he waited while I went through my start-up steps and motioned with his palm for me to go first. What a sweetheart. I blew him a kiss and lifted off. He remained in radio contact and said he was watching my rear—something the guys back in the office were probably having a hoot over—until he had to change heading toward his own destination.

Without passengers to entertain, my flight was a fairly

easy one. I kept the Skagway River in sight, then picked up the Klondike Highway, cruising along with steep, snow-capped mountains on either side of me until I broke out into the open meadows and spotted Cabin Three.

Two kids raced out to greet me and I brought the A-Star to a hover, making sure they would stay back before I touched ground. They bounced on the balls of their feet until their mom and another woman—I vaguely remembered that the two were sisters—came out. They kept an arm on each kid's shoulder until the rotors had quit spinning.

"Hey," I said, "you guys having a great time out here?"

"We are," said one of the women. "The kids have found some gold dust, we've hiked all over these hills, and Crystal and I are ready for a resupply of wine ..."

I laughed along with her. In addition to the wine, their supply list had included gummy bears and a sugared cereal, which ought to have those kids bouncing around even higher than they were at the moment. We offloaded boxes that included toilet paper, clean sheets and batteries. There was a cooler full of produce and some frozen salmon. The fresh bounty, along with one of those picture-perfect days, almost made me want to stay out here with them.

After asking if there was anything else they needed and making sure everything was functioning well in the cabin, I said I would get out of their way. They stood on their little porch, like a scene from *The Waltons*, waving and calling out as I lifted off.

I took my time returning. Drake's turnaround time was about an hour and if I could stretch out my own flight I wouldn't have to sit around the airport too long before he came in. On the other hand, in aviation, time is money and every minute in the air was ticking away in dollars, something I had to be aware of even though I wasn't flying our ship. I increased airspeed and radioed my final approach as I spotted the gold rush cemetery below.

Two cruise ships were in port this morning, so the other operator who ran helicopter tours up to the glaciers looked pretty busy. I held back, hovering over the inlet until two of their aircraft cleared the pads.

Setting the A-Star cleanly on its spot, I saw that Chuey was standing in the wide doorway to the hangar, staring at me. I gave a little wave and went into my shutdown procedure. When I looked up again he was gone.

Things went eerily quiet as I walked into the FBO. Earl Thespen was there and gave me a long stare. Surely he already knew about Kerby's and Lillian's plans for the day. Chuey brushed past him and rushed toward me, his face white, and I knew something was terribly wrong.

"It's Drake?" I said, my voice coming out in a croak.

He nodded. "Ray says he's getting an ELT signal."

"I didn't hear anyone trying to raise him on the radio," I said, grasping for answers.

"They're trying that now."

"What about the satellite phone?"

"Tried it. No response."

My mind went blank for a few seconds, then kicked into high gear. I rushed into the control room to see where the signal was coming from.

Ray looked up from a screen, his expression solemn.

"Can you tell if it was set off manually or automatically?" I asked.

"Not yet, FAA hasn't given me that data, if they know it."

If it was set off manually, then Drake had activated the

beacon; he was probably okay. The transmitter went off automatically when an aircraft went into water or crashed. I felt my breakfast rise.

"I've put SAR on alert."

That didn't help my peace of mind at this moment. I'd been on enough Search and Rescue operations to know that response time could vary from minutes to hours. I had flown that route to Cabin Two—the terrain was extremely steep and completely unforgiving to a small aircraft.

"I'm going out there to look," I said. "Chuey, refuel the A-Star for me."

"Charlie—"

I spun on Ray, ready for argument. A dot showed on his computer screen, flashing.

"I've got GPS coordinates for you," he said.

I wrote them down. "Keep trying the radio and let me see your satellite phone again," I said. I dialed the corresponding one that we carried in the JetRanger. Still no answer.

It doesn't mean anything, I told myself. The equipment might be damaged. Maybe he had a hard landing. People survive those all the time. Maybe he discovered neither the radio nor phone would work, there's an emergency of some kind with the people at the cabin, he needs medical help for them and figured this would grab someone's attention ... All this rushed through my head as I dashed back out to the A-Star, discarding most of those scenarios the moment I'd thought of them. Setting off your ELT was serious business—it put authorities on alert worldwide and wasn't something you did just because you couldn't make contact. Drake would try a lot of other things before he set all that in motion.

Which left the probability of a crash.

Chuey finished pumping fuel from the truck, unclipped the anti-static line, and started to get into the cab.

"I want to go with you," he said. "I'll grab a toolbox."

I tamped down my impatience. I wanted to leave *now*, but what he said made sense. It never hurt to have a second pair of eyes to watch the ground and, as Drake had chided me on many occasions, never *ever* head out without some tools handy.

Emotion threatened to well up inside me but I forced myself to think in small steps, with the goal that we would come upon Drake, safe and sound, and our million-dollar aircraft with the huge bank loan would also be in one piece. I had the rotors turning by the time Chuey came out, staggering under the weight of the red toolbox in his hand. Thank goodness—prepared for anything.

I programmed the GPS with the numbers Ray had given me and, after getting a priority clearance and building some altitude by going upriver, we cleared the surrounding peaks and faced two imposing ranges between ourselves and our destination.

"It'll be okay, Charlie," Chuey said. But his voice came over the headset so quietly that I got the feeling he was saying it as much to reassure himself as for my benefit.

I nodded but kept my eyes on the instruments. I couldn't help but think that the JetRanger was the one I normally flew. Had we followed that pattern I would have been the one on the way to Cabin Two and it could be me down there in the trees somewhere.

Stop it! I gave myself a stern little lecture. Anything can happen to any pilot. But I had to wonder, would I have been able to react correctly? Drake had so many more years experience than I did—and we didn't know yet whether he'd made the right choices either.

I had to steer away from that line of thinking or I would go crazy. I made it happen by talking to Chuey.

"We're within a mile or so," I told him with an eye toward the clouds that were building by the minute. "Start looking, try to see anything shiny. The blue or white of our paint scheme should show up against all the green down there."

The words sounded more certain than they really were. There were easily ten million trees below us, not to mention deadly high peaks covered in snow where a white aircraft would vanish into nothing more than a dent in the landscape. As always, flying over this vast wilderness made me feel microscopically tiny.

We narrowed the gap to our destination by another half mile.

"I don't see anything yet," Chuey said.

"Keep looking. We'll find him."

Another quarter mile. The cabin sat in a half-mile-wide clearing with an easy northbound approach. If he'd gotten close to that, we should see him. My gaze darted between the GPS readout, the other instruments and the ground.

"Anything?"

"Not yet," he said.

I circled the place on the ground where the GPS said the JetRanger should be. I could do this all day, if necessary. Well, at least until we got to that point-of-no-return mark where we had barely enough fuel to return to the airport.

"Anything yet?" I asked.

Chuey shook his head. I brought the A-Star to a hover and gave my stomach a moment to settle. The worst thing of all is to stare at the ground while the aircraft circles. It's like a prescription for puking. We both took deep breaths and I reached over to push my window open a little way.

"I'm giving it another pass," I said.

On the theory that flying circles in the opposite direction would help unwind my shaky inner-ear situation, I decided to do that. It doesn't really work that way, but at this point I needed something to concentrate on other than the possibility that I might have lost Drake.

Marriage to a pilot always means there's the chance that a morning kiss and have-a-nice-day might be the last. I know that. I can't focus on it.

"Charlie! I caught a flash of something." Chuey gripped at my forearm, pointing out the front window.

I pulled back and came to a hover.

"Where? Point to it again."

He looked a little confused. "I took my eyes off the ground. Let me see ..."

This time I caught it, a flash of light right in my eyes. I nearly cried for joy.

Drake always carried a signal mirror as part of his emergency gear. As the little light winked on and off I knew he was sending it.

I maneuvered toward the light, slowly, desperately trying not to lose sight of it. We cleared some high trees and came over a tiny clearing, and there was the JetRanger. I stared at the space in disbelief, amazed that Drake had been able to land it in such a tight space. There was barely enough clearance for the rotor blades. He stood near the nose of the aircraft.

There was no way I could bring the A-Star down beside it, but I saw another open space about five hundred yards away. I flashed the landing light toward Drake to acknowledge that we'd seen him, then headed for the other place. I locked down the cyclic and collective and left the rotors turning, flinging off my harness and running toward where I'd last seen him.

He came walking out of the forest and the first thing I noticed was blood, trickling down the side of his face.

"Hey, you," he said, pulling me to his chest.

"We were so scared!"

He held me at arm's length and I realized that I had mumbled into his chest and he hadn't heard a word of it. I babbled a lot more incoherent stuff and dabbed at the blood, most of which seemed to be coming from an inch-long gash on his temple.

Chuey, bless him, gave us a minute alone before he got out and walked over.

"Wow, man. What happened?"

He touched his face and looked at the blood on his fingers. "I got that from my travel mug. It kind of flew around a little when I had to make a sudden move. The aircraft—I'm going to let you check that out. I got an oil pressure warning. I know—weird—it was fine when I started out. After that, there was no choice but to do a forced landing."

"Let's go," said Chuey, heading toward the downed craft.

"I better see if I can get through to the FBO," I said. "They're about ready to call out everyone from Search and Rescue to the dog teams."

"Use your satellite phone," Drake said. "My radio crapped out and something's wrong with the phone I had on board."

I took a couple of steps and stopped dead in my tracks. What were the odds of that being a coincidence?

Chapter 28

Michael walked down the quiet residential street, a hazy afterglow still running through his body. Wow. He couldn't believe such a babe seduced him. It really was true, what they said about women reaching their sexual prime in their thirties. Maybe this recent birthday of his shouldn't have him freaked out at all.

At the corner of Seventh and State he paused and looked both ways, trying to remember which way he'd turned when he went to Geegee's house. Hell, no surprise he couldn't remember where he was staying; she'd made him forget all the other questions on his list, and that was his whole purpose in being here. Okay, so now it was *one* of his purposes.

The place where he'd rented the room was a block down, on the left. The roommate was gone now so Mike helped himself to an apple from the fridge and went into his bedroom where he tossed his backpack into the corner and fell onto the too-soft bed. At some point he kicked off his shoes, pulled the chenille spread over himself and slept. He didn't come fully awake until a shaft of sunlight hit him in the face. He groaned and rolled over.

A glance at his digital watch showed that it was four o'clock. That couldn't be right; he'd arrived in Skagway at three-thirty. And a lot had happened since then, he remembered with a smile.

Disoriented, he sat up and looked out the window toward the house next door. A big flowering tree stood between the two houses and birds perched all over it, chirping loudly enough to give any guy a headache. His stomach growled and he decided that hunger might be the cause of the headache. He'd eaten, what, a sandwich on the plane and an apple before he went to sleep. It must be four in the fricking morning. God, this place was just too weird.

He fell back onto the pillows but there was no way Jose that he would fall asleep again. Rubbing at his eyes he got up and pulled the backpack onto his lap, searching for his toothbrush.

In the bathroom he ran a long, hot shower, listening to this odd thumping sound the pipes made. The roommate pounded on the wall from the other bedroom.

"Hey, keep it quiet in the middle of the night!"

Hard to believe that argument when the rooms on this side of the house were bright with sunshine. Mike turned the hot water handle down a little and the noise went away. The shower refreshed him and he fluffed his hair—maybe this curly style would be cool after all—and padded naked and barefoot into the kitchen.

Taking care not to wake the other guy, Mike snitched a spoonful of his instant coffee and some sugar to make it drinkable, then carried his steaming mug back to the bedroom. Clothing spilled out of the backpack and he decided maybe he better hang up a few things. Didn't want Geegee to see him as a total slob, and he did plan to see her again. He had one ready excuse for calling. Fine as the sex had been, he reminded himself that his true mission was to find the family gold, and for that he needed information.

The pack contained two shirts—the dorky white one he'd worn to escape Vince's watchdogs and his favorite, a bright polyester with bold diagonals of orange and pink. He shook them out. Too wrinkled to impress Geegee. He draped them over hangers and put them in the closet. The blue and green flower print shirt from yesterday would have to work for awhile yet. He'd worn gray cords with it but had a pair of denims in the pack. Otherwise, there was his toiletry kit, two pair of boxers and the stack of letters and diaries he'd taken from the brass trunk at Katherine's.

He dressed, realizing that half the clothing he'd brought along had now been worn. Laundry never being high on his list of things to do, he decided he would think about that stuff later. He picked up one of the diaries, his notebook and his coffee mug and walked into the kitchen to top it off before the roommate caught him with a spoon in the coffee jar. He could hear the guy moving around in the other bedroom.

The living room had a couch and a chair and one lamp. No TV, no stereo. How lame was that? Mike didn't care; this would suit his immediate needs. He set his coffee on the table beside the lamp and opened the diary, flipping to the last of the entries and working his way backward through the pages.

The roommate emerged from his bedroom, sniffed the air and gave Mike the eye.

"Today's coffee, okay, I'll share. But by tomorrow you get your own."

Mike shrugged and gave the guy one of his charmer smiles. "Sure, absolutely." When the guy disappeared into the kitchen Mike aimed a finger his direction.

He turned his attention to the notebook and looked at the list of names he'd written down: Mrs. McIlhaney, Harry Weaver, Soapy Smith ... Mike had only made it as far as talking to McIlhaney and Manicot yesterday before he became distracted.

The memory of Geegee's soft thighs began to distract him again, and he decided he would have to touch base—hopefully home base—with her at least one more time. It wasn't even six a.m. yet. Should he tap on her door and hope that she greeted him wearing something filmy and with a sleepy look in her eyes? Or would she chew him out and slam the door on him for showing up when she didn't have her makeup on and her hair done? Women could be so hard to figure out.

Attention back on the diary, he reread the last few entries. Isabelle had apparently contacted someone other than Gertrude Manicot, a Wilbur Thespen. Mike added that name to his list. He chewed the tip of his pen and stared at the notebook. Okay, he had a couple more names to check out and could probably get more from Geegee. It was as much a plan as he'd ever made and he found his thoughts wandering again to the look of that long, dark ponytail that had brushed across his chest yesterday afternoon.

Movement at the kitchen door caught his attention as the roommate emerged, dressed and jacketed and obviously on his way out the door. The guy pointed an index finger, flicking it playfully like a pistol.

"Coffee. Food. Today," he said with what he probably thought was a joking tone. "Market opens in a half hour."

With that, he walked out and Mike saw him walk down the street.

Yeah, well, up yours. Mike decided he had to find another place to stay after this week. Of course, once he found the gold he had all the choices in the world open to him. He could stay in Alaska—could probably buy the biggest house in this little burg if he wanted. Or he might just go live in Europe awhile. Something about the Riviera had always appealed to him. Monte Carlo had that fancy casino where the men wore tuxes and the women were wealthy and glamorous.

Still, no point in getting into a battle here. He put on his new jacket and walked the four blocks to the grocery store where he very pointedly bought the smallest jar of instant coffee, along with some potato chips and a big bag of Oreos. Back at the house he put the coffee in the kitchen and the rest of his stuff in his bedroom. He closed his door and used the kitchen phone to call Geegee.

"Hey there," he said, starting off with compliments about how amazing she'd been yesterday and leading into his line about how he still wanted to follow up on the genealogy he had come here to work on.

"Come on over," she said. "I just got up so I'm afraid I'm not really dressed yet."

Oh, god. He rushed out the door so quickly he didn't

remember whether he'd actually replaced the phone on the hook.

This time there was no pretense for what the visit was all about. She greeted him at the door and pulled him inside by the lapel of his jacket. She wore some kind of kimono thing made of such slippery material that one tug of the sash and the garment just sort of fell off her. They were in her bedroom in less than thirty seconds.

She made some excuse for going into the bathroom and he scrambled out of his clothes and met her on top of the purple satin sheets, completely ready for action.

An hour later—what an hour!—she offered him coffee, which he accepted although he was already wired enough to be awake for a month. As she stood at her kitchen counter, elbows resting on its surface, hands cupping a warm mug, he remembered his official reason for being here.

"Families that have been in Skagway since the gold rush ..." she said, pursing her mouth in a way that made him want to nibble at it. "Yeah, there are some. Let me think."

"Wilbur Thespen—guy's older than dirt and lives in a retirement home now. Personally, I think it's a loony bin for people too far gone to know why they're there. Rumor has it the old man's father struck it rich in '98, started a bank and did enough things right that the family fortune kept on growing. Wilbur got voted to a few terms in the state legislature. But his son is around too. He'd be more our age."

Mike felt a secret thrill that she thought of him as her own age, not some kid.

"Let's see. McIlhaneys got into the hotel business."

He nodded. He'd already checked that one.

"Some Smiths claim to be related to Soapy Smith. I

don't know if that's true, but if you haven't heard the legend of old Soapy, it's worth a read at the library or in almost any tourist brochure."

He smiled, although he couldn't see himself spending any time in a library.

"Not everyone got rich," she said, turning to add more coffee to her cup. "The Connells were supposedly here way back in the day but they sure don't live like anybody with money. Got this ramshackle cabin out in the hills, with a pack of snot-nosed kids running around. The father runs guided hunts in the fall—far as I know that's their only source of income. Guess he feeds the bunch of them with whatever he can poach and whatever vegetables the wife grows out behind the place. I doubt they even have running water out there."

Sounded like a hard life. Mike couldn't imagine getting himself into a hole that deep, but then he remembered the thirty grand Vince wanted from him. He swallowed some coffee too fast and choked.

"Hey, baby, you okay?" Geegee asked, stepping around the end of the counter to pat him on the back.

He reached for the front of her kimono and there went that slippery sash again.

It was close to noon before they emerged from her bedroom the second time and he sensed that Geegee was a little impatient.

"I've got other things to do today," she said.

"Tomorrow?"

"I'm not sure. Call me in the morning if you want." She stubbed out her fourth cigarette of the day and handed him his jacket.

Mike wanted to be miffed at the brush-off but, man, the sex was so incredible. Geegee knew things Candy didn't know had been invented yet. If he played his cards right he could probably spend a little time with her every day he was in town. He placed a cool kiss on her cheek and slung the jacket over his shoulder before he sauntered away.

Out of sight of her house, he thought over the things she had told him about the older residents of Skagway. If he wasn't careful he would end up like some lovesick puppy, mooning and following her around and forget his true mission—getting his hands on that gold.

He went back to the house, where he had free use of the phone and the place to himself until the grumpy roommate got off work at five o'clock. He looked up retirement homes in the phone book; there was only one so he called it and asked if a Wilbur Thespen was a resident there. When the receptionist started in with questions, he made up a story about being related and said he wanted to come by and visit.

The address in the book showed that the home was about six blocks away—hell, everything in this town was only a few blocks away. No wonder people here weren't fat; they just walked everywhere they went. He ripped a couple of pages from the spiral notebook and stuffed them into a coat pocket. That way, he could check his notes without toting a lot of spare weight around. As he walked, he cooked up an elaborate set of relationships that would make Wilbur Thespen his great-uncle on his mother's side, a story he figured no one could easily check. As it turned out, no one even asked about that. A woman in a nursing uniform showed him down a hallway and into a big room with lots of windows.

From Geegee's description he'd expected Wilbur to be tottering on the edge of the grave, but the man who greeted him in the home's "day room" was probably not more than seventy.

"Hello, young man, do I know you?" he said when Michael approached him.

"Michael Ratcliff." He gave the explanation about how he'd come across the old letters and diaries and they sparked an interest in tracing his family history. "I was hoping to meet some people who might have lived here in Skagway at the time of the gold rush."

"Gold rush? Well, wouldn't that be something?"

"I meant the gold rush that happened in the eighteen-nineties." He did a little quick mental math. If this guy had lived here, he'd been a baby at the time. "Maybe your father was one who came up here for it. My great-grandfather did."

Wilbur's gaze had strayed around the room and he suddenly focused on Michael again. "Well, hello young man. Do I know you?"

Michael felt his smile freeze. What was with this guy? He repeated his story, watching for something to click. It never did. He itched to get out of the chair and finally made a brusque excuse, figuring the man wouldn't remember his rudeness thirty seconds from now.

At the reception desk a nurse stopped him. "Did you have a good visit with your uncle?"

"He doesn't seem to remember a thing. Is he always like that?"

"At this stage, there are still lucid moments. Not often. He remembers his son more than anyone else. I can sometimes get him talking about his days as a state senator but most of it's gone."

A shiver went through him. Life really could be worse than having a few mobsters tracking you down.

"I was hoping he might have been here during the gold rush. My great-grandfather came here then."

She shook her head, a sorrowful look on her face. "Even though he would have been very young then, he never says anything about it. I feel sure even those old, old memories are gone for him now. Even money and power can't buy some things."

"He has a son? Maybe he would remember old stories his father told him."

"A son and a daughter. The son has taken over the family banking business—biggest bank in the region and they've started to open branches as far away as Anchorage. The daughter went east to an Ivy League college, I believe. We don't see much of her."

Michael jotted down the contact information, including the nurse's name. It was the kind of personal reference that might get him in to see the man who ran the bank. It, as with everything else around here, was a few streets away, located on the main drag called Broadway.

He walked in and sized up the bank. A security guard greeted him and pointed toward a secretary's desk when he said he needed to speak with the bank president. The fifty-some-year-old woman in sturdy shoes and tight curls was immune to his charm, telling him that Mr. Thespen had no appointments available until the following morning. He chafed at that but let her write his name down for ten o'clock. He could see the guy—maybe forty, slim, with precision-cut hair and a suit that fit like it cost a bundle—right there behind the glass windows of a private office, but this old bat was *not* letting him through.

Fine, he thought as he walked out to the sidewalk again. He walked up Sixth Avenue a short distance, noticing a small parking lot behind the bank building. The newest car in the lot was a black Lincoln and he stationed himself where he could see it.

Banks closed at three o'clock, right? An hour, hour-and-a-half max. He could wait.

Michael's butt had a cramp in it from the wooden barrel where'd sat for well over two hours, pretending to soak up some sunshine and read a book. When the well-cut dark suit rounded the corner of the bank building, he stood too fast and had to work out the kinks in his legs. He strolled close to the big Lincoln.

"Mr. Thespen," he called out, tugging his jacket straight and hoping his jeans weren't too wrinkled.

The man paused, slightly puzzled.

"I went by to see your father today," Michael said. He rushed on with his story, fudging a little by adding that he and his grandmother had often talked about the close friendship between Joshua Farmer and a man named Thespen who'd been here during the stampede to the Klondike. He elaborated on how he had traveled all this way to Skagway specifically to meet the family and learn more about his own heritage.

Thespen had relaxed, leaning against the fender of the big car.

"Could I buy you a drink?" Michael offered, holding his breath a little.

The banker tilted his head, thinking. "Sure. What the heck." He pulled off his suit coat and tie and tossed them into the car. "The Red Onion's got pretty good happy hour specials. Four blocks, if you're up for a little walk. Myself, I find the office a bit stuffy by this time of day."

By the time the local man had two Scotches in him, he'd relaxed considerably. Michael felt sure this was a good time to bring up the real subject.

"So, I wonder what ever happened to all that gold they found. Grandma said that her father left his hidden somewhere around here. I wonder where."

Thespen laughed. "I suppose some did that. My grandfather bought the small bank that existed for the early miners. He always pressed people to put their cash into accounts or store their gold in the vault."

"Joshua probably did that." Michael felt his heartbeat pick up. "I should go by there in the morning and check his accounts."

The banker shook his head. "I can tell you right offhand that there are no accounts in the name of Farmer in our bank. My father and I both take pride in knowing our customers. Stop by if you like, but it's not there."

"So, if not in the bank, where would it be?"

The man leaned in close and spoke in a low tone. "There's an old story, the Legend of Gus's Gold they call it. Personally, I've never had time to check it out but I fully believe it's true. There's an old mine shaft—more of a cave, really." He glanced around the room, making sure no one else was nearby. Now his voice was barely above a whisper. "I know someone who can take you there. Meet us at Yakutania Point, across the river from the airport, in the morning—say, eight o'clock? It's a hike, mind you. Wear decent boots." He downed the last of his Scotch and stood up.

Michael hardly slept that night—picturing some old prospector, maybe Joshua Farmer himself, with a sack of gold almost too heavy to carry, putting the extra into this old cave for safekeeping. He woke as the sun began to shine into his room. In the bathroom the roommate was humming, probably just to let Mike know he was there and keeping an eye on things. His gaze fell on the letters and papers he'd brought with him from Katherine's place. It wouldn't be smart to let that guy get his hands on such private information. He gathered everything and went into the living room. The humming didn't stop.

The house had a detached garage. Michael had noticed it when he got there, the thought flashing through his head that something in there might be worth pawning for some extra cash, just until he found the big stash of gold. It might provide a hiding place where Mr. Nosy wouldn't check. He wiggled the hasp on the double doors and got inside. Shelves were full of all kinds of old crap—easy place to hide something.

A flowered cardboard box caught his eye, just the right size to hold most of his stuff. He jammed his spiral notebook and two of the diaries on the shelf, then put the letters into the box and shoved it in front. No one would think anything valuable could be inside. Plus, if he ended up staying in Skagway he would clear out of here real soon and buy something fancy for himself. He closed the garage door and went back in the house, pointedly making himself a cup of coffee from his own jar as the roommate came through and left for work.

Michael went into high gear and found himself at Thespen's designated meeting place a half-hour early, wearing boots he'd lifted from the closet of his roommate. No worry—he would have them back in place before nightfall.

Precisely at eight o'clock the Lincoln drove up. The banker and another man emerged.

"Mike, this is my son. He'll take you from here."

The teenaged boy had a serious look about him, not unfriendly, just intent. He showed Mike where the trailhead began and the two started walking. Away from even the minimal traffic in town, away from the airport and boats in the port and the ever-present murmur of tourist voices, Mike realized how utterly, utterly quiet it was up here.

Chapter 29

Drake led the way to the downed JetRanger, with Chuey at his side, the two of them having an intense conversation while I trailed along a few feet behind after shutting down the A-Star. There was no pathway or trail; we simply blazed our own through heavy underbrush. I finally began to catch glimpses of white—our poor disabled helicopter.

The clearing, which had appeared miniscule from the air, didn't seem so frightening at ground level. I saw that the break in the trees was easily twice the diameter of the rotor blades and that there was an open pathway at the south end of it where Drake probably set up his approach. Still, it was a scenario that probably would have panicked me.

The cowling covers were open around the engine. Clearly, Drake had spent his time already beginning to look for the cause of the engine failure. "There's a lot of oil," he said. "There has to be a leak somewhere."

With the care of a dentist probing around in a tender mouth, Chuey ran his hands over wires and lines, giving a gentle tug here and prod over there.

"You're right, it leaked like crazy."

He climbed down and headed back toward the A-Star for tools. Drake, meanwhile, had settled into the pilot's seat with the satellite phone in hand. He removed the cover to its battery compartment.

"Hon, look at this," he said.

I walked over. With a fingernail he flicked a tiny wire.

"This was tucked behind the battery so it wouldn't be visible. It's broken."

"Deliberately?"

"I can't tell for sure. I don't want to think that."

Chuey came back and Drake stood by to hand him tools as he worked in the engine compartment. It took him about twenty minutes to discover the problem.

"Look at this, Drake." He tossed down a foot-long length of rubber line and Drake caught it.

"See the chafing here?" Chuey pointed to a rough spot on the otherwise smooth surface. "That's not natural wear. There's nothing up there this should be rubbing on. And look here."

He pulled a tiny flashlight from his shirt pocket and shined its intense beam on the questionable area. "There's the hole. Wouldn't you say that's a little too perfectly placed?"

"Someone sawed it?" Drake's voice came out barely a whisper.

Chuey looked up at him, his dark eyes stunned. "I think so."

"Who had access to my ship?" Drake said. "The three

of us, Kerby, one of the other mechanics or pilots ..."

I knew he was running through the possibilities but they were limited. Although a lot of people came and went from the area around the helipads and the FBO, it would take someone with a knowledge of turbine engines to know how to do this.

Kerby and the other operator didn't always get along but to sabotage an aircraft? I'd never heard of even the most bitter rivals doing that to each other. Business feuds were one thing, but this ... this was attempted murder.

I looked back at the satellite phone Drake had left lying on the seat. "Somebody wanted you out of communication. I wouldn't be surprised if they tampered with your radio too."

Both men's faces were sober. A cloud blocked the sun and Drake looked up. "We better see if we can get this thing running."

Chuey considered the oil line and nodded. "I think I've got something." He headed through the woods to the A-Star again.

Drake couldn't stand still. He paced to the tail of the JetRanger and back. "If I hadn't been absolutely on top of this thing, there wouldn't have been time to set her down," he said. "If the engine had seized before I crested that peak, there would have been no safe place to land. I would've gone into the mountain."

No, *I* would have gone into the mountain. I realized it with a sickening lurch of my stomach. I, not Drake, normally flew the JetRanger. I was the more inexperienced pilot. I usually flew a slightly longer route to gain plenty of altitude before crossing the range, so the leak would have done its damage sooner.

And I was the person asking a lot of questions around town.

Chuey came out of the woods just then, noticed my expression, patted my arm. "We'll get her running and be back at the airport in no time."

I looked at the sky. The clouds had become a wide swath of dark gray.

"You could take the A-Star and head back now," Drake said, walking up to me as soon as Chuey climbed back up to the engine with a piece of repair line.

"And leave you out here, not knowing for sure you'll be able to start that engine. What if there's more damage than we know about?"

I had a point and he knew it. He squeezed my hand.

"Come here. I can't do much about the condition of your shirt but we can at least clean up your face a little." I led him to the aircraft and found a bottle of drinking water and some tissues. A bit of careful dabbing and he began to look less scary. The cut on his temple might leave a scar, a reminder of this little misadventure.

A gust of wind traveled through the trees, making a spooky swooshing sound that started a mile away and came toward us. I looked at my watch. We'd been on the ground nearly two hours and the storm was building fast.

"Okay, Drake, ready to try starting it up?" Chuey called out.

The two of them went into action as I stood uselessly to the side. Chuey went back to the toolbox and returned with three quarts of oil. It wasn't really enough but the engine might run long enough to get him home. I found myself holding my breath as the turbine whined to life. The rotor blades began to spin up and reassuringly held their speed.

"We have to get out of here fast," Drake shouted over the noise.

He was right. Any number of other problems could show up. I gave him a thumbs-up to take off, then Chuey and I dashed back through the woods to the A-Star. I wanted to keep the JetRanger in sight as we both flew back to the airport. He was far from being out of danger yet.

Chuey tossed his tools into the box and checked that all the cargo compartments were tightly closed while I ran through my checklist and started the A-Star's engine. The moment he climbed in and buckled up we were ready to go. As soon as I cleared the trees I began scanning the sky for the JetRanger. A dot in the distance was all the reassurance I got.

I kept him in sight, following his flight path and trying to ignore both the impenetrable forest below and the darkening clouds above.

"Chuey? You saw Kerby check both ships before he left this morning, didn't you?"

"Yeah. He did pretty good preflight checks on them."

"Look, I don't know how this happened, but can we not say anything about it?"

"I have to write it up."

He was right, of course. Strict rules existed for both maintenance and flight logs. An oil leak couldn't simply be ignored. "Can you write it so the sabotage isn't mentioned? Or at least not tell anyone else that we think it was deliberately tampered with?"

He started to say something but closed his mouth and nodded.

"At least for awhile. I need to do a little investigating."

Ahead, I saw Drake enter the Taiya River Valley and turn to make his upwind approach into Skagway. As I followed, my legs began to feel a little shaky. I could have so easily lost Drake today. Or he could have lost me. I forced myself to concentrate on my approach and landing and to ignore the wave of uneasiness that threatened.

On the ground, I turned to Chuey. "Thanks. I have no idea what we would have done without you."

He blushed a little and covered by unhooking his harness. "Just glad everything turned out okay."

The understatement of the year.

I glanced up. Near the door to the FBO office stood a small crowd. They all seemed to be staring right at us.

Mina led the way toward the JetRanger, a staff photographer striding along with her. Among the gathering were a dozen or more in Search and Rescue jackets, along with some of the tour flight pilots and a couple of mechanics and fuel truck drivers from their crew. Barney and Earl stood near the building and even Ray had left his dispatch post. As soon as Drake stepped out of the JetRanger they flooded toward him.

Celebrity is not my husband's strong suit; he prefers to do his work quietly and I've never seen him step forward to take the glory for the missions accomplished or all the lives he has saved over the years. His expression was cute to watch: surprise, followed by astonishment, overlaid with embarrassment as Mina began asking questions and jotting notes for what might be her front-page story of the week.

The photographer grabbed some great candid shots and the SAR folks stepped forward to introduce themselves and make sure he was all right. Ray shouted out a greeting before turning to get back to his radios. Even Earl stepped forward.

"I've already called Kerby to let him know that you got back safely," he said as I approached the fringes of the group.

"Thanks to my lovely and capable wife," Drake said, motioning me toward him, draping an arm across my shoulders.

Sure, right. Make sure I get equal treatment in the embarrassment department. But I couldn't be upset over it. I was too busy observing faces, trying to see if there was someone watching all this who was not happy to see me.

Chapter 30

Rain pelted the helicopters parked on their pads, the full fury of the storm catching up only moments after we got inside the building. The rain lashed out for ten or fifteen minutes then settled into a steady patter. Drake thanked the SAR people for coming out and they dispersed. I was ready to head home, myself, to find comfort food, the warmth of a fire and the easy love of a warm dog to snuggle with. Unfortunately, first came the paperwork.

I pulled out my logbooks and watched as Chuey went into the hangar to write up his own report. He would have to replace the makeshift line with one that was certified and approved, and there would be entries to describe all that. I could only hope that he honored my request to keep it low key and not mention the word sabotage.

Eventually, the fact of the tampering would come out, but I didn't want the perpetrator to know that his misdeed had been discovered. Let him think that the mechanic believed the wear on the line to be natural. He might let his guard down long enough for us to catch him.

There was one person I did plan to tell: Chief Branson. I quickly finished entering my own flight data and signaled Drake that I planned to wait in the truck. The rain had settled to somewhere between a drizzle and a mist. I sat in the passenger seat and pulled out my cell phone.

"You kids all right?" the chief asked after immediately taking my call.

I smiled. There was surely no more than a decade's age difference between Branson and Drake, but he did convey an air of fatherliness.

"We're fine. Luckily." I spilled it all. "I would have been at the controls of that aircraft, Chief, any other day of the week. It was purely chance that put Drake there. I don't know that I would have had the presence of mind or the skills to do what he did."

"You're saying ...?"

"That I've been asking a lot of questions around town recently. I must be getting close to the answers if someone wants to be rid of me this badly."

"Any particular names come to mind?"

"Barney Connell got pretty angry with me last night at the historical society soiree. He's around the helicopters all the time and somebody said he was pretty good with engines and mechanical things." I pictured the usually jovial mountain man. "I'm not making an accusation. I just don't know."

Branson mumbled something and I got the impression

he was probably taking notes. "Anyone else?"

"Kerby Allen, naturally, knows everything there is to know about the machines, the schedules and the terrain we fly over. He's made the trip out to Cabin Three so many times, he would know exactly when the helicopter would run out of oil. It's just that I don't see any pilot deliberately sabotaging another's flight. These guys can have big battles among themselves, but there's a line they don't cross."

"Okay, Charlie, you've given me two valid suspects and then proceeded to discount them as possibilities. Are they, or aren't they?"

"I don't know, Chief. My head is pounding right now and I can't think straight."

"Okay, fair enough. You've been through a lot. Go home and rest up, think about it. Be sure to call me if anything else comes to mind."

In reality, investigations of malfeasance with aircraft fall to the jurisdiction of the FAA. The fact that Branson had asked me to call him gave some reassurance that he believed my assertion that this was somehow related to our investigation into the murder of Michael Ratcliff and possibly to the older man in the cave as well. Clearly, I had struck a nerve with someone.

Drake drove and we stopped to pick up burgers—which Tootie comp'd us. Word spread fast around here. Mina was right about the newspaper being superfluous. We took our burgers and fries home in a bag and I slipped into flannel jammies, even though it was mid-afternoon.

A plan to spend a relaxing evening at home doesn't necessarily mean said plan will happen. Drake's phone rang almost immediately. Kerby, who was back from Anchorage and wanted a debriefing. I shook my aching head adamantly to the idea of going back to the airport and finally Kerby agreed to come by the house.

We had just finished our food when his truck rolled up out front. He carried a bag of chocolates that he said Lillian insisted upon, and he seemed genuinely happy to see us alive and well. Drake told him about the worn oil line and, respecting my wishes, left out the discovery that it had been done purposely. On the chance that someone at the FBO was involved, I had taken the damaged line from Chuey's toolbox and brought it home with us. It was now in a plastic bag under our mattress and we would turn it over to the authorities once we knew who to trust.

My phone rang while the men were talking and I went into the kitchen to take the call.

"Is this Charlie Parker?" asked a smoke-roughened voice. "It's Gert Manicot. I don't know if you remember me."

"Yes, certainly."

"I remembered something about the man you were asking about the other day, Michael Ratcliff. It was a lot of years ago, and I only ever knew him as Mike." She paused, looking for words. "Well, he did come here looking for information and, oh gosh, it sounds silly now ... We—he and I—had a little fling. A couple days of fun is all it was, really. I suppose I should be embarrassed to say that I barely remember him."

I sat down at the table, completely unsure where she was going with this.

"He'd come to town with an old diary of his grandmother's in hand, and I got the feeling he was way more interested in gold than in learning about his ancestor's adventures, even though that's what he said it was about. The same kind of inquiry that Mother and I fielded for years. I showed him Mother's notes from way back—same one I showed you—but I forgot to make a card to document his visit." She laughed in a way that turned into a cough.

"A girl wouldn't exactly want to document what we did for those couple of days," she said. "But I had written down his name and some contact information in case I ever came across anything else, and … well, it all became misplaced."

I could easily see that happening—I'd been to her super-cluttered house.

"Yesterday I decided to rearrange some of those old research records—don't ask me why—and I came across some Xeroxed copies."

I rested my forehead in my hand, wishing I had grabbed some aspirin when we first got home. Would she ever get to the point?

"I don't even remember where I got these copies but they look like they came from some old magazine. It's an article about the legend of a large quantity of gold hidden in the mountains near here. Gus's Gold, they're calling it. I guess I had copied this article with the idea of sending it to Mike—my note with his name on it is paper-clipped to the thing—but then I never did."

"I haven't run across that particular legend," I said.

Drake came into the kitchen to grab a couple of beers from the fridge, and I took the moment to have him get me a glass of tap water while I found a bottle of painkillers.

Gertrude had kept talking. ". . . says in some small cave in the region of Mount Clifford."

My attention jumped back to her. "Mount Clifford?" The same area as our cave with the two bodies.

She came to the end of the article and I hated to admit

that I'd missed a big portion of it.

"Can I come by tomorrow and pick up that copy?" I asked. With any luck, there might be more specific directions. This might be the very reason Joshua Farmer and Michael Ratcliff had both gone in there.

We made a plan and by the time I went back to the living room with the idea of giving Freckles whatever was left of the fries, my headache had begun to subside. Kerby must have gotten the hint that we were ready for an evening alone—he slugged the last of his beer and left a few minutes later.

"He says he'll take tomorrow's flight," Drake told me. "I think he's feeling bad that we ran into problems today. We never did get the supplies delivered to Cabin Two, so he'll do that too. Chuey worked on the JetRanger this afternoon and I want to give it a thorough test flight in the morning."

At the moment all I wanted to do was settle in and sleep for a long time. Toward that end, I made sure to pull the blackout drapes in the bedroom when I crashed completely at eight o'clock.

Early to bed, early to rise—okay, but midnight was pushing the wake-up time by a little too much. I gave it another hour, during which I rolled over a half-dozen times. Finally, I grabbed a spare blanket and went to the couch so I wouldn't keep waking poor Drake. That solution wasn't much better—I dreamed of flying a helicopter with missing parts and having to land on a precarious mountain peak. At five o'clock I woke with an edgy feeling.

Freckles was restless in her crate, wakened by my moving about, probably picking up on my unease. I let her out and sneaked into the bedroom to retrieve my clothes so we could take a long walk.

Although Gert and I had agreed that I would come by around nine, as Freckles and I passed her house I spotted the older woman outside watering some potted geraniums on her front porch. I waved and she called out for me to come on in. She offered coffee but I declined. Freckles was way too busy sniffing into corners of the living room and I didn't want to spend any more time than necessary in the lingering haze of the woman's cigarette. She'd left the magazine clipping on an end table so I took it and called my dog away from whatever critter she had spied.

At a small park, I unclipped Freckles's leash and let her run full-out for a few minutes, chasing and retrieving the tennis ball I'd carried in my coat pocket, while I took a look at the article titled "The Scintillating Saga of Gus's Gold."

The body of the piece was written in the same flowery language as the title, reminding me more of a rousing fictional adventure story than a news article. The way in which it had been clipped, with no heading or date, meant it easily could have been fiction. But I had to admit that it painted a picture of a treasure worth going for.

Supposedly, Gus Garrett, an early miner who'd gone to the Klondike, had found so much gold he couldn't carry it all. He had braved winter storms and crossed icy rivers with his trusty sled dog team, becoming lost in a blizzard. Unable to find his way back to the Taiya River, he ended up in a small valley surrounded by imposing peaks. His dogs had died, all but two, and his sled had fallen apart under the weight of the gold. He fashioned packs for the dogs and one for himself and loaded them with more than a hundred pounds of gold. They made their way into a nearby cave to wait out the weather.

The following spring he struggled into Skagway, a tiny

settlement of no more than a dozen people on the inlet, alone but for a pouch full of nuggets that weighed close to a pound, which he gave to the doctor who took him in. The doctor treated him for severe frostbite and Gus said that, having barely survived off the flesh of the two dogs, he had hidden the bulk of his gold and would go back for it when his health was restored. Old Gus died and the gold was never found.

I folded the pages and stuck them into my pocket, calling out to Freckles. I seriously had to wonder if there was any truth to this wild tale. The terrain was rugged up there and *if* there was any validity to it, I could only imagine how daunting it would be for a man alone and with a heavy load in the days before highways and airways. It would make sense that old Gus had to leave the gold behind. It was definitely the kind of story that might have easily attracted men to search for it.

Back at the house, the yummy scent of bacon greeted me.

"Hey, girls," Drake said. "I wondered where you'd gone."

I gave him a kiss and explained about my sleepless state and the long walk.

"Breakfast will help." He tipped the skillet up to scoop scrambled eggs onto two plates and added a couple slices of bacon.

"I'm heading to the airport soon. Chuey got that oil line replaced so I'll give her a good test flight. Want to come along?"

I didn't especially, but he gave me that "you've got to get back in the saddle" look and I knew he was right. I couldn't let one malfunction scare me away from flying. I was too jittery to sit around the house and I was really feeling at an impasse in solving the two murders. I'd gone through my suspect list pretty thoroughly yesterday with Chief Branson but no new ideas had come to me.

At the airport, an hour later, I walked along on Drake's careful preflight inspection, paying attention to the areas that he double-checked. Scary, how someone had managed to inflict the damage that went unnoticed by either of us last time. Chuey stood near the hangar door, and I imagined he had his fingers crossed inside the pockets of his jacket.

"It'll be fine," Kerby said to me as I took a spot near the building. "Look, I'm heading up to Cabin Two to take those supplies. Will you be around for awhile?"

I nodded and watched him walk to the A-Star at a helipad a few spaces down from ours. Drake lifted off and I caught myself listening, making sure the sound of the engine was reassuringly strong. Chuey gave me a thumbs-up and went back inside the hangar. I decided that I could make use of the next few minutes by checking with Mina and making a plan to go over our notes together. She picked up her phone right away and I told her about my visit to Gert Manicot this morning.

"Ah, the old legend of Gus's Gold," she said. "We were told that story as kids, more of a fairytale than something we believed in. I never realized anyone had written it up as an article."

"I'm surprised Gert didn't tell me that when she gave me the copy of it."

"Maybe she was just having some fun with you. So, Chuey got the helicopter up and running again?"

"Drake's on a test flight now."

My attention got distracted by someone waving an arm

in my direction. Barney Connell came toward me with a note in hand so I told Mina I needed to go.

"I just booked some people who want to take Cabin One for a week. They're coming in on the Norwegian cruise ship this afternoon and I guess they worked a deal where they can stay ashore a week and go back home with the ship when it heads south on its way back. First time I've heard of anyone doing that but Kerby won't complain about the extra business."

"I'm sure he'll be thrilled. What time does he get back?"

"I'm not sure, but I'm thinking that I could go up there and get the cabin ready. Can you or Drake fly me up there?"

"Sure." Kerby would probably be pleased that we employees had taken the initiative. I looked up the inlet to see the JetRanger coming in on final approach. "Are you ready now?"

Barney rushed off to get his things and I walked out to the ship as soon as the skids hit the tarmac.

"Your turn," Drake said when I told him Barney's idea. He locked down the controls and I took over his seat.

Barney came out a minute later, wearing his mountain-man red plaid jacket and carrying a huge box of food staples. Chuey followed with another box. "Good thing the cabin was cleaned a few days ago. I think I can get it ready without too much effort."

I was happy to see that Barney had regained his cheerful attitude and didn't seem to bear any of his previous anger toward me. Mina was probably right—it had been the drink talking the other night. Supplies safely stowed and my passenger in the seat, I lifted off.

The aircraft ran in top form, smooth as silk, and in eight minutes we slid through the pass between Mount Clifford and A.B. Mountain and saw the cabin a half mile ahead. I circled to make the approach and noticed something odd.

Kerby's A-Star sat on the ground out front, in the spot where I would normally land. He was supposed to be at Cabin Two or on his way back.

As I made the big loop I saw Kerby, Lillian and Earl step out from behind the cabin. A few pieces of the puzzle fell into place. I clicked the radio, calling out on the base operator's frequency but I could only raise a bunch of static, repeating my concerns and my location. I did not like the look of this.

Chapter 31

I shut down the engine and got out. "Kerby? I thought you were at the other cabin."

I walked toward the trio. Barney followed. Lillian and Earl stood close together. In their casual clothing the resemblance between brother and sister was more apparent than usual.

Kerby gave me a cocky smile. "We had a little business here. Why are you here, Charlie?"

A chill passed over my arms. Had I just stepped into the midst of the enemy camp? Had Barney lured me up here, and there really was no customer coming to the cabin this afternoon? I turned to look at the mountain man but I couldn't get a reading from his expression. I decided to play it upbeat and innocent.

"There was a call from a customer who wants to come

up later today, Kerby. I brought Barney to get things ready and greet them."

Kerby's moment of uncertainty showed on his face as his gaze darted toward Barney. Barney's expression only registered the same confusion as my own. Reassuring to me—they had not cooked up this plan together.

"We can't let anyone come up here, Kerby. Call it off." Earl's voice was more forceful than I'd ever heard it.

"That's right," said Lillian. "My great-grandfather's legacy is not public property. Not any more."

Great-grandfather's legacy? It took me a half-second but the final piece clicked into place.

"He was Mick Thespen, wasn't he? And your father was Wilbur?"

Lillian's face grew hard.

Earl's went red with fury.

"You! You people come in here and all want a piece of us! Where did you get those letters? *Where!?*"

The letters. I had to mentally backtrack, quickly.

"Joshua Farmer wrote a series of letters to his wife in San Francisco. How does that tie in with you?"

"Don't play stupid. He bragged about it, didn't he? Boasted about how he didn't have to put his life in danger going up to the Klondike, how he would just wait around town and take someone else's fortune, the fortune they'd worked hard for."

Joshua had not quite admitted that in writing but the gist of it was there between the lines.

"But Joshua Farmer ended up dead, murdered right here on this property," I said. "And that happened well before your time. So what are you saying, Earl?"

"He's saying that we know the real story," Lillian said, a

snarl twisting her features. "We were told the story of how our grandfather's hard-earned fortune was taken from him."

"Dad lived to be a very old man and he used to remember every minute of that time, when he was a little kid and Grandpa Mick told him about the theft of the gold."

"And this story was passed down to you and—you decided to do what? Your family didn't grow up poor. I'm guessing that the story of the gold being stolen was only half of it. Mick Thespen never included how he had killed Joshua Farmer and taken that gold back, did he?"

Earl averted his eyes but Lillian stared defiantly at me.

"And then Joshua's great-grandson showed up. It's been a long time ago but I'll bet you remember him. Michael Ratcliff." Katherine might have wanted to believe he came up here looking to verify family history, but I'd picked up plenty of clues from his own notes that he intended to find this big stash of gold he believed was rightfully left to him by Joshua Farmer.

Earl turned on Kerby. "I *told* you that Ratcliff woman wasn't here in town innocently. I *knew* she'd be the start of a bunch of trouble!"

Kerby started to growl something in response but Lillian stepped in between her husband and her brother.

"Stop it!" she snarled with her teeth nearly clenched. She gripped Earl's arm. "You never told me anything about this Michael Ratcliff."

"You were off in New York, getting yourself a husband. I was working in the damn bank," Earl hissed.

I verbalized the thoughts that came rushing at me. "The bank that your great-grandfather founded with the gold he took back from Farmer. Which, unfortunately, wasn't all his for the taking. Part of it belonged to Alistair Connell. Now that's the family who should be angry over this whole thing, not yours. The Connells didn't have the advantage of a bag of gold to start themselves a profitable business."

Lillian stared defiantly at Barney Connell, who seemed stunned. Apparently, tales of the gold rush crimes hadn't been passed along in his family.

He spoke so quietly I could hardly hear him. "All I ever heard was that Alastair Connell came up here to find a fortune and he failed. My father and grandfather seemed to have that branded into them, the word 'failure' and the idea that no Connell would ever really get ahead in this place."

"Your greed is astounding," I said to Earl. "Your family had it all and it still wasn't good enough. You had to get rid of—" The picture of Michael Ratcliff's skeleton wearing its sorry polyester shirt came at me. "Did you do it yourself?"

Even Lillian was looking warily at her brother now.

"Me? No! I had nothing to do with him." But the look in his eyes said otherwise. He would have been in his teens when Michael arrived, and he must have brought him to the cave.

Somewhere in the far distance I caught the very faint sound of rotor blades. Kerby tapped Lillian on the shoulder and started to turn toward his aircraft.

"No!" shouted Earl. "We aren't done here."

He pulled a pistol from his waistband and took a firm stance, aiming it first at Kerby and then at me.

"We need these two out of the way," he said, referring to me and Barney. "They'll go back to town and tell the authorities."

"I think—" Kerby closed his mouth when the pistol turned back his way.

"Get them up to the cave," Earl said. "The place has

been thoroughly searched already. No one will go up there."

"Earl, that's not going to work. What will you do with my helicopter? Unless you learned to fly in your spare time as a banker, you can't get both these machines out of here."

An evil smile formed on his face. "This is even better ... Kerby, strap them inside, douse the thing in gasoline. They just crashed here."

That steady whop-whop grew a little louder but no one else had picked up on it.

"You really think Kerby and Lillian want murder charges on their heads, just because you already have one? They won't help you." I kept raising my voice to cover the sound of rescue.

"They don't have to," Earl said, a tiny note of desperation creeping into his voice. "I can—"

I saw the gun waver for a second and I rushed him. But Earl was slightly quicker. He squeezed off two shots and Barney fell to the ground. That and Earl's crazed stare stopped me in my tracks. Lillian let out a small shriek. Barney was screaming and clutching at his leg.

"You really did kill that young man, all those years ago." Lillian sounded stunned. "Even that time you got drunk and bragged about it I never believed it was true."

"He went on a long hike. That's all."

And ended up stabbed in the gut. Earl was on the edge, I could tell. He still had three people to cover with the gun and the two he'd believed to be allies were quickly turning. However, the magazine in that pistol still had at least eight rounds in it. He could get rid of Lillian and me and force Kerby to fly him out.

"Earl, you need to put down the gun," Kerby said, working the same salesman voice I'd heard him use with the customers. "Charlie, can you tend to Barney over there?"

I could try, but I'll admit that nursing is not among my best skills. Besides, I really wouldn't mind if Barney kept up the noise for another two or three minutes. I could see a distinctive shape coming up the valley and we could use a little lead time before Earl realized he was up against the wall.

Earl turned the gun on me again. "Yeah, either you shut him up or I will."

So, okay, nursing it would be.

I dashed over to Barney and tried to reassure him in a low voice while I made a show of looking at the leg wound without really *looking* at it. His cries quieted to a whimper and then the rush of rotor air and the blast of sound could not be ignored.

With a pilot I didn't know at the controls and Chief Branson in the passenger seat, one of the glacier-tour ships came roaring in. He found the perfect landing spot, close to the little tableau of people, and set it down. Branson took in the scene at a glance and emerged with his service pistol drawn, aimed squarely at Earl. I had a feeling his shot would be far more accurate, especially when I saw that he'd brought another officer along. My heart leapt when I saw Drake get out of the backseat.

Earl slumped and dropped his gun. Kerby had already distanced himself from his brother-in-law; now Earl raised his hands in surrender. Lillian squared her shoulders and tried to act as if she hadn't really been here, hoping perhaps the police chief would treat her with mayoral deference.

Drake came to my side. "The FBO heard your radio call and Chief Branson insisted we come. Apparently, he's been piecing together a case against Earl Thespen for awhile now."

"I'm fine but Barney's injured. I don't think it's life-threatening but he's in a lot of pain. Can they get him to the clinic?"

He spoke quickly to the pilot, who got out and together we got Barney into the back seat of the green and white A-Star. I climbed in and helped him stretch across the four back seats and strapped two seatbelts around him.

"Lie as still as you can," Drake said. "They'll have you at the clinic in ten minutes."

I backed out to find that Branson's officer already had Earl in cuffs. Lillian and Kerby Allen were suddenly all cooperation and Kerby volunteered to fly the prisoner back to town. Chief Branson would ride along to be sure Kerby didn't pull anything.

Already his officer was directing where each of them would sit. Drake and I found ourselves alone with the JetRanger as Kerby started up his machine. I stepped to the side window where Branson sat.

"I'll be along in a little while," I said. "There's some cargo we need to offload."

He gave a nod. I opened the cargo hold and took out the first of the boxes Barney had loaded.

"This isn't the real reason I wanted to stay," I told Drake as we carried boxes into the cabin. "There's something else I want to check out. Grab a couple of flashlights."

He followed me up the narrow trail to the cave where this whole mess had begun.

"I can't let this summer get away without at least trying to verify one old story," I said. "We're this close."

I had already guessed that Joshua Farmer's body ended up here as a matter of convenience. He had come up this trail for some reason, probably connected with the Thespens' allegation that he had stolen their gold, and the cave had made a convenient hiding place for his body. Perhaps he had led someone into the cave—or vice versa—and that was the place where his skull had been bashed with a rock.

Michael Ratcliff had come looking for the gold he believed his great-grandfather had legitimately discovered in the Klondike. I couldn't be sure how he came to be on this trail but Earl Thespen's admission about Michael made me believe that Earl had either brought Michael up here himself or had hired a killer. Earl and his father were probably the only two who had ever really known.

Perhaps Earl had explored these hills as a kid; maybe he even knew about the older skeleton and thought of the cave as a perfect hiding place. The longer Michael's body remained in the cave the more likely the evidence would erode with time. No one in 1975 would have had any idea how easy it would be to prove the relationship of the two sets of bones when they were eventually found.

"Earl might have been in here looking for a far bigger stash of gold than what Mick Thespen ever found. There's an old legend." I told him the story of Gus's Gold as we made our way by flashlight deeper into the cave.

"Earl and Lillian were raised on that story, and with his insatiable need for money I can't believe he would simply ignore the chance to find such a haul. A hundred pounds of gold—it would be worth a couple million or more by now. Earl probably explored caves all over the place, including this one, until that cabin was built. I'm sure he wasn't at all happy that his brother-in-law started bringing tourists up here."

"But he couldn't very well suggest that Kerby's crew block off the passages inside the cave, because they would have found the two skeletons. It was better to keep the cave secret."

"He could have moved them," I mused as we ducked to enter, "but maybe there wasn't time. Or maybe even a killer finds some things distasteful."

We passed the areas where each skeleton was found and edged our way through a narrow spot beyond. Passages branched off in three directions.

"Is this safe?" I asked Drake.

He shined his light around all the surfaces. "It looks natural, as opposed to a mine shaft where people have cut into the rock."

We pushed onward taking the right-hand opening, mainly because footprints on the ground indicated that it had drawn the most interest already.

"He's been poking around in here," I said, showing Drake some fairly fresh chisel marks in a spot where the rock was full of natural indents anyway.

"Yeah, but I don't see that he found anything."

I didn't either.

"Let's think about this logically, unless you want to spend weeks in this place." Poor Drake, he'd been walking bent over and was already getting a crick in his neck. I wasn't too fond of the musty damp of it either.

"You're right. A man with nothing at his disposal but 1890s technology, a man who has already been on the trail in brutal conditions, whose dogs have died in the effort to haul this gold—he's not going to lug it an extra mile inside a mountain, right? He's going to look for a place that's reasonably convenient to the entrance but hidden from plain view."

Which probably meant someone else had come upon it

a long time ago.

He read my thoughts. "Let's not give up yet, but we should try to keep things simple."

We backed out of the tunnel Earl had already been working. Back at the wide spot, a beam of light indicated that the tunnel on the left was too small to walk into, no more than a small den. The middle tunnel was the largest and seemed undisturbed, without a current-day footprint in sight. Or an old footprint either. With no wind, rain or traffic to erase them, even really old prints would show.

I steered Drake back to the small, left-hand tunnel. "Look at these piles of rock. They very well might have fallen here but a few of them seem like they could have been deliberately stacked in position."

We set our lights on the ground and began moving rocks. I was astounded at how heavy they were—even those the size of a breadbox were a chore for the two of us. Clearly, I had watched too many films with Styrofoam-prop boulders. We got six of the heavy monsters rearranged before I caught a glimpse of something light-colored.

"Look."

Drake moved one more shoebox-sized rock, which revealed a glimpse of pale tan cloth. I gave a tug but it stayed firmly in place. Smart man, he pulled out his pocket knife and slashed it with an X. The fabric still wouldn't rip, but between the cuts we could see the distinct glitter. Gold.

My heartbeat quickened. "Oh my god. It's really here."

"Well, mother nature didn't just place it in this spot, wrapped in canvas. Somebody put it here." Drake reached into the small opening and what came out was a gold nugget roughly the size of a golf ball.

I tossed another of the rocks aside, joining Drake in the

effort, uncovering more of the canvas bag, until something thunked me on the shoulder.

"Hey, careful," I said.

"What?"

"Tossing those rocks. That hurt."

"Hon, I didn—" Fine dirt sifted down onto our heads. A deep moan came from somewhere to my right.

"We gotta get out of here!" Sharp stones cut into my knees as I scrambled backward out of the small space.

"Run!" Drake shouted, grabbing my arm and dragging me along at his side.

Behind us, the moan became a rumble and ragged stones skittered across the floor and zipped past us. One flashlight was long gone and the other did little to guide us, bobbing along as we scrambled over the uneven ground and dodged outcroppings that could knock us senseless. My feet skidded several times.

Finally, through the cloud of dirt, a light patch showed ahead where daylight came from the entrance. We reached it and kept on running as dust plumed and rocks bounced out the mouth of the cave.

Chapter 32

A week passed before the nightmares ended. Facing down Earl Thespen and his pistol was nothing compared to the knee-knocking, brain-numbing fear that coursed through me in those final yards before we emerged to freedom. We'd stumbled down to the helicopter and collapsed, lying on our backs on the grass for a good thirty minutes before either of us felt steady enough to stand, another half hour before Drake wanted to take the controls and fly us out of there. That night, there had been survivor sex, a desperate coupling of the animal sort. We'd slept with our limbs entwined; being more than a few inches apart seemed to reinforce the near miss that would have permanently lost us to each other.

Now, I stacked the last of our suitcases beside the front door. Drake had been carefully packing the truck all morning. The JetRanger, with a lot of its gear stowed inside, waited at the airport. We would spend one last night in Berta's house before hitting the road in the morning, our Alaskan adventure at an end.

Kerby's business was shut down the day after the arrests; front page headlines about how he had scammed tourists with promises of riches and a contract which guaranteed they would never keep their findings pretty well cooked that golden goose. Just another of Mina's articles to go national.

Earl would stand trial for first degree murder, a charge Chief Branson felt would stick because he had located a man named Bobby Manning who, in exchange for a lighter sentence, was willing to testify that he had helped Earl hide Michael Ratcliff's body. Lillian didn't have much choice about stepping down as mayor once the citizens made enough noise and the borough assembly met and voted her out.

I boxed the groceries we hadn't used and set it on the kitchen table. I would give Berta the unused cereals, soups and a half-dozen eggs, among other things. I looked toward her house and saw Mina crossing the lawn toward my kitchen door.

"Hey, girl. Big congratulations, I hear?" I gave her a hug as I let her in.

She blushed a little. "Best Investigative Journalism from the Western Newspaper Association, for my story that led to Katherine Ratcliff and the identification of the bones. I think there was a qualifier in there about its being a small-town paper or something."

"Well, none of us care about that. We're proud of you."

"I'm putting out job feelers. Maybe something big-city will come my way."

"How does Chuey feel about that?"

She wrinkled her mouth a little. "I don't know. First, I think I have to see whether a job actually comes through."

She saw the box on the table. "So, you guys are packing up. It's going to feel a little empty without you here."

I laughed. "Ten thousand tourists a day, out there prowling your streets. This town won't feel empty until the season's over."

"Yeah but ... I never get attached to *them*."

Drake peeked into the kitchen to see if there was anything else ready for the truck.

"Look, you're busy," Mina said. "I'll let you go. Don't forget, Mom wants you to come to dinner tonight."

How could we forget? Berta had instructed me to bring the champagne so we could make a big deal of Mina's journalism prize.

Drake helped me check through the house. I'd kept my toothbrush out for tonight, and of course the dog crate and dishes would be the last thing to load. I came across a large brown padded envelope.

"Oh, that reminds me. A couple of errands before we leave." I showed him the envelope. "The report to Katherine Ratcliff, along with her grandmother's diaries and the letters. Even though her brother's interest in family history wasn't real, she may want to read these someday."

"And?—two errands?"

"I thought I would stop by to see Barney. I feel badly that I suspected him for awhile. His family really did get the short end of the stick in everything, it seems."

"I'll go along with you." He whistled to Freckles, who was more than happy to hop into the truck for the short ride to the cabin near the gold rush cemetery.

The Connells lived simply but the little cabin was clean inside and the two kids greeted us politely with only a slight prompt from Sissy. Her hair was still a wild mass of curls but she had it back in a ponytail rather than the attempted glamor-do she'd worn at the fundraiser. Clearly she was much more in her element in jeans and a sweatshirt—as was I.

"He's in front of the TV," she said. "Seattle Mariners. He can't stay away."

"We won't stay long," I assured her, handing over two packages of cookies that I'd swiped from the food box. They seemed more like a gift than the leftovers we were giving to Berta. "How's he doing?"

"Other than being unemployed again, he'll be fine."

"I'm so sorry the investigation led to Kerby's business getting shut down." I said.

"Oh, that's no problem. Barney was always a little uneasy around the Thespens anyway. I guess it's a thing that goes way back. He's got a job lined up to drive the little shuttle bus around town, once he can do it without pain from the leg."

Drake had drifted to the living room and taken a seat on the couch beside Barney's recliner chair. Both men were intent on the televised baseball game.

"We can't stay long, Barney," I said, "but I wanted to thank you so much for being there that day. Not too many friends have ever taken a bullet for me."

"Well, I won't go so far as to say it was my pleasure, but I do have a great story now for the kids. It impresses the heck out of my brother's boys."

I nudged the back of Drake's seat. "We better head back."

Drake stood and reached into his pocket. "Got a little something for you," he said to Barney. He held out a closed hand.

"Call it a good luck charm, or a token of thanks, or next month's mortgage if that helps."

Something dropped into Barney's open palm. The gold nugget he'd taken from the cave, right before we'd run for our lives. I'd forgotten all about it. Barney stared at the lump and Sissy slapped her hand to her chest with a little cry.

"That was so much the right thing to do," I said as we pulled out of the Connells' driveway. "They seem like a family who could use a break."

I found myself thinking more about that huge cache of gold the next morning as I flew over the rugged peaks east of Skagway. I'd won our coin toss so I was airborne, while Drake and Freckles took the first leg of the return trip to New Mexico by highway.

On all sides of me loomed range after range of snow-topped mountains, blue-purple in the distance. How many of those hills had abandoned mines or caves in them? In how many had someone stashed the fruits of their labor, planning to come back, and how many of those dream-filled men had ever done so? In one small cave in one fairly insignificant mountain, beside a cabin that would disintegrate with time and weather, I had been blessed to witness the outcome of only one of those legends. The cache was still there. The story would live on, no doubt, and no one would ever come as close as we had to finding the whole, magnificent treasure.

It was a memory that I knew would stay with me all my days.

Author's Notes

Alaska, the land of such magnificent natural beauty that it is hard to fathom it all, was long a dream of mine and I went there with an eye for a place where a story could unfold. Skagway caught my eye, and my heart, and two trips there were not nearly enough. But that's what I had to work with.

So many resources came my way, both during and after my travels. *The Skagway Story* by Howard Clifford painted many pictures for me of daily life on the streets of the town during and after the gold rush. The visitor center and chamber of commerce provided a bounty of maps and answered questions I didn't even know I would run into while I was actually on site. (Who knew that over 6,800 abandoned mines exist in Alaska?) The local newspapers helped tremendously with both historical and modern-day facts, as did our friendly and helpful guides (I am so sorry I didn't get your names).

Despite the research, please keep in mind that this is a work of fiction. Aside from the events and names documented in history, this entire story comes from my imagination. No real modern-day people are mentioned here. The events surrounding the death of Jefferson Randolph "Soapy" Smith, the funerals and burials of Smith and of Frank Reid are well documented in history, although there were discrepancies in some of the accounts and I could only choose one of them.

My sense of what Skagway must be like when the tourist season ends is just that—a guess based on my own experience having lived in places that rely heavily on tourism for their livelihood. Any given person you ask may feel differently. In other words, the opinions expressed by the characters in this book are not necessarily those of the author.

Mainly, I hope you will sit back and enjoy this little adventure along with Charlie and Drake. I feel incredibly lucky to be able to pass it along to you.

---Connie Shelton
October, 2014

Sign up for Connie's free mystery newsletter at
www.connieshelton.com
and receive advance information on new books, along
with a chance at prizes, discounts and other
mystery news!

Contact by email: connie@connieshelton.com
Follow Connie Shelton on Twitter, Pinterest and
Facebook

Made in the USA
Charleston, SC
19 November 2014